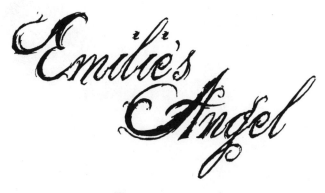
Emilie's Angel

BOOK 1
LOVE IS HELL SERIES

BY SONIA BRANCHAUD

Copyright © 2011 Sonia Branchaud

ISBN: 1463749201
ISBN 13: 9781463749200
Library of Congress Control Number: 2011912950
CreateSpace, North Charleston, SC

I would like to dedicate this book to my husband, Marc.
I never would have come this far without him.

Acknowledgements

Many people helped make this book possible. Firstly I would like to thank my husband. He has been there to help me from the moment I began conceptualizing the story of Emilie and Dante. He was my first reader, my harshest critic, and even my first editor. His love of science fiction and fantasy novels helped me with the realization of the Beyowan world. Some of my best chapters were written at his prompting. I should also thank my boys, Nathaniel and Xavier, for growing up faster than necessary while I was engrossed in my writing. I wasn't able to give them all of the attention they deserved. They could have become bitter, but they've been very supportive.

I would also like to thank one of my best friends in the world, Sherri Thompson. Through her input I gained valuable perspective into the characters and the story. She has been by my side from the very beginning, and I owe her a considerable debt of gratitude. I've also relied heavily on my new sister-in-law, Sandra Houillier, my self-proclaimed biggest fan. She has been an excellent sounding board, and her advice was most appreciated. My outstanding friend, Felicia Staub Brassard, has also been a strong source of support throughout this process and has encouraged me even in my darkest hours. I can't forget to mention my friend and fellow author, Chris Gregg, who was a real help with the writing and the publication process. He was able to relate to my pain and struggles on an entirely different level.

Lastly I would like to thank all of my friends and family. I have been incredibly fortunate that so many people have encouraged me not to give up on my dream. I couldn't have done this without you all.

Chapter 1

"Would you guys please cut that out!" Lei barked. "Some of us are actually working here."

Dante looked sheepishly over at his friend Jude. They both started laughing quietly under their breath. Dante was bored and impatient. It was Saturday, and it had been a long week. He really wanted to go home. "Hey... If I say that we'll be here at five then have the shipment ready at five. Otherwise, if you make us wait, then we'll have to find something to do to pass the time," Dante explained, trying to sound self-important.

Lei just shook her head disdainfully. "If you guys break anything in here, it comes out of your pay check," she warned. "Am I making myself quite clear? I don't care which families you belong to."

Jude ignored her and whipped another paper clip at Dante, who smiled to himself, tracking it carefully in the air. He easily caught the clip on his magnetic gauntlet. Dante found all of the protective gear necessary for his job uncomfortable. He had on a bulletproof vest with his dart gun holstered to his shoulder, and long, leather, fingerless gauntlets with six-inch-wide, thin magnetic strips wrapped around each forearm. Plus he wore big, heavy, steel-toed leather boots covering half of his calves. Overall it was hot, bulky—and absolutely necessary.

He shot Jude a speculative glance and ducked behind one of the two large rectangular tables in the center of the laboratory. As he peeked over the table top he saw Jude gesturing confidently to him, challenging him to throw the paper clip back.

Dante tried to figure out a way to hit Jude, which was a formidable task because there was no one in the world faster than Jude. Dante leapt up from behind the table, faked a high shot, and flicked his wrist, sending the clip down toward Jude's legs. Jude leapt gracefully into the air, allowing the clip to slide under the counter behind him.

"Hey, you have to get that one!" Dante complained. "That's our last one! Now what are we going to do around here?" He leaned over, trying to estimate where exactly the paper clip had disappeared.

"Maybe you guys can act like grown men for a change," Lei grumbled.

"I guess we're just going to have to learn how to knit or something," Jude commented sarcastically. He was on his hands and knees, attempting to fish his prize from under the counter. He spun quickly around and flicked the paper clip at Dante, who was taken off guard. Jude was just too fast. Dante sucked in his breath, reflexively jumped backwards, and brought his magnetic gauntlets up in front of his face. He managed to catch the clip, but he crashed into Lei, who was on her way over to start packing up what Dante hoped was the last of the day's shipment into one of the two large, insulated, plastic medical transportation cases.

Dante reached out and grabbed Lei before she fell over. "Well now," he purred seductively. "I can think of something I'd rather be doing to pass the time."

"Let go of me, you animal. You're not my type," Lei commanded, laughing softly.

"I'm hurt..." Dante whimpered, letting Lei escape from his grasp. "You know I only have eyes for you." He flashed her his sad puppy dog look, deliberately batting his long lashes. Lei was just too much fun to flirt with.

"Oh please..." Lei mumbled. "Does that ever work for you?"

"You might be surprised what works for me, baby," Dante replied, smiling mischievously.

Lei groaned in disgust. "Anyway, your big brown eyes are not the problem. If I ever decide I'm interested in men, you'll be the first to know. Deal?"

"I'm ready whenever you are," Dante responded, allowing his eyes to run indecently over her lab coat-covered body. The other three girls working in the lab had stopped what they were doing and were giggling behind their hands.

Dante had a strict policy of never getting romantically involved with anyone from work, but he had developed a reputation for being an incorrigible flirt, and he thoroughly enjoyed the attention that he often received from women as a result. It was surprising just how bold some people could become if they felt there was little personal risk involved.

Lei rolled her eyes. "One of these days, you're going to catch me in an experimental mood and then you'll actually have to put out or get out."

"Promises, promises," Dante taunted. He had known her for a long time and had every confidence that she would never be interested in men, especially rogues like him.

"Don't get him too lathered up now, Lei. Some of us still have work to do around here," Jude grumbled, obviously feeling left out.

"I'll take Dante in the back and keep him busy for you," Lei's assistant Sunisa offered.

Dante laughed. *Case in point*, he thought to himself. He particularly enjoyed flirting with Sunisa. She was a feisty little girl. "Oh, I think I could handle the both of you at the same time," Dante boasted, pulling himself up to sit on a table top.

"See, that kind of attitude just makes me glad I'm a lesbian," Lei countered, grimacing distastefully.

"Maybe I'll take both you and Jude in the back so Lei can get her work done in peace," Sunisa challenged, bouncing her eyebrows at Dante.

He burst out laughing, rocking himself backwards on the work top. Jude doubled over with laughter but managed to choke out, "Wow...Aren't you ambitious! You would really have your hands full!"

Dante was still laughing crudely to himself, watching Lei finish packing the second case, when he noticed something out of the corner of his eye. The smile slipped off his face as he searched the space above the table where the first of their shipment cases was waiting.

Dante had the ability to travel through inter-dimensional space, and like others of his kind with this ability, he could see if someone was standing in an inter-dimensional doorway, looking out into this space. No one else in the room would be able to see anything out of the ordinary, but he had definitely seen someone hiding. This could only mean one thing: They were about to be attacked.

This was the perfect day of the week and the perfect time of the day for it. This was his last shipment of the week, and he was headed home to the Montreal Council Office, carrying the most valuable cargo. If he were a thief, this would be the one he would try to intercept.

Dante jumped down and walked around the other table to see if he could confirm his suspicion. As he came around the table, Lei put the second case down next to the first and then walked quickly to the back of the lab to get the paperwork ready. He spotted something moving.

"Everyone, get down, now!" he yelled at the top of his voice, glancing around with concern.

A figure dressed from head to foot in black stepped out of thin air, towing another with a rope. The lab's alarm system went off, and the deafening sound of sirens could be heard through half of the Bangkok Council Office. Dante knew that security officers and paramedics would be on their way. Hopefully they could avert a serious situation.

The first thief grabbed the handles of both shipment cases as the second started spraying the room with bullets from the two automatic weapons in his hands.

Dante only had seconds to save the shipment. The man with the cases just needed to take one step and he could disappear back into inter-dimensional space, pulling his partner with him. Dante crouched down and swiped out with his leg as the thief started the crucial step. Dante smiled to himself as he managed to trip the other man. Dante hoped the thief would be distracted enough to let the doorway close and not stumble through it back into inter-dimensional space.

As the thief toppled forward, Dante quickly peeked over the table to see if Jude was ready. No big surprise— he was. He had his dart gun out and was firing at the man with the cases. Dante heard the shot and ducked back down behind the table, looking up at the thief. Jude's aim was true, and the man disappeared into dust, dropping the cases onto the floor of the lab.

The gunman was now trapped in the lab with six other people. He was facing away from Dante and focused on Jude, who was on the other side of the room. Still crouching on the floor, Dante glanced over to make sure that Lei was down on the ground. She was crawling quickly into the back.

Dante rolled across the floor and took cover in front of the table, taking his own dart gun out of its holster as he went. He steadied himself, popped up from behind the table, and aimed. The gunman turned, and they both fired at the same time. Dante felt a horrible burning pain tear through his abdomen. He dove across the floor, trying to take cover behind the table he had been sitting on before. He popped his head up quickly and saw the gunman disappear into dust.

Dante sighed with relief as he sat down hard on the floor, leaning his back against the skirt of the work table. He was in serious pain. He reached down and felt his side. There was a nice neat hole in his vest about three inches up from his right hip bone. *Great...shot again. What's the point of wearing a vest if the bullets go through anyway?* He reached around his back, where he found an even bigger hole. At least the bullet had passed through his body, but he was losing blood fast.

Jude came over to check on him. "You don't look so good," Jude teased, yelling to make himself heard over the alarms.

"I don't feel so good," Dante replied, trying to laugh, but the pain was too intense. "You don't look so good yourself." Jude had a nasty wound under his own vest, in the right shoulder just below the collar bone.

"I'm fine. Nothing vital hit. I don't know about you though." Jude's tone of voice had lost its humor and sounded deeply concerned. Then the alarms shut off and they could suddenly hear much more clearly. "Dante's been hit! I need the medical kit now!" Jude yelled, standing up to assess the damage to the rest of the group.

Dante tried to take a deep breath but his side ached. At least he hadn't collapsed a lung. *Now that really hurts,* he thought to himself, remembering another injury.

Lei dashed around the table with a roll of gauze in her hand. She crouched down and examined Dante carefully. She reached for the clasps holding the vest closed. "Don't touch me, I'm fine," he muttered, snatching the gauze from her hands.

"A minute ago you were all over me like a rash and now you say don't touch me. Men…all talk and no action," Lei teased, but she was looking a little too worried for Dante's taste.

He stuffed the gauze into the hole in his back and tried to laugh but could only let out a groan of agony instead. "Hey, you had your chance. It's too late now," Dante mumbled, trying to catch his breath. He was starting to feel faint.

Lei snickered quietly next to him. Jude was checking everyone else for injuries. Dante noticed a gurney rolling toward him. Someone bent down and asked, "Did the bullet go right through?"

"Yeah…It's messier on the other side," Dante explained as he was lifted up onto the gurney.

"Whatever they're paying you, it isn't enough," Lei announced, her features etched with worry. She watched the medic take Dante's vest off and put a big pad on his back before laying him back down onto the gurney.

"Yeah, I know. I quit!" Dante replied, trying to sound stronger than he felt.

"You can't quit," Lei said. "We'd all be screwed. I'm just glad you're so young. Thankfully I'll be long gone before you are, because I wouldn't want to work in this business without you and Jude."

"Thanks...But seriously, this is my last year. I swear it. I don't need the money and I don't need this," Dante grumbled. He saw Jude stretched out on another gurney but was glad that all four girls were unharmed. The last time this had happened, three other people had been shot, and one of them had died from a bullet to the head.

"I'll be back tomorrow for the shipment. This time, be sure it's ready for me," Dante ordered as he was being wheeled out of the room. "I hate working weekends..."

"We'll be ready. You just take it easy," Lei scolded.

Sunisa ran up and took his hand in hers. "Thanks for the warning, Dante. You saved us all."

Dante smiled a crooked grin. She really was a sweet girl. "It's no big deal. I'm just the messenger. Nothing special."

"You're so much more than that, and you know it too!" Sunisa declared, patting his hand firmly before releasing it. Dante blew her a kiss on his way out. He was sick of this job. There had to be more to life than this.

୴

Emilie Latour turned to her friend Caroline and announced, "I think that's the last of them."

Emilie put the box down on the kitchen counter. Now she just needed a couple of days to unpack. She sat down hard on one of her kitchen chairs. Moving was hell. She couldn't wait to start school though. She was beginning a master's degree in anthropology at McGill University.

"Are we done for tonight?" Caroline asked. She took the seat next to Emilie and tucked her long russet hair behind her ears. "I'm starved," she added with a sigh.

"Let's go somewhere good tonight. You deserve it. You've been such a big help," Emilie said, but she felt as though she couldn't rise from her seat to go out anywhere.

Caroline Grissom had moved from Vancouver to Montreal in July in order to set herself up before school started. Montreal was a great city in which to be young and carefree in the summer time. Emilie had been forced to wait until September to move in order to take care of the sale of her parents' house in Vancouver.

Emilie didn't like to think too much about it. At twenty-three years old it was hard enough coming to grips with the fact that she was an orphan without also having to sell the house in which she had spent so much of her childhood. Walking out of their house for the last time had forced her to accept her parents' deaths. Living there had created an illusion of normalcy, allowing Emilie to pretend that her parents were simply away on another back-country camping or ski trip.

If only they hadn't driven home from Whistler on that terrible night in the snow. The Sea to Sky Highway was very dangerous. The highway patrol had eventually closed the roads, but not before her parents' car had been hit by a drunk driver and everyone had been killed in the resulting fire.

Almost two years had passed since the accident. Some days it felt like an eternity, and others felt like the blink of an eye. The shock of her sudden loss had forced Emilie to take a reduced course load and graduate from the University of British Columbia a year later than expected. Taking her time had been a good decision and had worked out for the best, because she was here now.

Emilie had been so happy when she had been accepted to McGill. She had been born in Montreal, but her family had moved to Vancouver when she started middle school. For some reason, she had always felt drawn back to this city.

As much as Emilie loved and missed her parents, she was glad that they had taught her how to be independent at such a young age. They had been biologists as well as wildlife photographers and so had been away from home much of the time.

Her parents had been told not to get their hopes up about having a child together. Emilie had been their little miracle, but her birth had not affected their active lives. They had continued with their work and their favorite sports, leaving Emilie in the loving care of her grandmother in their absence.

Being an only child could have made her spoiled and lazy, but Emilie had learned how to be self-sufficient and run a household earlier than most. This had proven to be quite an advantage after the accident, and consequently the wrapping-up of her parents' estate had been a much less painful process. Now a new chapter of her life was about to begin.

Her best friend Caroline had decided to follow her to Montreal and earn her master's degree at McGill as well. Emilie was glad for the company. She would have hated to come here all by herself. She was a bit of a loner but not a hermit. Caroline, on the other hand, had an extremely outgoing and adventurous personality, which brought out the best in Emilie. She just wasn't as social. She had always been a bit awkward, but she had still been reasonably popular. The two were not mutually exclusive. She considered herself fairly attractive and had taken dance lessons with many of her classmates throughout high school. These things, combined with her friendship with Caroline, had helped Emilie to fit in quite comfortably at school.

Emilie and Caroline were both single women, starting their lives fresh in a new city. Luckily Caroline had not found her true love in Vancouver. She was still on the prowl and was eager to discover what opportunities were available.

Although fortune had not been particularly generous as far as Emilie's love life was concerned, she'd had some great sex. Privacy had been the primary advantage of having parents who were often away from home. She considered herself a modern woman and had been open to the occasional casual fling, but she longed for something truly intimate. Hopefully living in a new city would change her luck with love. Maybe she would finally find someone special with whom to share her life.

"I know a great club," Caroline declared. "We should go out and celebrate getting your new apartment...

mostly…set up," she added, gesturing to the partially unpacked disaster spread out all over Emilie's kitchen. "There are a lot of hot guys in Montreal. There's one especially cute bartender at one of my favorite dance clubs. I'll have to take you to meet him." She started sniggering to herself. "You always seem to attract the naughtiest of the bad boys in a room. Maybe if you don't turn his head, then he'll be safe for me. What is it about you anyway?"

Emilie sighed heavily. She didn't know what to say. She needed to find herself a nice, safe, uncomplicated man. She glanced around her new one-bedroom apartment with cheerful optimism. Perhaps her luck was about to change.

Chapter 2

Emilie quickly settled into her apartment and her new university routine. It was only a couple of weeks into the semester and already she had more work than she could handle. Fortunately her advisor had convenient office hours and a relaxed, open-door policy.

"I'll see you on Thursday," Emilie said to Professor Ashton as she began to slowly back out of his office. She could hear voices talking and laughing quietly outside the open door, which made her feel pressured to get out of there as quickly as possible. She was just about to turn around and be on her way when she bumped into someone. Whoever it was had been standing at the office door and she, in her clumsiness, had walked right into them.

Fortunately she had been moving so slowly that their bodies had barely touched. She was embarrassed, but at least no harm was done. She could feel the color rushing up her face. She was about to turn around and apologize when all of a sudden a strange sensation raced up her spine. It was a gentle feeling, like a feather softly brushing against her skin, yet powerful. It didn't stay on the surface but somehow penetrated her body and went deep into her chest. As it spread, she sucked her breath in sharply. She had never experienced anything like it before. Goose bumps rose all over her skin, as if she had taken a sudden chill.

She managed to pull herself out of her shock quickly enough and started moving again. She turned slowly around to face the unseen person and got a second shock. She found herself looking into the face of an angel.

He seemed as surprised as she was. He had obviously turned around at the exact same time and at the exact same speed, because they had gone from back-to-back to face-to-face in one fluid movement. *And what a face!* she thought. *He's positively breathtaking.*

For the second time Emilie involuntarily gasped for air. He was examining her face with beautiful brown eyes flecked with gold, and it appeared as if he had somehow shared her strange sensation. He wasn't smiling and wore a bewildered expression.

Wow! She couldn't help but stare. He wasn't your typical tall, dark, and handsome. He was young, maybe slightly older than she was. His skin was light golden brown and flawless, as if he had a perfect tan. His hair was dark brown, almost black, and it was longer than most men wore it. It was cut in perfect wavy layers and flipped back like a rock star's. He was tall, at least six foot two. His long, thick lashes blinked over those lovely brown eyes.

As Emilie tore her gaze from his face, she noticed that he was wearing an unusual tan-colored long-sleeved shirt, covered in Egyptian hieroglyphics, which fit his gorgeously sculpted body perfectly, accentuating his muscular form. *Man, he's in good shape!* She snapped her jaw shut and tried desperately to compose herself.

It felt as if time had stopped, but in fact only a few short seconds had passed. Emilie's attention was drawn away from the angel as Professor Ashton walked around his desk toward them. Through the haze in her mind she heard him say, "Emilie, this is my son, Dante Ashton. Dante, this is one of my grad students, Emilie."

Reflexively she brought up her hand for Dante to shake. He took it in both of his, but he didn't shake it. He just held it gently but firmly. Surprised, her eyes flicked back up to his face. He was still looking at her with the same confused expression, as though he knew her but couldn't quite place where they had met.

Emilie felt the color rising in her cheeks all over again. He was staring a bit too deeply into her eyes for comfort. It felt almost intimate. Not what you would expect from a stranger you were meeting for the first time.

A silly and embarrassed grin spread awkwardly across her face as she studied the floor in order to sever his gaze from hers. She tried in vain to take her hand out of his, but he refused to relinquish it.

Emilie was startled out of her daze by Professor Ashton barking, "Dante! You're being rude!"

Only then did she notice that the angel was not alone. There were two other men standing behind him, laughing uncomfortably. One of them was even slapping Dante on the back, trying to snap him out of his stupor. Dante's hair swayed perfectly back and forth against the sides of his face with each blow of his friend's hand against his back.

Realization hit Dante suddenly and he quickly released Emilie's hand. She wouldn't have believed it possible for him to get any more gorgeous if she hadn't seen it with her own eyes. He smiled. A grin of embarrassment raced across his face before he composed himself and said, "Nice to meet you. Sorry, what was your name again?"

His voice was soothing and magical, almost like music. *Maybe he is a rock star,* she thought. "Emilie. Emilie Latour. Nice to meet you too, Dante," she answered shyly, desperately trying not to stare.

Dante turned around to introduce her to his companions. He raised his hand and pointed to the first of the two men. "This is my good friend Jude," he said, smiling widely. He reached over and slapped Jude gently on the cheek, a rebuke for his previous abuse.

Jude was huge. He made Dante look small and delicate. Jude was at least six and a half feet tall and was built like a football player. He had large, broad shoulders with a thick, muscular chest stretching his long-sleeved shirt. He appeared to be Middle Eastern or North African, maybe Egyptian or Moroccan, with very dark hair and eyes. His skin was a rich color and he wore a bristly goatee on his face. His hair was cut short and gelled up into a prickly style, making him seem even more intimidating. He was worth admiring, though preferably from a distance.

Jude had the eyes of a man with a good sense of humor. They were almost black but sparkled with mischief. They lit up as he said in his own magical voice, "Nice to meet you, Emilie."

Dante then turned to his second companion and introduced him as Colin.

Although handsome in his own right, Colin presented an entirely different picture altogether. He was a touch shorter than Dante and his body was thinner. Where Dante was broad and muscular, Colin was lithe and athletic. To call him fair was putting it mildly. His long blond hair was almost white. His skin was flawless and very pale, almost translucent. Colin's eyes were quite the opposite of his friends'—a very liquid shade of blue with a darker circle around the cornea. They were haunting, almost cold. Emilie found it disconcerting to meet Colin's gaze. She felt as if he could see right into her mind. His body language suggested that he was uncomfortable with the whole situation of meeting her and anxious to be about his business.

"Hi," he said politely.

Emilie nodded to him. She was already walking around their group, on her way out the door. She could see Dante watching her in her peripheral vision. Jude was shoving him gently from behind, trying to get him to move out of the way and into the office.

She started off down the hallway, then decided to risk a quick glance back. Colin was gone, but Dante was craning his neck out the door, still watching. Jude shrugged his shoulders apologetically and shoved Dante more forcefully.

The last thing Emilie saw was Jude's grinning face as he winked at her in a flirty sort of way.

She turned quickly, started marching off to class, and thought, *Wow…What a miraculous day. I've met an angel.*

ψ

Dante leaned back, trying to watch the girl walk away. *Emilie…*She moved so gracefully and seductively that he was tempted to chase her down the hallway. She glanced back at him over her shoulder with those bewitching aqua eyes. He shivered and took a deep breath, inhaling her scent. Definitely human, but there was something different about her, something foreign yet familiar.

Dante's shoes slid on the floor as Jude succeeded in shoving him into the office. Dante locked his memory on Emilie's face and scent. He was determined to see her again. Jude wasn't going to get in his way next time. No one was.

"Wipe that look off your face, you animal!" Dante's father snarled. "You leave my students alone."

Jude burst out laughing. Colin just rolled his eyes and shook his head.

"I'm not doing anything," Dante muttered, trying not to meet his father's gaze. *Yet,* he thought to himself, suppressing a smile. *Emilie's coming back here on Thursday. Interesting…*

"What was that all about?" Dante's father demanded.

"I don't know…There was just something about her," Dante replied irritably. "Let's just forget about it."

"Yes, what an absolutely fabulous idea. You'd better forget about her. I know how you get when you find something you like," his father continued, wagging his finger at him.

Dante rolled his eyes. "I didn't come here to get lectured. What am I going to do with a human girl anyway? I'm an Angel."

Jude sniggered crudely and Dante shot him a scathing glance.

His father snorted angrily. "The way you were looking at that girl was anything but angelic. I was actually expecting your eyes to start glowing red."

"What?" Dante hissed. "Don't be ridiculous!"

"You have too much of your grandfather in you," his father scolded. "It would break my heart if you turned out to be a demon like him."

"Hey now! Let's not get insulting," Dante grumbled. This conversation was getting out of hand. "Keep Dorian out of this. I have less of his blood than my mother did—and she was an Angel."

"Keep in mind, Graham," Colin sneered, locking eyes with Dante's father. "You must have made Delilah's eyes glow at one point while you were still human."

"I guess nobody's perfect," Graham conceded, smiling wistfully. "Although in my opinion, no one was closer to perfection than Dante's mother."

Silence...Everyone paused, temporarily lost in their memories of her.

"Listen, people, can't we just move past this?" Dante asked, losing patience. "I'm getting depressed."

"Why did you come here?" Graham asked. "You hate coming to the university. Too many eager little human girls. Your words exactly, if memory serves."

Dante shuddered in agreement, but he had to stop and think for a moment. He really didn't know why he had come. "Since I had the day off, I just thought I would take my old man out for lunch. I haven't seen you in a while," he explained, almost more for himself than for his father.

"It's true..." Graham agreed, looking at him more affectionately. "I haven't seen you since earlier this month, when you got back from Bangkok, after you and Jude got shot."

Dante was glad to be finished with the subject of humans. "Good times..." he grumbled sarcastically.

"Why did you drag poor Colin here with you? He looks like he's going to lose consciousness. Is he even breathing?" Graham asked with concern.

"Let's stop talking and get going," Colin stated, getting up to leave. "I'll feel better with a full stomach."

Dante had no need to stay any longer. He only had a few days to wait. He would return on Thursday to find that enchanting girl. *Emilie...*

"What's your schedule like on Thursday, Dad?" Dante asked innocently as his father locked the office door behind them.

"I have meetings all morning. Why do you ask?"

"Just curious," Dante answered. He was curious all right, but not about his father's schedule.

ॐ

Caroline and Emilie were relaxing over a cup of coffee. Caroline was nattering on about her classes and the books that she had yet to buy. Emilie was too preoccupied to pay much attention. She couldn't get Dante's face out of her mind. She had never seen anyone like him in all of her life.

"Are you listening to me at all?" Caroline asked with an irritated chuckle.

"I'm sorry. I'm just a little distracted."

Caroline looked Emilie over curiously and leaned forward. "Is it a guy?"

"What gives you that idea?" Emilie asked, surprised at how transparent she could be to her friends.

"You have a love-struck expression on your face," Caroline explained, leaning back in her chair.

"Have you ever met Professor Ashton's son, Dante?"

"He's a bit of an urban myth around the anthropology department," Caroline began. "He isn't seen very often, but he's supposed to be absolutely gorgeous. Not many people have actually met him. I wonder if he's as good looking as they say, or if his reputation has been exaggerated in the constant retelling by so many desperate women."

Emilie could tell by the determined line of Caroline's lips that she was planning on wringing out every drop of information. "I met him today," Emilie taunted, allowing a mischievous grin to spread across her face. "In Professor Ashton's office." She wanted Caroline to sweat a bit before she got into the details.

"So what does he look like?" Caroline whispered, leaning toward Emilie again. She put her elbows on the table and rested her chin in the palms of her hands.

Emilie rolled her eyes dreamily and drew in a long, ragged breath. "I have never, in my life, seen anyone as unbelievable. I'm going to have many warm and fuzzy dreams about him."

"Wow…Okay, but what does he look like?" Caroline asked again, with an edge of annoyance to her voice this time.

Emilie desperately tried to put into words the image in her mind. "Tall, dark, and handsome. I don't know… He looks like a model or a rock star." After a reminiscent pause she added, "His two friends were gorgeous too. I bet the three of them get a lot of attention around campus."

Caroline leaned back in her chair and finished her coffee in one gulp. "I don't think any of them are students here. That's why they aren't often on campus. I believe Dante only shows up when he needs to talk to his dad." She winked at Emilie and asked, "You didn't by any chance get his phone number, did you? I sure would like to see him for myself."

Emily snorted incredulously and glanced at Caroline as though she was completely insane. "I could barely get my jelly brains to say 'hello' to him. I doubt I could have formulated as complex a question as 'Can I get your phone number?'"

Caroline laughed. "Plus Professor Ashton would probably fail you if you slobbered all over his son right in front of him like that. Although for an older man he's quite handsome. Do you find much of a resemblance between father and son?"

Emilie's eyebrows furrowed in concentration as she tried to visualize Professor Ashton in her mind. She had never paid much attention to him before. He was, after all, in his fifties or sixties. "I really didn't get a chance to compare, but if pressed, I would have to say no. I think he must look more like his mother's side of the family. I don't know what happened to me in that office, but I really had the feeling I knew Dante from somewhere. It's going to bug me all day."

"It doesn't matter anyway," Caroline remarked absently. "You'll probably never see him again."

Emilie knew Caroline spoke the truth, but for some reason it hurt to hear those words. Emilie couldn't understand why she had been so bizarrely affected by this random meeting. Perhaps the answer was as simple as too much caffeine, but somehow she suspected it was much more complicated than that.

Caroline's voice dragged her out of her musing. "Let's go to the bookstore. I'm already behind in my reading."

Emilie stood up slowly, feeling sad and empty inside. She really hoped to see that angel again.

ॐ

The next evening, Emilie and Caroline went out dancing with a group of people from the university. Emilie sat by herself at the table, keeping watch over everyone's belongings. She just wasn't her usual, enthusiastic self. Normally she loved to dance. It didn't help that one of the guys who had tagged along with their group had hands like an octopus. Emilie wasn't the least bit interested in him, but he didn't seem to want to take the hint.

Caroline walked up to Emilie and urged, "Come and dance with us."

"I don't really feel like it right now."

"Dante Ashton is not going to walk through that door, so you may as well try to enjoy your life until you see him again," Caroline teased.

"I know, silly, I wasn't thinking about him anyway," Emilie lied. She had found herself thinking of Dante quite a bit. It was weird. She wasn't usually this obsessive. There was just something about him. "I'm just avoiding that eight-armed jerk, Nick."

"Sophie, Melissa, and I have all told him he needs to keep his hands to himself. You're not the only one he's harassing."

Emilie rolled her eyes impatiently. "You have more tolerance for idiots than I do."

"What do you think of the bartender?" Caroline asked, obviously distracted.

Emilie turned toward the bar. The man was handsome, but nothing spectacular. *Not like Dante,* she thought sadly. "He's pretty cute. You should definitely go for him. He hasn't even looked in my direction so he must be safe," she teased.

"Ah, but that's where you're wrong. You're just not as observant as I am. He was watching you quite a few times. He just doesn't watch you when you're not dancing."

"Whatever...I'm not interested," Emilie grumbled.

"Suit yourself. But Dante Ashton isn't coming, and you'll have to get into your big cold bed all by yourself tonight."

"I told you that I wasn't thinking about him," Emilie snapped defensively. "Even if he was here, he'd be dancing with his super-model girlfriend. Guys like that never get into cold beds by themselves."

"Okay, fine. I was just teasing you," Caroline soothed. "I'm going to get back to the girls. There's safety in numbers. This place is a meat market tonight. You'd better be careful here by yourself. You'll be under attack in no time."

"I'll be fine. You go ahead." Emilie was actually looking forward to crawling into her big cold bed. She had a lot of work to do and had all sorts of things due by the end of this week. She shouldn't have agreed to come out in the first place, but Emilie felt that she counted on Caroline too much for company and wanted to make some new friends.

Emilie glanced at her watch. It was still too early to leave. She would stay a while longer, make her excuses, and then go home. Alone.

Chapter 3

D ante sat in the Montreal Council chairman's office. The chairman, Dante's cousin Purson Maxaviel, sat behind his desk, talking on the phone. Dante was curious about why he had been called in for this meeting, but whatever it was had better not interfere with his plans for Thursday morning. He had resolved to wait in his father's office for Emilie. *Why should I give a damn about a human?* he scolded himself. *Speaking of which, I will most certainly be damned if I do.*

Dante sighed heavily and tried to focus on the purpose of this meeting. Perhaps it had to do with the empty council seat in Bangkok. Purson had been dropping hints about Dante taking the vacant Thailand seat. Dante had already made it quite clear that he wasn't considering it, even if his grandfather had held a seat there until his death.

Purson and many other councillors around the world had been asking Dante to do little favors for them over the years. Dante wasn't oblivious to their intent. They were testing his abilities. The council wanted to gauge the soundness of his advice and see how he reacted in crisis situations. Purson wasn't the only councillor who wanted to see Dante on the council. Dante just wasn't sure why. He was far too young for a seat, and he wasn't ruthlessly ambitious to the same degree as some of the other, more experienced candidates.

Yet the council's curiosity worked to his advantage. Even though he charged an astronomical fee for any "consulting" he did for them, his time was still in high demand and he made a tidy sum every year on top of his already substantial messenger income.

Dante couldn't shake the unease he felt inside. He expected Purson to try to enlist his help in dealing with some of the problems the Montreal office had been having in recent years with human organized crime in the city. Dante wasn't privy to all of the details, but the instability among the different crime rings was common knowledge. The problems weren't between his species and the humans. It was a battle among the humans for control, not of the entire city, but for the honor of being the council's distributors for their human customers as well as some of their satellite offices. Once the humans were done battling each other, everyone would breathe a little easier.

"You must be curious about why I've called you here," the chairman began.

"I'm at your service, sir," Dante replied.

"I'm glad to hear it. We need someone with an object-ive eye to assess a particular situation for us."

"Really? What kind of situation?"

"We need to find out if one of our potential new partners is performing their own transformations."

Dante nodded contemplatively, but he was quickly filling with dread. This was a serious offense. Humans could only be transformed into changelings by going through the council first. There were strict protocols to be followed and no exceptions were made. The repercussions of making forbidden transformations were serious indeed, and Dante wasn't excited about being placed in the middle of a situation like this. The last thing he needed was for some over-anxious criminal to spray him full of bullets.

"A great deal of money has been changing hands in this city, and unfortunately the councillors are divided as to what action is needed and with whom we should be doing business," the chairman explained.

In other words, some of the councillors' opinions on certain matters may not be as objective as they should be. Dante wasn't at all comfortable dealing with human criminals even if they were an essential part of everyday operations. Fortunately this type of situation was uncommon, because the humans usually took care of their own. Crime lords didn't want anyone cutting in on their profits, but there had been so much infighting in Montreal that chains of command were beginning to break down. Many valued business partners were coming to the council for help.

This put the council in a difficult position. Who should they help and how far should they extend their reach? The council had a strict policy of never getting involved in human business. By showing no favoritism they were rewarded with the loyalty of whoever was in charge. This also helped preserve security and secrecy for both species. But it was getting to the point where security was already being compromised. Too much violence drew unwanted attention, and the council couldn't afford having anyone with sensitive information being brought before human authorities for questioning.

If the rumors were true, crime lords were adding changeling mercenaries to their armies to give themselves an advantage over their rivals. This in itself was acceptable, but it considerably increased the risk of a security breach. It would be disastrous to have a changeling brought in for questioning or, worse, killed by human police. *What a mess*, Dante thought.

To add unauthorized transformations to the mix was only taking matters from bad to worse. For countless millennia, changing humans had always been done through the council. Unauthorized changelings running around major cities were just far too dangerous and needed to be handled swiftly and without mercy. Fortunately, transforming a human required a willing volunteer with the physical strength to survive the procedure. Plus the availability of the pure venom required was strictly regulated. The price of the venom made it an expensive way to enhance your ranks, and the high failure rate meant the costs usually outweighed the benefits.

The medical techniques for transformation had also been strictly guarded since the Fall of the first Angels. Unless a crime lord had purchased this information from someone with a serious death wish, they were using trial and error, which had never worked well for humans in the past. There were too many intricacies involved, including two commonly known factors.

First, transformation required a willing human. No one could be forced, and even many who thought they were willing died. The second was venom, but the exact dosage was still a mystery—too little venom meant a failed transformation and too much meant certain death.

Another obstacle was the freshness of the venom used. All venom had an expiration date, and age affected its effectiveness. It could be frozen to maintain freshness, but as soon as it thawed it began to lose its potency.

The council sold venom in various levels of purity to partners around the world. Some was used in the cosmetics industry as a secret ingredient in beauty creams. Some was used in the food industry in energy drinks and power bars. Dante often wondered if the makers of Red Bull were customers of the council. Red Bull's slogan "it gives you wings" would be much funnier if the drink contained the venom of fallen angels.

Venom-enhanced humans were common in organized crime. Low-grade venom was mixed in a mineral oil formula and sold to individuals in easy-to-consume gel caps. Small doses of venom could be used to give loyal men physical advantages without the effects being permanent, but it was expensive. Dante wondered how many governments bought caplets in bulk for their armies. The council's customers were kept very secret, so he could only speculate.

He roused himself from his musing and asked the chairman, "So what do you want me to do?"

Purson sighed heavily. "Well, we've done a great deal of reconnaissance of the situation, and it seems that a man by the name of Miguel Marquez is currently in charge around here. He controls other smaller cities around the world and has been requesting recognition from the council for quite some time. We haven't been taking him seriously, but I think that's about to change."

This type of thing wasn't part of Dante's job description. As the council's primary venom transporter, he served an invaluable role. They had a great deal to lose if his life was unnecessarily put in danger. He already faced injury and death on a regular basis. There was so much money to made in the venom trade. Moving it from one location to another opened opportunities for thieves, but inter-dimensional travel made the interception of shipments much more difficult.

Dante wasn't interested in becoming an intermediary between the council and human crime bosses. He had enough to worry about from people of both species wishing to see him removed from the equation. "You didn't answer my question," Dante said. "What exactly do you need me for?"

Purson leaned across his desk. "I'd rather not put you at risk, but we need someone with some sense to evaluate the situation and advise us as to what role we should play. It's also essential for us to determine if they have any unauthorized changelings in their employment."

"So you want me to meet with this Marquez?"

"No, he trusts us about as much as we trust him. At this point, he only sends his henchmen. You'll have to meet with a subordinate."

"Great..." Dante grumbled. "But I want twice my usual fee."

The chairman rolled his eyes. "Fine."

"I'm taking both Jude and Rodney in with me, and I want a team outside to intervene in case I need assistance. I don't want to walk into any traps."

"Don't worry. Marquez is new to this business, and he doesn't have much information about us. He won't know who you are. Remember, he wants a partnership. I doubt he would be stupid enough to provoke us."

"I don't make any assumptions when it comes to humans," Dante grumbled.

"You'll get whatever you need. You just let us know when you're ready."

"I can have a team assembled for this afternoon, if you can make the necessary arrangements on your end."

"Great! I'll be in touch."

Despite the seriousness of the council's request, Dante hoped that this little diversion would distract him from obsessing about Emilie. She had become a regular feature in his thoughts. She was only human and a few moments alone with her would probably be all it took for him to realize his mistake. Then he could wipe her from his memory and get back to his regular routine. Right now, he needed to focus on work and forget about her.

❦

Dante stood with Jude and Rodney outside the door to a changeling club called A Basement. Dante really enjoyed the irony behind the name. Whoever this Marquez guy was, he had a sense of humor. The council traditionally turned a blind eye to the many unauthorized clubs around the world, run by humans and catering mostly to changelings. As long as they were run by legitimate business partners who managed their affairs with an iron fist.

"Can you tell Jordano Gomez that Dante Ashton is here to see him?" Rodney asked the human guard at the door.

The man didn't seem impressed. Dante had a bad feeling about this. He looked back at the van in which they had arrived. There were five armed men ready in the back, and another five were taking up strategic positions close to the club. At the first sign of trouble, they would spring into action. They were all extremely well trained and experienced at cleaning up sticky messes.

Dante's group only had to wait a short time before a lovely young human woman came to collect them. As they entered the club another guard stepped toward Jude, wanting to pat him down for weapons. Jude's eyes flashed bright red and he growled menacingly. The man thought better of it and ran off to report that their guests were coming to the meeting armed.

Meanwhile Rodney was admiring the young lady waiting with them. She was average height for a human and looked about twenty years old. She had long blond hair and was wearing a provocative red dress. Her figure was slender and she had an ample bosom. She seemed very impressed with Rodney and ran her eyes over him suggestively. "Were you born or made?" she asked.

"We were all born," he replied proudly, gesturing to the others in his group. His answer appeared to bump them all up in her estimation.

This girl's lack of experience with pure-bloods wasn't surprising to Dante. Members of his class didn't frequent places like this, but there was a great deal of money to be made from clubs through the sale of blood and sex. He didn't know how much information these people had about the venom trade, but there was still some money in the sale of individual venom caplets to select human customers of the club.

It was three o'clock in the afternoon, and most of the handful of customers had slipped quickly out the back as soon as they had seen Dante's group, leaving the staff with little to do. A homely human girl was pole dancing and a ragged collection of waitresses and dancing girls were standing around, all under the watchful eyes of quite a few armed guards.

Their human companion ran her eyes over Jude, but he was intimidating on a good day and looking particularly dangerous today. She turned her attention to Dante. "Are you in charge?" she asked, and reached over as though she was about to run her fingers down his tie.

Jude's hand snapped over and seized hers. "Don't touch him," he hissed, releasing her distastefully.

Dante laughed softly as she looked him over with greater appreciation. "I am," he answered.

"You have a beautiful voice," she purred, rubbing her wrist and shooting Jude an angry glare.

"Thank you," Dante replied with a crooked grin. His mother's mother had been from the Enasvant family. They were considered to have the purest blood of his kind and had the most original traits. Dante's voice may have been inherited from her. He would have preferred her venom, but unfortunately that hadn't been the case.

Has this human girl been sent to beguile us? Dante wondered. *I hope not.* Just because many changeling men were willing to abase themselves in places like this didn't mean that all men of their species could be so easily distracted. Underestimating your opponent was a serious error.

It didn't take long for the guards to come back to collect them. As they walked through the club, Dante's heart sank. *What a seedy establishment,* he thought as he examined the place more closely. It was nothing like the clean and well-organized clubs run by the council. *You get what you pay for, I guess.* He had to keep in mind that not everyone had the money to afford services from the council. These people did offer a viable alternative and kept changelings out of the human population. This was also one of the reasons that the council tolerated them.

Jude threw him a concerned glance. "Nice place," he whispered sarcastically.

Dante laughed softly but kept further comment to himself. A well-dressed man approached, looking rather pleased with himself. He was flanked by two armed guards of his own. Changelings by the smell of them, but something didn't smell quite right about this Gomez. Dante couldn't quite place it. *Interesting,* he mused. *Maybe he has some level of mixed blood.*

Dante stood between Rodney and Jude in one of his best suits, trying to appear relaxed and confident. In his world, everybody knew his rank and abilities and treated him accordingly. For all this man knew, Rodney was in charge.

Dante had no idea how to behave in these types of situations and had been given minimal instructions. This was surely part of the chairman's test. Dante wasn't sure what qualities the council required of their candidates, other than ruthlessness and ambition. He hoped his inexperience wouldn't lead him to make any serious blunders.

"Mr. Ashton, my name is Jordano Gomez, it's a pleasure to meet you." He extended his hand to Dante.

"It's nice to meet you too," Dante replied, shaking his hand. "These are my associates, Jude Kamin and Rodney Saddan."

Gomez shook each man's hand in turn and introduced his own security detail as Leonard and Sid. Then he gestured toward a room at the end of the hall, which turned out to be his office. This room was much tidier and better decorated than the rest of the establishment.

"You'll have to forgive me, Mr. Ashton. I've been given the run around by a great many underlings from the council office who lack the authority to help us with our problems. We have been getting quite frustrated."

"Yes, well...I don't know how much help I'm going to be," Dante replied. "Why don't you briefly outline your most significant issues and I'll make sure to report everything back to the council."

Jordano Gomez sighed irritably, and one of his guards grumbled, "Oh great! They've sent us another pencil pusher with no balls."

Dante laughed softly and shook his head, but Rodney was more offended. He got right up in the man's face and growled, "How dare you speak so disdainfully about Dante! He's so far above you that you're just lucky your eyes can still focus on him."

Dante jumped up and put a soothing hand on Rodney's shoulder. "Easy, Rodney! These people don't understand how things work."

Gomez ran his eyes over Dante with greater appreciation. "Please, forgive Leonard. He often forgets to think before he speaks."

Leonard growled menacingly at Rodney but he had gotten himself under control and refused to be baited.

"Tell me, Mr. Ashton. How do you get that kind of loyalty from your men?"

Dante wasn't surprised by the question. Gomez was hinting that he had difficulty controlling his changeling soldiers. The transformation affected each individual differently. Adapting to their new bodies and instinctive drives was a challenge for some. Many became more emotionally volatile and aggressive. Also changelings tended to be self-serving. Loyalty for them was something to be bought and sold. Even among men with breeding, loyalty could be bought, but social class and family honor made the price vary considerably.

Dante thought carefully about his answer. "Jude and Rodney were trained by the council. Plus they are both sons of gentlemen and know how to behave as such." Both Jude and Rodney stood up taller. "Respect is earned in my world in the same way it is here. My birth is the only real difference. It automatically sets me above some others."

"Are you a nobleman, Mr. Ashton?" Gomez asked.

So this man has a basic knowledge of the class system. "Yes, I am," Dante answered carefully. He could tell that Gomez was gathering as much information about them as they were about him.

Gomez turned to his associate and said, "See, Leonard, they are taking us more seriously. They've finally sent us someone with some breeding." Leonard didn't look impressed, but Gomez sure did. "So tell me, Mr. Ashton. What exactly is your position with the council?"

Dante needed to be careful. He didn't want to paint himself as a target. "I'm a *malak*, a messenger."

"What?" Leonard snarled. "That's a step down from a pencil pusher!"

Rodney was affronted. He growled deep in his chest and flashed Leonard with his eyes.

"Rodney!" Dante commanded, and Rodney was instantly quiet. The other changeling guard, Sid, was sizing Jude up, but he didn't seem confident about his odds.

Gomez was watching everything with fascination. "What does *malak* mean?"

"It's an Aramaic word," Dante began. "It represents many things, but mostly it means a supernatural messenger, either an angel or a demon."

"Really?" Gomez murmured. "Does that make you a supernatural being?"

"Yes, it does," Dante answered, locking his eyes intently on Gomez.

Leonard snorted disdainfully, and both Jude and Rodney instantly began growling under their breath, their eyes glowing red with anger.

Gomez examined their faces with undisguised curiosity. "What causes the glow?"

"Changelings can make their eyes any color, including red, but the glow itself is genetic. Some can do it, but not many. It's thought to come from the blood of the Fallen," Dante explained.

"Leonard, could you please leave us," Gomez said. It was not a request.

Jude and Rodney grinned victoriously, making Leonard appear even less enthusiastic about leaving. "But they're all armed," he argued. "I can't leave you in here with just Sid."

Gomez laughed softly. "Leonard, if you can't behave then you can't stay. You should speak when spoken to," Gomez hissed. "Truth is," he added more soothingly, "any one of these men could kill all three of us without even drawing their weapons."

"Oh please...even that stuffed suit?" Leonard sneered, indicating Dante.

Rodney lost his composure and barked, "Dante is a world kick boxing champion. Plus he can travel in mesay, you moronic vampire! He doesn't even need us here. We're just for show."

Calling someone a vampire was the most extreme insult imaginable, and everyone knew it. Leonard, furious, charged Rodney, but he was more brawn than brains and was easily wrestled into submission. Dante stood with Jude close at his side, their eyes locked on Sid and Gomez. It only took a few short moments for Rodney to pin Leonard to the floor, clearly enjoying grinding Leonard's face into the carpet and listening to his joints and bones groan painfully.

"Enough!" Dante commanded. "Let him up so he can follow orders." He regretted his decision to include Rodney in this outing. He was one of Dante's favorite martial arts students and had a great deal of potential. Rodney was young and enthusiastic, but was still in training as a security officer. Dante had thought him ready for his first assignment, but obviously he had maturing to do in order to gain greater control.

Rodney released Leonard and jumped back, analysing his movements carefully. Leonard stood, brushed himself off, and shot Rodney an angry glare as he walked out of the room.

"Mr. Gomez, I apologize for Rodney. I certainly wouldn't appreciate any of my guests speaking to me or any of my employees so contemptuously," Dante said, shooting Rodney a scathing glance. Rodney's expression instantaneously went from smug to sheepish.

But Dante was losing patience. "Mr. Gomez, I trust you have better control of your other men. I'm beginning to wonder if we should have as much confidence in Mr. Marquez's ability to retain his position in this city."

"I'm the one who should apologize, Mr. Ashton," Gomez muttered. "We've gotten off on the wrong foot here, but we're in full control of all of our territories around the world. Some individuals are more volatile than others." He glanced at Rodney, who hung his head in shame. "I can assure you. They're the exceptions and not the rule."

"I hope so for your sake," Dante began. "But speaking of exceptions, all changelings need to be registered with the council. All of them."

"I see," Gomez replied evasively. His eyes flicked almost unnoticeably to Sid.

"We consider our security among the human population to be of the utmost importance, and we take responsibility for all of our own. If there are individuals among our numbers who are not under our control, then we're unprepared to accept responsibility for them, although their actions could be detrimental to us all."

"I see…" Gomez repeated.

Dante leaned in more closely and pointed his finger at Gomez. "I need to make myself very clear. If our security is in any way compromised by an unauthorized being then the wrath of Hayl will descend upon the individual responsible."

"Don't you mean the wrath of Hell?" Gomez asked.

Dante laughed and Rodney snorted disdainfully. "Ignorant human," he grumbled, too quietly to be heard by Gomez.

"I can understand your confusion, but in our legends Hayl was married to Satan's daughter Varenya. He won her hand in a tournament and went on to become one of Satan's top generals. So when we say Hayl's fury or the wrath of Hayl, we're referring to the full power of the armies of darkness," Dante explained.

Gomez was obviously enthralled. "Really? How wonderful...I mean...terrible. I would love to have you come to my home and tell me more about your legends. I've been studying your species my entire life. There really isn't very much information available, for obvious reasons."

Dante hesitated. The last thing he wanted was to socialize with human crime lords. "I could see if something could be arranged."

"Rodney mentioned another unusual word. Something about travel. What did he mean?"

Gomez was obviously trying to divert the conversation from the topic of changelings. Dante growled and shot Rodney another scathing glance. He didn't know if he was allowed to divulge this information, but Rodney had put him in an awkward position. "He was referring to my ability to travel in mesay. It comes from another Aramaic word, meaning 'in between.' We believe it refers to the manner in which the angels travel between Heaven and Earth to bring messages or to guide souls. But they are also said to travel between realities, as well as through time and space. We're not so fortunate, but there are those among us who can travel from one position on the globe to another almost instantly, as did the original Fallen. This ability is what makes me supernatural and why my title as a messenger makes me so important."

Gomez's mouth fell open and Sid sucked in his breath, giving away the fact that he must be a human creation because any council-created changeling would have been familiarized with all of the intricacies of their new world. "Teleportation…Really?"

Dante could almost see the target expanding on him. A dreadful feeling crept into his soul, making him anxious to leave.

"Are there many like yourself?" Gomez pried.

"My ability is not uncommon, but unfortunately we have had issues among our own kind, and over the years many have been killed, leaving the number with my ability at a minimum."

"I see…" Gomez mumbled, fascinated. "Are you a family man, Mr. Ashton?"

"I'm not married and have yet to father a child," Dante answered. *Are you plotting to use someone close to me in order to force me into serving your crime boss?* Dante wondered but kept silent. *I hope not for your sake because there's no hiding from people with my ability.*

Dante wanted to get back on track. "What would Mr. Marquez like the council to do to help him get established here in Montreal?"

"Men, for one thing," Gomez answered. "And venom."

This is where it gets interesting, Dante thought. "We can provide security for our side of venom distribution but we don't interfere in human turf wars. If Marquez can't hold this territory on his own then it isn't any of our concern. We deal with whoever is in charge. We don't ask questions or offer advice."

"Can we hire men from the council to help us...get organized?"

In other words, Gomez wanted to bolster security for his clubs. The safer his customers felt the more of them would come, especially women. "I'll mention it to the chairman."

"Do you know the chairman personally?" Gomez asked.

"He's a blood relative of mine, on my mother's side."

"Really?" Gomez looked as though he was gaining insight into just how high up the chain of command Dante was.

"About the venom, are we talking about pure venom or marketable capsules and darts?" Dante asked. The answer to this question was crucial.

"All of the above," Gomez answered casually. Far too casually. Pure venom was not easily accessible because of its rarity and price. Plus the council didn't trust humans—for good reason.

"Why do you need pure venom?" Dante inquired, deliberately letting his eyes stray to Sid.

Gomez paled and hesitated.

Do you think I can tell the difference between unauthorized and authorized changelings? Dante wondered. They all smelled the same. Perhaps Sid and Leonard had been included in this group to test how much the council could figure out. Hopefully this would discourage further transformations.

"We like to keep venom on hand in case of emergencies," Gomez explained.

"Oh…so we're talking about the fatal venom and not the venom for transformation," Dante said, playing dumb.

Gomez smiled. He knew that he was being backed into a corner. "Both would be great, if possible."

"The dosage of venom per capsule is monitored by the council. We don't care if humans want to consume more than one at a time. But we're not issuing manufacturing rights to venom capsules. We collect, process, and sell venom. Human middlemen can distribute it. Period. There are some very good synthetics out there. We turn a blind eye to that industry and leave it to you humans. Whatever emergencies you have should be covered by synthetics."

"Harsh words…" Gomez grumbled.

"Listen, if you want to turn some of your men, then make an appointment with the council. They will be changed safely and properly…for a price. Everyone wins. Why do you have to make illegal monstrosities?"

Gomez shot Sid a worried glance. He was growling softly under his breath. "Some men prefer to have complete control over their affairs," Gomez answered as though he didn't agree but was left with little choice in the matter.

"I hope you realize that, in the manufacturing process, we deliberately make the dosage necessary for transformation impossible for the human body to consume in capsule form. It's difficult to separate the venom from the mineral oil mixture. Too much oil induces vomiting. We do it on purpose. Plus the capsules dissolve rapidly in stomach acid and the venom is quickly absorbed. Too much venom in the blood becomes painful, preventing the victim from consuming enough capsules to cause a complete transformation. This recipe has been used for thousands of years."

Gomez looked as though he found Dante's little rant amusing but not particularly informative. Perhaps he was the man responsible for the experimenting. Dante didn't know how they were transforming these people, but he knew that it had to stop. Perhaps the human recipe for synthetic venom was getting closer to the original. Could a combination of the two be effective? The council would have to do some digging. If he recommended the strategic placement of council employees, much information could be gleaned.

"I'll let the council know of your concerns," Dante said. "We'll see what we can do. Have you received all of the paperwork about quotas, procedures, contacts, and sales figures for this territory?"

"Yes, we have everything. We just need time to get established and get used to the rules of the game."

Dante stood to leave. He offered his hand to Gomez. "It was nice meeting you. I hope you get up and running soon."

"Thank you for coming, Mr. Ashton. I have more confidence in our partnership after this conversation."

Gomez walked them partway down the hall. The young human girl who had met them at the door smiled warmly at Dante. She had been joined by several others. Gomez cleared his throat. "Mr. Ashton, Amber and her friends would like to show you a different level of hospitality, if you and your men have a few moments before you leave."

Jude started laughing softly under his breath and Rodney looked shocked that Gomez would try to bribe them so blatantly. Dante suppressed a grimace of disgust. "I'm very grateful for the offer, but I'm afraid I can't accept. I myself am bound by my religion."

"Religion?" Gomez asked. "Your people are religious?"

"Not all of the children of Satan are demons. Some of us long to return to Heaven," Dante explained, watching the girls look both disappointed and embarrassed.

"Really?" Gomez asked, fascinated. "What's the name of your religion?"

Dante smiled. How could he possibly explain his beliefs to such a malevolent creature? "I'm considered a Dark Angel because, although I have the blood of

Heavenly Angels, I was born in darkness and shame here on Earth. I have to earn a place in the Light."

"So in your world there are both angels and demons?"

"Yes."

"How remarkable...Are there many of you?" Gomez asked, his face ashen, as though realizing for the first time just how much he had underestimated his guests.

"No, unfortunately. Most of us are...demons." Dante smiled and resumed walking toward the exit.

"I beg you to excuse our ignorance," Gomez called. "And I want to apologize for offending you in any way."

"Don't worry, it's a common misunderstanding," Dante replied. "Have a nice day."

"You too."

Dante was pleased to hear the door close behind Rodney as he followed Jude up the steps into the light of day. He sucked in a deep breath, trying to get the smell out of his nostrils. *I hope I never have to darken this door again.* He focused his thoughts on something more pleasant. *Emilie...I'll see you tomorrow.*

Chapter 4

Thursday was a beautiful late summer day. The morning had started off cool and fresh. Now it was approaching noon and the temperature had risen, making Emilie feel warm in her jeans.

People were bustling around the campus, many out enjoying the fine weather. Days like this were special. Fall was coming. There were only at most a few weeks of nice weather left. By Thanksgiving it would be cold and wet.

Emilie was hurrying to Professor Ashton's office. He was rumored to be a tough professor, and she was grateful to him for giving her an extension on her thesis proposal. He expected it by lunch today, and she was determined not to be late.

Emilie was both exhausted and starving. She had stayed up half the night finishing off another assignment. She still couldn't believe her terrible luck this morning. She had been all set to print everything out when her stupid computer stopped working—or so she had thought. Once she had stopped swearing and jumping up and down, the problem had become obvious. The printer had simply run out of paper. She would have figured it out a lot faster if she hadn't been so tired and stressed out.

But her bad luck hadn't stopped there. She couldn't find a scrap of paper in her apartment and had torn the place up like a burglar trying to find some. In the end, she had been forced to make an emergency run to the store. *Days like this make me wish I owned a car*, she thought. As conveniently located as she was, walking everywhere was a pain when you were in a hurry.

By the time she got back, there was just enough time to print out her stuff and run. *Thank God for e-mail!* She had sent everything else off, but the proposal was to be dropped off personally as promised.

Unfortunately there had been no time for breakfast and most importantly: coffee. Emilie couldn't make it through the day without it. She would call Caroline as soon as she was done with her delivery. Perhaps they could meet for lunch.

Thankfully Emilie's apartment was only a five-minute walk from the university, so it didn't take long for her to reach the hall to Professor Ashton's office. A couple of girls were outside the office door, looking in. *Good*, she thought. *There are others waiting, so he hasn't left yet.* She quickened her pace.

As she approached, the two girls smiled at her and quietly pointed into the office. Emilie peeked around them to see what they were on about. The angel was back. Dante was leaning back in his father's office chair, stretched out with his expensive-looking shoes on the desk. He appeared to be asleep with the headphones of his iPod plugged into his ears, his face beautifully peaceful.

Emilie didn't want to wake him, but she needed to put her proposal on the desk, shoes or no shoes. She walked in, much to the frustration of the angel's admirers. They disappeared as soon as they saw her head in. Emilie realized too late that she should have taken the proposal out of her backpack in the hallway before walking in, because now she was going to have to rustle around in her bag to find it. She stood in front of the desk, staring at Dante as she scrambled to make a decision. Should she back out, get the proposal, and come back in or just make a bunch of noise and risk waking him? He had headphones on, so perhaps he wouldn't even notice.

Emilie didn't have long to contemplate. The angel's eyes opened and he looked straight at her as if he had been staring at her the whole time. Then he smiled. He quickly pulled his shoes off the desk and the earphones out of his ears.

"Emilie, right?" Dante asked in his magical voice.

Could my luck get any worse? she cursed. The most gorgeous man in the world actually remembered her name, and she was an absolute disaster. She hadn't showered, had barely brushed her hair, and she wore no makeup. Her sloppy T-shirt and baggy jeans desperately needed laundering, and the black bags under her eyes were so large that they could only be described as luggage. At least she had brushed her teeth. Blushing with embarrassment and tongue-tied, she tried to compose herself.

"Hello, Dante," Emilie finally managed to say, trying not to meet his watchful gaze. She was on the verge of tears, and crying would only compound her humiliation. She remembered the purpose of this visit and added, "I was supposed to meet your father here to give him something." She picked up her bag, tossed it on one of the office chairs, and started rummaging through it.

"I'm meeting my dad for lunch, but I think he's stood me up," Dante explained. He was watching her every movement and making her feel horribly self-conscious.

She managed to retrieve the proposal and was about to put it on the desk when the angel said something completely unexpected. "Are you hungry?"

Emilie stared at him in complete shock, not knowing how to answer.

"I hate eating alone," he continued. He wore a sad-puppy look on his face and seemed genuinely hopeful.

Emilie's stomach growled, and he smiled broadly. "That settles it. I'm taking you out for lunch." He jumped up from his chair, walked around the desk, and gestured for her to precede him out of the office.

"Okay," she responded as she dropped the proposal on the desk, picked up her bag, and started for the door. *Maybe my luck isn't so bad after all*, she mused.

As they walked down the hallway, Emilie scrambled to think of something to say. "I didn't get any breakfast this morning," she mentioned.

"I have to eat regularly or I'm just not myself," he replied, and chuckled as though he had made a little joke.

Emilie's brain was running at half capacity. With little sleep, no food, and especially no caffeine, she wasn't feeling particularly sharp. But she wasn't prepared to ask him to explain himself. She also didn't want to baffle him with any stupid questions, and so she decided to talk as little as possible. Her general appearance was bad enough; she didn't want to make matters worse by giving him the wrong idea about her intelligence and personality.

Emilie wasn't in the habit of going out with random men. Her internal safety mechanisms were flashing warning alarms in her brain. She understood enough of social psychology to know that there wasn't a general stereotype for psychotics. *Look at Paul Bernardo, for instance; he was supposed to have been fairly good looking and charming. And one of the biggest psychopaths ever convicted in Canadian history. How many women had he murdered? Didn't he murder his wife's little sister?*

She scolded herself for allowing her thoughts to meander down such a dark path. There couldn't be anything strange about a beautiful, probably wealthy and successful man like Dante asking a homely university student, who he's met only once for two seconds, out for lunch. Alone. *Oh boy!*

Emilie scanned Dante as discreetly as possible. He was something to behold. He walked with grace and confidence, ignoring all of the girls staring at him with obvious admiration. Why did she have to be seen in her current state next to him? *Great!*

He was wearing black jeans and a black T-shirt. He also had on a black, long-sleeved silk shirt with a thin Chinese dragon stitched in gold, white, and red wrapped around the back hem. *Lucky dragon*, she thought to herself, watching it wriggle over Dante's behind as he walked. He looked phenomenal. Somehow these loud and unusual clothes suited him, and not just anyone could pull off this kind of fashion statement.

Emilie had remained silent for longer than was polite. They were already on their way out of the building. She had come in the campus entrance, but they were leaving by the door out to the street. Emilie saw Dante's two friends sitting together on a bench by the doors, looking bored.

Jude, she remembered was the big guy's name, was playing with a hand-held video game. Colin was reading a book. She couldn't see the title, but he seemed fairly comfortable behind it. Jude noticed them first and jabbed Colin in the ribs with his elbow. Colin was obviously irritated as he glared first at Jude and then in Emilie's direction. They watched uncertainly for a moment as she and Dante approached, and then Jude started getting up as though he was planning to join them. Emilie noticed Dante shake his head almost imperceptibly and motion, as discreetly as possible, for Jude to sit back down.

To her surprise, Jude complied, but watched them pass with a very puzzled expression on his face. Colin just stared with his mouth hanging slightly open, as if he'd just swallowed a bug and was gasping for air.

"I spend way too much time with my friends," Dante said casually to her.

Emilie didn't bother to disguise the bewildered look spreading across her face. Dante bent down and whispered directly into her ear as though trying to prevent Jude and Colin from overhearing. "The three of us share a condo here downtown. Don't worry about them. We've been living together for so long they've forgotten we're actually three separate people."

"I see," Emilie remarked, smirking. Either he was completely insane or she was. *What am I doing?* she thought.

Dante stopped in front of a sporty red convertible. Emilie saw a wildcat hood ornament and assumed it was a Jaguar. He unlocked her door and held it open for her. He must have sensed her hesitation because he said, "Don't worry, I don't bite." A huge, mischievous grin decorated his handsome face.

Somehow his words did nothing to comfort her, and against her better judgment she got into the car. *I hope I don't regret this decision,* she scolded herself. *I know what they say about curiosity.*

Dante shut the door and walked around the car, laughing to himself. He got in and smiled at her again. "I promise to keep my hands on the wheel," he explained, starting to look sheepish. "I'll leave the top down so you can jump out if I don't behave myself."

"I don't usually get into cars with strangers," Emilie admitted, but she didn't want to sound rude.

"Good policy," he replied. "Look, if you're not comfortable with this, you're free to leave. I'm not going to drag you off against your will." Dante brought his hands up as though surrendering to her. "I do know a great place to get a steak, and I'm starved."

"Steak sounds good," Emilie said, although she was still wondering if she was making a mistake. He was just too enticing for her to refuse him anything. She had been thinking about him practically non-stop since they'd met. She wasn't going to pass up an opportunity to spend some time with him. She would take her chances and stay, but she would be on her guard. There was something odd about this guy, but her curiosity couldn't be denied.

Dante appeared satisfied with her response. He put on a pair of really dark sunglasses and slipped the key into the ignition, making the engine roar.

"Are you sure?"

"Yes, but I've got my eye on you," Emilie warned.

"Okay, then. Let's go," he said cheerfully as he pulled out into traffic.

Soothing classical music was playing on the stereo. Something Emilie recognized but couldn't place. "What's playing?" she asked.

"Vivaldi's 'Four Seasons,'" he answered. "I love to listen to this on days like today. It's so beautiful out. We're still in summer but there's a hint of fall in the air." He looked over at her and flashed her a dazzling grin. "I can't wait for the leaves to start changing colors."

"Montreal is spectacular in the fall," she remarked, starting to feel more relaxed. "I missed the fall colors when I lived in Vancouver. Vancouver doesn't really have fall. They just have a long summer then it starts raining and doesn't stop until spring," she explained nostalgically.

"I've been to Vancouver. Nice city." Dante was concentrating on the road so his voice was somewhat distracted. "I travel a lot for work."

"Oh really? What do you do?"

"I'm a messenger," he answered.

Messengers must get paid a lot better than she thought. Emilie examined him with a critical eye. He was dressed in what she assumed were designer clothes. She wouldn't actually know because she couldn't afford any. He was also driving what she assumed was a fairly new car, but then again, she knew nothing about cars. She had always thought Jaguars were more for old men, but this one was very young and sporty.

"What kind of messenger are you?" Emilie asked. She hadn't meant for her confusion to be so apparent in the tone of her voice.

"Obviously not the kind you're thinking of. No bicycle shorts for me," Dante answered with a chuckle.

Emilie was pleasantly distracted, imagining his muscular body in a pair of tight shorts.

"I work for a private organization," he explained. "I take packages and documents to their offices around the world."

"I didn't realize that people still sent documents any way other than by e-mail or fax."

"The people I work for are very old-fashioned," he said, laughing to himself again. "Anyway, many contracts still need to be signed by all parties involved, and it's easier to have the documents brought to them. Faxing back and forth is fine for most things, but sometimes documents are important enough to require my services. Plus you still can't fax a package."

"Being your kind of messenger must pay pretty well," she commented and quickly regretted it. She had been horribly rude. It wasn't polite to discuss personal income with perfect strangers. She had just blurted it out without thinking. She needed some caffeine fast or she risked embarrassing herself further.

Dante laughed uncomfortably. "There aren't many people in my line of work who are as..." he paused, cogitating. "I think the word I'm searching for is 'efficient' as I am. Supply and demand. Have you studied any economics?"

"No, but I know what supply and demand means. When the supply of a good or service..." Emilie gestured to him when she mentioned the word service, "...is low and the demand for that good or service is high, then the price goes up."

Dante seemed impressed. "Exactly," he stated, obviously satisfied with her answer.

She hadn't been paying the slightest bit of attention to where they were going and didn't have the foggiest clue where they were. She really wasn't thinking very clearly today. Truth be told, she hadn't been in Montreal long enough to know her way around very well yet.

Dante managed to squeeze the car into a rather small parking spot. He jumped out and came around to open the door for Emilie, who was busy digging her wallet out of her backpack. She tried to climb out as gracefully as possible with him watching her so closely.

"The restaurant is just around the corner," he said, beeping his car alarm over his shoulder.

At the restaurant, he held the door for her. Emilie decided that if he was a psychopath, at least he was one with good manners. The restaurant was bustling. As she glanced around, she became concerned about whether or not they would get a table. There seemed to be a couple just leaving and the waiter asked them to wait as he cleared the soon-to-be unoccupied table.

"Smells good in here," she said, uncertain about what to say next.

Dante's phone went off. He picked it up and checked who was calling. "I'm sorry, I have to take this." Emilie just nodded blankly as he answered, "Hello."

There was a pause while he listened, his face expressionless. "I'll get back to you later, okay?"

She could hear someone talking very loudly on the other end of the phone.

"Thank you for your concern, but I have everything under control," Dante continued. The voice on the other end was getting louder still. "Okay then." Dante glanced at his watch and Emilie could have sworn it was a Rolex. "I'll see you in about two hours. Good-bye." He put his phone away, rolling his eyes apologetically. "Some people are so impatient," he added.

Emilie had the impression that he had hung up on the caller. His phone went off again. He glanced at the number but didn't answer. "I'm so sorry about this," he said and poked at the phone until it stopped.

The waiter had come back for them, and Dante continued poking his phone on the way to the table. He smiled and said, "Sorry about that again." The phone bleeped quietly, and Dante just rolled his eyes and didn't even look at it.

They stared at their menus in silence for a while, until the waiter came back to take their drink orders. Emilie desperately needed some caffeine and ordered a Coke. Dante ordered a beer. She didn't know if she was happy about him drinking when driving, but a body his size could surely process one beer. She tried to remember if she had enough money in her wallet to take a taxi if Dante drank too much. She wasn't going to get back into his car if he did. They couldn't be too far from the university. They hadn't been driving for very long at all.

They sat quietly together for a few minutes as they took in the atmosphere of the place. It was very busy indeed. She felt a great deal more comfortable being out in public and was looking forward to getting better acquainted with Dante. She peeked at him from behind her menu a couple of times. He was just too handsome to resist, making it difficult for her to concentrate on anything other than him.

Emilie scrambled to fill up some of the silence. "I'm addicted to caffeine, I'm afraid to say. I haven't had my fix yet today," she said. Although she didn't want to draw too much attention to the fatigue on her face.

"Caffeine doesn't affect me much," Dante replied dismissively.

They sat quietly together for a bit longer, and Emilie busied herself with the menu. She was trying to figure out what to say next when the waiter came back with their drinks. Emilie ordered a chicken salad, not wanting to be seen as too much of a pig.

Dante ordered a steak as predicted. "I want it very rare," he explained. "I like 'em still mooing." When the waiter was out of earshot he added, "Well, you've asked me about what I do. How about we talk about you now?"

"Okay…" she answered. "What do you want to know?"

"Why are you studying anthropology?"

"It doesn't seem to be a very practical career choice, does it?"

"You're talking to a messenger, remember? I'm not one to judge someone's career choices. What is it about anthropology in particular that interests you?"

"I find human cultures intriguing. Over time we've changed so much, but even today people are very similar in some ways and very different in others. I enjoy the basic comparisons. Like, for example, a woman's role in society. Religious mythology is also very interesting. Religion is one of the things we have most in common with each other, and yet it can still drive us so far apart."

Emilie laughed uncomfortably and paused. "Well, we shouldn't talk about religion or politics. Those are two of the most controversial subjects, aren't they?" She suddenly felt embarrassed. "I'm talking too much. I'm so sorry."

"You're doing fine," Dante soothed. "Don't worry about me. My father's an anthropologist, remember? Are you thinking of becoming an academic?"

"Probably not. I'm actually more interested in forensics. I find skeletons fascinating, but I'm too squeamish about blood and guts to be a doctor. Though I do find a good mystery irresistible. Forensic anthropology has come a long way in recent years, and there's more demand for that kind of expertise. I'm thinking of taking a psychological profiling course next year. I'll have to see. I really haven't made up my mind yet."

"Sounds a bit gruesome to me," Dante remarked, smiling broadly. "Out of curiosity, where were you born?"

"Here in Montreal, at the Royal Victoria hospital. How about you?"

Dante smiled slyly and replied, "I thought we were talking about you?"

Emilie smiled back at him uncertainly. "I was just asking."

He nodded quietly. "I was born in Thailand, in Bangkok. How long did you live in Vancouver?"

She was confused by his terse reply. He didn't seem to want to talk about himself. Was he deliberately trying to force the conversation back in her direction by distracting her with questions about herself or was he just being polite? "My family moved to Vancouver when I started middle school, and then I went to UBC for my undergrad degree in anthropology. I wanted to come back to Montreal for my graduate studies." Emilie decided that she would play along with his game and end her statement with a question about him. "You don't look Asian. What was your family doing in Thailand?"

Dante paused as if he suspected her of being up to something. "My father was in Thailand doing research. Would you consider yourself superstitious?"

Emilie laughed. She didn't know if he was doing it on purpose or if it was unconscious. He was answering her questions quickly and then asking her a question as though trying to change the subject. His evasiveness was only creating an aura of mystery around him, adding one more thing to the list of reasons she already liked him. "Superstitious? No, I would not consider myself superstitious. But I would have to say I'm careful about how I live my life because I do believe in karma. How old are you?"

He appeared taken aback by her question, or maybe it was her answer. But she was distracted by the waiter's arrival. The smell of food made Emilie remember her hunger, and she was happy to pause to eat. Besides, it was his turn to ask a question, so the pressure was off of her.

After a few bites Dante asked, "How old do you think I am?"

So he had been surprised by her question and not her answer. She must have taken him off guard, because he only asked her a question without answering hers first. She examined him carefully, exaggerating her appraisal before saying, "Twenty-six. Am I right?"

"You're good," Dante purred with a mysterious grin. "I'm definitely twenty-six. How many boyfriends have you had?"

Now it was Emilie's turn to be taken off guard. If she didn't know better, she would have thought he was asking her a personal question to throw her off somehow. He was definitely stepping things up a notch. She took her time answering, using her food as an excuse to avoid his question. Finally she said, "I've had a lot of boyfriends, but only two more serious relationships. How about you?"

He grinned broadly and contemplated his response while he chewed. "I haven't had any boyfriends. Do you currently have a boyfriend?"

Emilie laughed. Dante was smarter than he looked. And he wasn't gay. "How's your steak?" she asked, making a bit of a disgusted face while staring at his blood-soaked plate.

He was already almost finished his meal. The meat sure was blue, but he had ordered it that way. *Oh, I've broken out of our pattern*, she realized. She had avoided his question. He had thrown her off guard.

The way he was staring at her suggested he'd also noticed the shift. "My steak is excellent as always. How's your salad?"

From the way in which he had crinkled his perfect nose, she could tell he didn't think much of salads. "Not too bad. Are you going anywhere interesting on business soon?"

He smiled, as though pleased with her response. "I'm going to Beijing on Saturday. Do you currently have a boyfriend?"

Emilie had to smile and shake her head at Dante's persistence. She had hoped he hadn't noticed her omission. She wanted to steer things away from personal questions. She felt some tension building between them and wasn't sure what it meant. He couldn't possibly be interested in her romantically. Maybe, in her current physical condition, he couldn't believe that *anyone* would be interested in her romantically. She toyed with the idea of asking about his favorite sexual position. Although she was concerned it would only lead into an even more uncomfortable conversation. Plus she still hadn't decided if he was a psychopath, so she figured she'd better keep it clean. Emilie had a great alternative though. "Not currently. Are you asking me out?"

He stopped chewing and gawked. She was so confident in his romantic disinterest that she wasn't worried about his answer. Flirting was always so much easier and more relaxed when you knew nothing serious was going on. Dante sat blinking in shock, struggling for a response.

Emilie just smiled sweetly and cocked her head, waiting for his answer. His hesitation gave her some time to scarf down more of her salad.

Dante thought about his reply much longer than she would have expected for innocent flirtation. Perhaps he was interested. His phone went off and snapped him out of his contemplation. He checked the incoming number then snarled in an animalistic way. He poked the phone angrily and put it away. "I'm sorry," he soothed in a calm and musical voice that didn't match the strange noise he had just made. "I've turned it off so we won't be interrupted again. Now where were we?"

He's avoiding the question, Emilie thought to herself. She didn't know what that meant. Should she let him get away with it or should she pursue it further? Maybe he didn't want to hurt her feelings. She decided to let him out of it for now. "I just can't remember. Are you sure you can't remember?"

He seemed pleased by the fact that she was allowing him out of the previous question. He said slyly, "No, I'm afraid not." But his beautiful brown eyes were twinkling. "Do you want any dessert?"

Emilie tittered quietly behind her hand. She was starting to like this guy, a little too much for her comfort level. She hoped to see him again and not just because he was easy on the eyes. She found him interesting. He had a good sense of humor and a sharp mind, not a common combination. "No, thanks. I'm full. Am I going to see you again?" she asked rather boldly, her eyes locked on her plate. She picked at the remains of her salad with her fork, afraid to meet his gaze.

"I think I would like that. So are we friends?"

Emilie still wasn't looking at him, and she wasn't sure how to answer his question. The waiter came back and took Dante's empty plate and asked them if there was anything else they wanted. Dante shook his head and asked for the bill. Emilie let the waiter take away what remained of her salad.

Friends…It's a good start. Better than nothing. She decided to repeat his answer back to him. "I think I would like that. Can men and women ever truly be friends?"

He sat and smiled at her for a bit, considering what to say next. "Now there's a good question. I've never had any female friends. What do you think?" He rested his elbow on the table and put his chin in his hand. He blinked at her through his thick lashes.

She was having a hard time concentrating, and she suspected that was his intent. "I've had quite a few male friends. It seems to work okay as long as everybody knows the rules. Do you have any requirements?" She rested her own elbow on the table and batted her aqua eyes at him just as mischievously.

Dante responded to her copy-cat flirtation with a devilish grin. "Due to my inexperience in this department, I'll have to think carefully about it and get back to you next time. Do you have any rules for me?"

"I'm pretty easygoing, but if you cross the line, I'll let you know." Emilie pointed her finger at him for emphasis. "Now how much do I owe for my salad?"

Dante had taken the bill as soon as the waiter came to the table. He had discreetly stuffed some money into the folder and sat with it under his elbow. He smiled sweetly and said, "I told you that I was taking you out for lunch. Shall we go?"

Emilie scrambled to think of another question to ask him. "I'm ready whenever you are. Can you take me back to the university?"

He laughed. There was a long pause before he said, "It would be my pleasure. Will you give me your phone number?"

It was Emilie's turn to laugh, but she was ready with an answer. "It would be my pleasure. Do you have a pen and paper?"

He patted himself tentatively but found nothing. "I don't, but I'll put it in my phone. Do you want my number?"

He took out his phone and she went to do the same but realized she'd left it in her backpack in the car. *Aack!* Her concentration was shattered. She couldn't think of anything else to say. Emilie rolled her eyes in frustration and growled, "Damn it! You win this time."

Dante smiled graciously. "I didn't play perfectly myself. I would call it a tie."

"You're being generous."

"I haven't enjoyed a conversation this much in a very long time," he said. "Normally I don't have to be on my toes so much while making small talk."

Dante entered her phone number into his cell, then stood up and gestured for her to precede him, rushing to hold the door open for her. They walked around the corner to the car while Emilie tried to come up with something interesting to discuss.

"Thank you very much for lunch. I really had a good time," she said. She needed to remember her own manners.

He unlocked the car and opened the door for her. "Oh! That reminds me," he exclaimed. He stood on the sidewalk, took out his wallet, and started ruffling through it. He found what he was looking for, put his wallet back, came around to his side, and sat down beside her.

"I wanted you to have this." Dante handed her his business card. It had a beautiful graphic of a griffin with its wings spread and its claws outstretched on the right-hand side. His name, number, and the word *Messenger* were in the middle.

"It's very nice and simple," Emilie commented, trying to be sure to convey the compliment intended by her statement.

"I could be considered almost self-employed, but I work for one organization almost exclusively. They call whenever they need me, so I don't have one of those nine-to-five jobs. I get some flexibility, but travel takes a lot of time, so I'm often away." He started the car and pulled out into the street.

"So you'll be in Beijing on Saturday. How exciting."

"You have no idea what crowded means until you've been to China," he replied, shaking his head thoughtfully. "It's such a beautiful country. Did you know that many of our most popular garden variety flowers were first grown in China?"

"I had no idea," Emilie answered. She was genuinely envious of his travels and was losing herself in the fantasy of accompanying him on his journey. "Do you have room for me in your carry-on luggage? I would love to go to China one day."

"Unfortunately I tend to travel light. I do get a lot of travel miles though. Maybe I'll take you someday."

Emilie allowed herself to believe in his sincerity. "Excellent. I promise not to get in your way." She sighed dreamily. "Where else have you been?"

He looked a bit nervous as he answered, "I've been all over the world. But it's a big planet. I haven't seen everything yet."

"It must be so nice, travelling all over the world and actually get paid for it." She could only imagine how wonderful it would be to spend all year jetting from one country to the next.

"It can be fun, if you have someone to enjoy it with. I'm always happier when I travel with Jude or Colin. Otherwise it can be lonely."

"Do you work with Jude and Colin?"

He cleared his throat, his brows furrowed suspiciously. "I guess you could say that they work with me."

They had arrived back at the university. He stopped in front of the entrance to the building containing Professor Ashton's office. Their quick return was a disappointment. Emilie wasn't ready to leave him just yet.

She felt fairly confident that Dante wasn't a psychopath. He was gorgeous and mysterious. Everything a woman could want, and want him she did. Unfortunately she didn't know if she would ever see him again.

"Thanks again for lunch. Call me when you get back from China if you find yourself alone for lunch sometime." She undid her seat belt and gathered up her belongings.

"No problem. It was fun. I'll definitely call you when I get back."

As Emilie opened the door to leave, she glanced over at Dante. She really wanted to lean over and kiss him. She wasn't brave enough to try and he made no move toward her, so she just slid out as gracefully as she could.

"Thanks again. Good-bye!"

Dante waved to Emilie as he pulled out into traffic. She watched him drive up the street and turn out of sight. A deep sadness crept into her stomach as he disappeared.

ψ

As Dante reached the top of the street, he checked his rear-view mirror. Emilie was standing there watching him drive away. He was tempted to turn the car around and pick her up again. It was still early on this beautiful day. They could find something to do together. He growled longingly to himself. He definitely knew what he'd *like* to do with her.

He stomped on the gas pedal in frustration, flying a bit recklessly around the corner. *Damn it! Get a grip. She's only a human. Nothing special,* he scolded himself. But having to admit that a human could get to him like this only irritated him more.

He stomped on the brake suddenly. In his distracted state, Dante had almost driven through a stop sign. *Focus!* The last thing he needed was to be stopped by the police. *Come on now...It isn't far to the condo.*

Emilie's scent still lingered in the vehicle. Even with the roof open he could smell her. He took a deep breath, filling his lungs almost to bursting, savoring every second of it. Unfortunately it wasn't making it any easier for him to focus on the road. *Human girls aren't supposed to smell so good, unless you're really hungry...*

He shook his head and blinked his eyes, trying to redirect his thoughts. Thankfully he was almost home.

He arrived at the condo, punched in his code to open the garage, zipped into his spot, and jumped out of the car. He beeped the alarm over his shoulder and headed for the stairwell. Once there, he looked all around and listened carefully. No one.

Dante liked having the ability to travel through inter-dimensional space. It made getting around in a hurry so much more convenient. But he couldn't let himself be seen doing it. He stepped through the doorway in space and came out in the entrance of his condo. *Home sweet home!*

Jude leaned back in the couch and stared angrily at him. Colin looked up from his book and appeared to be assessing Dante's mood. Dante tried to radiate his irritation to discourage either man from initiating any kind of lecture.

Too bad that Jude couldn't take a hint. "Have fun?" he sneered.

"Yes and no," Dante answered evasively, walking to his bedroom.

"Where are you going now?" Jude called from his seat, completely disregarding the agitation pouring off of his friend.

"I'm going downstairs to run a couple of hundred miles," Dante growled as he changed.

Jude leaned over to Colin and said, "He likes her."

Even from his bedroom, Dante could hear Colin's disappointed sigh. "I have to agree. How unfortunate for us all."

"And I was just getting used to Montreal," Jude complained. "The weather is great here. You almost never have to be outside."

"Will you guys cut it out? I can hear you!" Dante snarled as he emerged from his room wearing his track clothes. "Do you want to come or are you two going to sit up here and gossip like little old ladies while I'm gone?"

Jude laughed and stood up. "At least you've calmed down a bit."

"I have to," Dante muttered. "It would be different if she was one of us."

"You'd better believe it. She's a human civilian. Off limits," Jude replied with a surprising amount of sympathy in his tone considering the seriousness of the situation.

"Hurry up, Jude. I can't wait all day," Dante grumbled. "I need to burn off some of this energy fast." He took a cleansing breath and held it for a moment before letting it out slowly.

Dante was upset with himself. He should have known better than to tempt himself in such a way. Spending time with Emilie was supposed to have made him realize that she was just like every other human. *Why do I feel as though I've been somehow bound to this girl?* he wondered. *I was hoping this was all just chemistry or some passing attraction.*

But it was much more complicated. Emilie was beautiful, perceptive, intelligent, exciting, and forbidden. He definitely couldn't see her again. It was too risky. He did like this girl. He liked her a lot. That was the crux of the problem, because he could never have her, and Dante was used to getting what he wanted.

ॐ

Wow...What an incredible day, Emilie thought cheerfully. Lunch with Dante Ashton. She shook her head incredulously. He wasn't just drop dead gorgeous. He had a playful sense of humor and he was intelligent. He was interesting and definitely mysterious. He was absolute perfection. These thoughts only made her miserable, because she didn't have a snowball's chance in Hell of getting him.

Why is it that I always fall for the unobtainable ones, she cursed. She had a bad habit of choosing emotionally unavailable men. Caroline was right. Emilie did attract bad boys. *Why are bad boys so good in bed?* Some of her relationships had been short but hot. She had been burnt by love, but never very seriously. She had always protected herself, in every sense of the meaning. She had never entirely given herself over to a man.

Her most serious relationship had ended because he had felt her reluctance to commit to their relationship. Jeremy Forbes was a good guy. Emilie had loved him, just not in the way he needed to be loved. It had turned out for the best because long distance relationships rarely worked out.

I wonder if Dante is a bad boy? she mused. *He's probably a playboy and I should just forget about him.*

She was on her way back to her apartment and felt totally drained. It was almost two-thirty, and she had one lecture from four to six. It seemed like a lot had happened already and yet it was still early in the day. Maybe she would nap for an hour before class.

She took her phone out of her bag to check for messages. Caroline had called. Emilie dialled her number. She couldn't remember when Caroline had class on Thursdays. She wasn't answering. Her voice mail picked up, and Emilie waited for the beep. "Caroline, you'll never in a million years guess who I had lunch with today. Professor Ashton's son Dante! Call me and we'll talk."

Caroline would call as soon as she got the message. Emilie just wasn't sure what she would tell her friend. Probably everything...as usual.

ૐ

Through the fog of sleep, Emilie heard the phone ring. She rolled over and grabbed it off of her night stand. She checked who was calling. It was Caroline, of course. It was also four-thirty, and Emilie was missing her lecture. *Damn it...*

"Hello," Emilie mumbled.

"Wow…You've got to be kidding me, right?" Caroline demanded.

Emilie couldn't help but smile. She still couldn't believe it herself. "No. I'm definitely not kidding. I had lunch with him today."

"Wow, that's incredible. What are the chances of running into him twice in one week?"

"I don't know. Math has never been my strong suit. I just scraped through statistics, remember?" Emilie replied. "I ran into him in Professor Ashton's office and he asked me out for lunch."

"So tell me everything!"

Emilie ran through every detail from the minute she had walked into Professor Ashton's office to the minute Dante had dropped her off at the university.

"You've got it bad for this guy already. I can hear it in your voice."

Emilie sighed. "I don't know. I'm a realist. With the way I looked today combined with the fact that I had to make conversation without sleep or caffeine, it will be miraculous if I ever hear from him again. Anyway, he said we could be friends. It's what you say to people you're not interested in."

"One way or another, keep yourself under control. I don't want to see you get your hopes up and get hurt. There are plenty of good men in this city. You haven't been here for long, so give a few others a chance to make an impression on you. They aren't all like Nick the octopus," Caroline suggested with a chuckle.

"I know. I know. But for today, I'm going to enjoy warm and fuzzy feelings about Dante Ashton's big, flirty brown eyes."

"Yeah…Like it's only his eyes you'll be thinking of," Caroline teased crudely.

"Hey! I said I'm a realist, but I'm allowed to have an imagination."

Chapter 5

Dante sat at his office desk in his home in Bangkok, lost in thought. He had finished a long day's work in Beijing but travelling in mesay meant that, even if he worked in one city, he could easily return home to an entirely different location. Dante felt truly at peace in his grandfather's Thai mansion and had come here to settle his nerves.

He was absently twirling a small jade bracelet around his finger. He had bought it for Emilie from a street vendor in Beijing. He and Jude had been out for lunch, and as soon as Dante had seen the bracelets, he'd thought of her. He didn't know why he had stopped and bought one. He just had to.

Jude had lectured him all through lunch, but Dante had only paid the barest amount of attention because he was already chastising himself over the fact that he had just given himself a reason to see her again. Everything inside him and everyone around him was telling him not to see her again. Why was he torturing himself over this girl?

Dante was debating whether or not to call her. No matter what he was doing, he couldn't get her out of his mind. He had worked for twelve hours transporting cases of high-grade venom from Beijing to smaller offices around the world with no in-house supply of their own. He was exhausted and should be in bed resting up for another long day, but he just couldn't relax.

A servant knocked softly on the door and opened it. "Colin is here to see you, sir."

"Let him in, Renard, and thank you," Dante replied.

He quickly tucked the bracelet into his pocket and opened some computer files to give the impression that he had been sorting through some of his investments instead of indulging his romantic delusions about some insignificant human girl.

Colin poked his head into the office and said, "Listen, I know it's late, but I just left the temple and I thought I would drop by to see you."

Dante gestured for him to come in and have a seat. He tried to act oblivious about the reason for Colin's visit, but he knew exactly what this was about. He already regretted Colin's involvement in this situation. Things would be so much easier if Colin was blissfully unaware. Jude was bad enough, but Colin wasn't going to leave this alone, and Dante was feeling particularly sensitive about this subject. "Sure, Colin. What's bothering you?" he asked.

Colin seemed hesitant to begin. He kept his gaze locked on the desk as he said, "I need to talk to you about what happened the other day."

"Okay..." Dante muttered, bracing himself for a lecture.

"Dante, I've known you since the day you were born, and I've never seen you look at a human like that before.

As a matter of fact, I doubt I've ever seen you look at any woman the way you look at her."

Dante rolled his eyes. "It's nothing, Colin, seriously."

"I'm worried about you," Colin admitted.

"I haven't seen or talked to her since, so don't worry."

Colin was visibly relieved. "Are you planning to?"

"I won't call her, don't worry."

"What if she calls you?"

Humans had stricter rules regarding personal relationships. They had more gender inequality. Therefore women, on average, were less bold and consequently less likely to be the first to call a man. "She's not gonna call me, Colin. Stop worrying."

"What if she does?" Colin repeated.

"I don't know. It depends."

"Just let this go, Dante. Please."

"I've got everything under control," Dante lied, but with every intention of rectifying the situation. "Just give me a little time to work this through my system. Okay?"

"I don't know," Colin began. "What exactly do you need to work through?"

"I'm just curious about her. It's completely harmless." Dante sighed heavily. "Just give me a chance to realize that I'm wasting my time."

"You can't be wandering around with this girl. Without Jude. It's not safe."

"I know. I know. I won't let myself get too predictable. I just need to do this."

"Why? She's a human."

"I know, but if I don't get her out of my system, it's going to eat me up inside. It won't take long, I'm sure."

"Just don't do anything stupid."

Dante could barely bring himself to look into Colin's concerned face. His blue eyes were sincere and pleading. Colin had taken Dante under his wing at an early age. Colin was a high-ranking nobleman, a devout Angel, and a dedicated spiritual advisor. Throughout his teen years Dante had been torn between embracing the life of a Dark Angel and following in his grandfather's demonic footsteps. It had been a difficult time for Colin, and Dante didn't want to disappoint him after they had come so far. *What can I possibly say to make this acceptable? Nothing.* Dante knew he should feel offended by Colin's lack of faith in him, but somehow he was just as worried as Colin. "Come on," Dante replied. "What do you think I'll do?"

Colin clamped his jaw shut, his muscles bulging in his cheeks. "I don't want to go there," he muttered through gritted teeth.

"Please..." Dante hissed. Now he was offended. He was just curious. He wasn't an idiot. "You can't be serious."

"You're right, I'm sorry," Colin soothed, but his jaw muscles continued to twitch as though he was struggling to hold his tongue. "But I'm going to be keeping a close eye on you, just in case."

"No problem," Dante said. "There's nothing going on, so I've got nothing to hide." He felt dirty inside as soon as the words slipped from his mouth. He had feelings for this girl, and he was going to put them both at risk if he chose to pursue her. Maybe he would be lucky and she would just forget about him. Although he didn't know how long it would take for him to forget about her.

૭

The twenty-fifth of September was Emilie's parents' wedding anniversary. Her parents had met later in life. They had both attended a mutual friend's photo exhibit and been completely inseparable from that day forward.

Emilie felt particularly nostalgic today. It was probably just loneliness. She took out her phone and dialled her grandmother's number.

Evelyn Gagnon was ninety-two years old and dying of liver cancer. Emilie had every reason to be lonely. She was going to lose all three of the most important people in her life in a matter of years. She had come close to refusing her admission to McGill because of her grandmother's deteriorating health. They had a particularly close relationship, and Emilie didn't want to be so far away under the circumstances. But her grandmother had been furious.

"Hello," Evelyn answered weakly.

"Hi, Grandma," Emilie cheered.

"Oh, it's so good to hear your voice."

Emilie sighed heavily. "I should be there with you."

"Let's not get into that nonsense again, child," her grandmother scolded.

"But Grandma…"

"I'm already dying, girl. Let me take my time about it."

"What?"

"If you had stayed here because of me, I would have felt obliged to get on with it so you would have a chance to make something of yourself. You're young and bright, and you've lost enough time in grief. It would kill me to be the reason you put your dreams on hold yet again."

"Oh, Grandma…"

"Listen," Evelyn interrupted, "I know how you feel about me. We've always been close where it counts. Now enough of this. Tell me about Montreal."

"It's Mom and Dad's anniversary today."

"I was trying to distract you."

Emilie laughed. Her parents had only ever had one fight, and it had been a doozy. "Remember the stories of their trip to Alaska?"

"You mean the Big Fight?"

"Yeah…" Emilie replied. Her mother had called her father's most recent series of photographs self-indulgent and over-intellectualized. He had stormed off in a huff and had fallen into a crevasse, breaking his ankle and severely spraining his knee. "I can't believe Dad just sat there in the cold and the dark until Mom called him on the walkie talkie to apologize."

"Your father was the most stubborn old goat on legs."

"Yeah…I get my stubbornness and impulsiveness from him. He was lucky not to have lost his leg. It took more than twenty-four hours before the rescue team could extract him."

Her grandmother spoke on about the incident, but Emilie's attention had waned. She was staring at the opposite wall of her living room where she had hung a collection of black and white photographs her parents had taken over their careers. She stood up and walked over to one of her favorites. It was a ptarmigan hen camouflaged in the tundra, sitting on her nest of eggs. The mountains were in the backdrop and the sun was rising behind them. It was a beautiful picture.

"Emilie?" her grandmother asked.

"I'm still here, Grandma. Sorry. I was just looking through some old photos."

"Why don't you tell me a bit about Montreal."

Emilie obliged her grandmother by nattering on about all of the small things that had come to make up her everyday existence. Her sadness and loneliness faded as the moments passed.

Until her grandmother asked a pivotal question.

"Have you met any nice guys?"

"I don't know about nice," Emilie taunted. "I've met some pigs and some cute guys."

"Anyone special?"

Emilie thought of Dante. She was always thinking about him these days. She wondered if he was back from China yet. An entire week had already passed since they'd had lunch together. She had wanted to call him but didn't have a good enough excuse. He was supposed to call her, but she wasn't well known for her patience. "I have met someone special, but don't get your hopes up. I'm sure not."

"Oh, well. I'll keep my fingers crossed for you. Listen, the nurse is here with my medication. I should go."

"I love you, Grandma," Emilie said sadly.

"I love you too, sweetie. Take care."

"You too."

Emilie put down the phone and looked back at her photos. She needed to get out of this apartment. She snatched up the phone and sent a text to Caroline.

How's it going?

It took longer than expected to get a response.

Tired. What's up?

Emilie was confused. Caroline should be in great spirits. She was out having a late lunch at the pub with a cute engineering student she had met at a beer bash.

What r u wearing?

She waited again.

Not much.

*Oh, Caroline...*Emilie scolded and typed:

U'll never get a boyfriend if u act like such a slut. ;)

Emilie knew she shouldn't be getting into a debate with her friend at this moment in time, but as much as misery loved company, she didn't want Caroline to be lonely too.

I thought I told u I hadn't had any boyfriends. I'm not gonna start now.

"Oh my God!" Emilie cursed aloud, slapping her hand over her mouth. "I dialled Dante Ashton by mistake!" His number was the one immediately following Caroline's in her cell phone directory.

Emilie burst out laughing. She was so embarrassed. How could she have made such a terrible mistake? Now Dante probably had the impression she was an inconsiderate, desperate woman hoping to get into his pants. She laughed again as she thought, *One out of three isn't bad.*

OMG! Sorry, dialled the wrong # by mistake.

Her phone vibrated and she snatched it up like a woman possessed. Emilie groaned as she read:

LOL! Thinking of me, were u?

What have I done? But before she could reply, she received another text.

I was thinking of u. ;)

Emilie was still reeling. She didn't know what to make of his comment or how to answer his question. *And what's with the wink?* Was Dante winking: I'm just kidding? Or was he winking: I'm naked in bed and thinking of you?

What was she supposed to say now? She typed:

Freudian slip, I guess. Where r u?

Dante replied:

Speaking of Freud, I'm in Bangkok. Now tell me what ur wearing.

Emilie closed her eyes and chuckled. *Perfect!*

Ur a bad boy. Aren't u?

She wasn't quite sure why she had sent that message. She already liked him more than she should and her fondness for bad boys had already been well established. Why tempt fate?

U have no idea. Want 2 get together on Sun?

Emilie's heart raced. She was thrilled at the thought of seeing him again. This was working out better than she had expected, but warning bells were sounding in her mind. Yet she typed:

Yes.

She stared at the phone, waiting for his reply.

Call me Sat. L8.

No problem, she thought as she put her phone away. The rest of this week was going to drag by. Emilie had no idea what she wanted to do with Dante—besides the obvious, but that was out of the question. They were supposed to be friends. She wondered what time it was in Thailand. It was probably the middle of the night. *How embarrassing!*

Saturday came, but Emilie was having problems defining the word "late." "Late" was too subjective. Did Dante mean after dinner or before bed? She didn't even know what she was going to say to him for that matter.

It was nine in the evening and she had hardly gotten anything done all day long because she'd spent all of her time watching the clock seemingly tick backwards. Emilie couldn't wait any longer. Nine was late enough. She picked up her phone and dialled. It rang for a long time and was about to go to voice mail.

"Hello," Dante's magical voice sang in her ear.

"Hello...it's me, Emilie," she answered, flustered. "I hope this is late enough."

"It's fine. I'm jet lagged anyway," he replied, laughing softly.

"So how was China?" she asked, eager to embark on a lengthy conversation.

"Crowded. How was Montreal?" he answered in a distracted whisper.

Emilie wondered if he wanted to play another game with her. He was following their answer and question pattern from last time. "Boring as hell...Are we playing a game?" she asked, mentally preparing herself. She had consumed a lot of caffeine over the course of the day and felt particularly alert.

Dante laughed uncomfortably before saying, "No. I'm too tired for games. Another time maybe."

His voice had been filled with humor, but now there was nothing but silence on the line. Perhaps it was time to come to the point. "What do you want to do with me tomorrow?" she asked.

There was a pause. An uncomfortable pause. "Hello?" Emilie asked, wondering if they had been disconnected.

"Sorry...I was distracted. How about a movie?"

Emilie sensed a hint of irritation in Dante's voice. Perhaps he was in the middle of something and she had interrupted him. She decided to wrap up the details quickly so he could get back to whatever he was trying to do. "Sounds good to me. Where and when?"

They made their arrangements and Emilie put her phone away. She felt foolish. She had waited for days to spend a couple of minutes on the phone. *How anticlimactic*, she grumbled under her breath. But Dante had just returned from Asia, and he did sound exhausted. She had to cut the poor guy some slack. Emilie resolved to focus on the positive: she would see him tomorrow, and she couldn't wait.

❧

"You have gotta be kidding me!" Jude barked.

Dante sighed heavily. This was not off to a good start. "Lucifer's legends, Jude. I'm just going to a movie."

"Oh no you're not!" Jude insisted.

"I have to agree with Jude," Colin grumbled.

Dante tossed his magazine on the coffee table and crossed his arms angrily across his chest. He took a deep breath and let it out slowly. "Come on, guys, it's just a movie. It's a public place. There will be no bloodshed. I promise you both."

Jude sniggered rather crudely, making Colin throw Dante an accusatory glance. "Aw, Jude. You're just making this worse for me."

"I don't want to leave you alone in the dark with a human," Colin growled. "A lot can happen…"

"We won't be alone," Dante argued.

"That's right!" Jude snapped. "Because I'm coming with you."

"Give me a break!" Dante hissed. "I won't be gone for long."

"It doesn't take long for something bad to happen. You can't just go out into the civilian population and act like you belong. You're already enough of a target," Colin argued. "I'll never understand why you insist on transporting venom. Assassins of both species have been trying to take you out forever. In my opinion, the council hasn't been doing a very good job of protecting you, so you should be particularly diligent," he added. "I'm going too. Between the two of us, we'll keep you out of trouble."

"I'm not thirteen," Dante complained. "I don't need a chaperone...or two."

"You're not thinking clearly," Jude insisted. "You need someone to remind you just how dangerous it is involving yourself with humans. Have you even thought about the danger you're putting this girl in?"

"I haven't so much as touched her," Dante growled. "Nothing is going to happen."

"Jude isn't talking only of the danger you represent to her. He's thinking of your enemies. You've become such a key player in this horrible industry, and there are many who wouldn't hesitate to use an innocent civilian to bend you to their will. The council itself might kill Emilie if they find out. They can't afford to lose you. Plus you're a Dark Angel, Dante. Unless you've decided to embrace your inner demon, you shouldn't be snuggling up with any human girls," Colin explained.

"It's just a movie," Dante grumbled. It didn't matter. They would come along whether he wanted them to or not. Maybe next time he wouldn't bother mentioning where he was going in the first place. He growled angrily. If he was lucky, there wouldn't be a next time.

ψ

Emilie loved living in downtown Montreal. Commuting by foot was so easy, especially underground. The weather in this city could be less than desirable. The summers were steamy, hot, and humid. The fall and spring could be fresh and rainy. But the winters were long and bitter cold.

Today was one of those rainy fall days when you could feel winter coming up fast. Emilie rushed down University Street to jump into the Metro station there. Once inside, she would be able to work her way toward the theatre easily without having to be out in the elements.

She didn't know why she had bothered to dress so nicely or put on any makeup. The wind and rain were ruining her appearance. Once inside the Metro station she tried to straighten herself out. She ran her fingers through her hair in a vain attempt at saving what was left of her hairdo. *What a waste of time,* she scolded herself. She dabbed her fingers tentatively under her eyes to see if her mascara was streaking down her face or not. It didn't seem too bad, but she was desperate for a mirror. Emilie hoped to have some time to fix her face before Dante arrived. She was running a bit late so she decided to quicken her pace.

Emilie couldn't figure out why she was trying so hard to impress this guy. Dante was way out of her league. She was also uncertain about where they stood. He didn't seem interested in her romantically, but somehow they seemed to be more than friends. He was flirty yet distant.

Who was she trying to kid anyway? She felt ridiculous. It must be all in her imagination. She had to be reading something in those beautiful brown eyes that she wanted to find—not something real.

Caroline had been warning her not to get her hopes up, and Emilie was starting to feel foolish. Maybe she was going to have to confront Dante about this. *Yeah, right…*she thought. She could barely form a coherent sentence around the guy. She doubted her ability to speak to him about something so delicate. She rolled her eyes, imagining him bursting out laughing.

By the time Emilie finally reached the theatre, she was just about discouraged enough to turn around and call him to cancel. She did have a lot of work to do. She couldn't afford to waste precious time slobbering after this rock star.

Then she saw him.

All of Emilie's preparations, all of her self-deprecation, and all of her neglected school books were worth it just to look at him. Dante wasn't even doing anything special, just leaning against a column playing with his phone. He appeared to be posing for a magazine spread. *Every hair on his head is in the right place,* she thought as she unconsciously ran a hand through her own hair. His outfit was high-fashion and well coordinated, especially his long black trench coat. At least he had enough common sense to dress for the weather, unlike herself.

Emilie stared at him like a starving woman looking through a window at a buffet table. He was attracting a respectful amount of attention for someone who wasn't even trying. A group of high school girls were openly ogling him and giggling over by the concession stand.

She was happy for the distraction because he looked up curiously from his phone. His beautiful face lit up as if he was happy to see her, but he held up his index finger for her to wait a moment and quickly turned his attention back to his toy.

She reached him just as he put away his phone. Dante said, "Sorry, I have some meetings coming up and I needed to get organized before I forgot." He smiled broadly at her. "You look nice." He reached out and touched some of her wet, dishevelled hair with his long fingers.

Emilie assumed that he was making fun of her appearance. Her heart pounded in her chest, just having him touch her in any small way. She blushed bright red and grumbled, "Very funny!"

He stopped playing with her hair and laughed softly, sensing her irritation. "No, seriously." He sounded sincere.

Dante handed Emilie a ticket. "Do you want anything to eat?"

"Thanks," she replied, taking the ticket from his hand, "but no thanks. I'm not hungry."

"Do you want to get a seat?" he continued, shrugging in the direction of the theatre door.

"You go ahead and save us some seats. I'll be just a minute," she said, turning toward the washrooms.

"Okay," he replied cheerfully and headed toward the theatre.

The bathroom mirror didn't lie as convincingly as Dante. Emilie's hair and face were both bordering on horrific. It would take much too long to complete full repairs, so she just made a few minor adjustments and rushed back out.

She walked into the theatre, scanning the seats for Dante. She found him in the middle about halfway up, but he wasn't alone. On one side sat Jude, stuffing his face from an enormous box of popcorn, and on the other side was Colin, looking sullen as usual.

Emilie's heart sank. She should have realized that this wasn't a date. After all, they were just friends. Somehow she managed to wipe the disappointment off of her face. She waved to them pleasantly, as if she wasn't at all surprised to see them all together. She started up the stairs, wondering if she should sit next to Jude or Colin. She decided to sit with Jude because he was closer, and he had food.

As she squeezed by the other people sitting in their row, Emilie saw Dante pat Colin on the shoulder and motion for him to move over a seat. Colin shot him a pained expression and seemed about to start arguing with Dante, then Jude burst out laughing. Colin got up and moved over, but he sat down hard and slumped in his seat as though he was sulking.

There was hope for Emilie yet. This wasn't a date, but at least she would get to be close to Dante for a couple of hours in the dark. Best of all, she wouldn't have to try to say anything intelligent to impress him. She could just sit and relax.

Emilie sat down as gracefully as she could with the eyes of three of the most gorgeous men watching her every movement. She must be the envy of every unattached woman in the theatre.

"So did you have to walk far in the rain?" Dante asked, trying to make a little small talk in order to break the uncomfortable silence haunting them all.

"No, I mostly stayed underground. I really hate this time of year," Emilie answered conversationally.

Mercifully the lights dimmed and the commercials and previews started up on the screen. Dante not so discreetly stretched up and slipped one arm around Emilie's shoulders. She suddenly couldn't breathe. *Maybe this is a date*, she speculated. She tried to act like nothing had happened, but felt as if every hair on her body was standing on end. She shot a quick glance in Dante's direction, but he was smiling smugly to himself, eyes fixed on the screen. Beyond him she could see Jude snickering into the fingers of one hand.

She glanced quickly away and stared back at the screen, but in her peripheral vision she could see Colin glaring through her at Dante. Emilie couldn't understand what she had ever done to Colin to make him dislike her so much. All she wanted to do was sit in the dark and fill her mind with happy fantasies about the man attached to the arm around her shoulders. Colin was ruining it with the negative energy steaming off of him.

Emilie noticed Dante lean back and mouth something in her direction. At first she thought he was speaking to her, but she quickly realized that he was looking behind her head and not at it. His words were directed to Colin, and if she wasn't mistaken in her lip reading, Dante had said, "You are not my mother." He had also punctuated his statement with a most facetious grin.

Emilie was confused and became even more so as Dante proceeded to run the fingers of the hand around her shoulders through her hair. A little chill ran through her body from his touch, but somehow she felt dirty rather than aroused. Something was going on between these two men, and she suspected it had to do with her. She glanced over at Colin. He had slunk down even further in his seat and was staring angrily at the screen with his face hard and tight, as if he was using all of his self-control not to jump up and throttle Dante.

Emilie threw Dante a questioning glance. He just made a face, shrugged his muscular shoulders, and rolled his eyes as if to say, "Sorry, what can I say."

Jude had been laughing so hard that he had actually inhaled a piece of popcorn and started to cough. The couple next to Jude glared at his noisemaking, although not many people would have the nerve to say anything negative to a man as massive and intimidating as Jude.

Dante had his smiling-but-smug face back on and was pretending to pay attention to the screen. Emilie couldn't help but smile along with him, although hers was far from smug. She was perplexed. *What's going on here?* she wondered. If this was a date, why did Dante bring along his friends? And if this wasn't a date, why was he taking such liberties with her body?

Emilie felt Dante's arm jerk roughly behind her and heard him let out his breath sharply. She looked over just in time to see Jude pulling his elbow out of Dante's rib cage. Dante started laughing quietly but took his arm away from her.

Emilie's disappointment grew astronomically.

Dante brought his other arm down around Jude's shoulder and cuffed him roughly on the back of the head. Jude just continued snickering. Over the sounds of the screen Emilie could just barely hear Dante sighing deeply as he adjusted himself with his hands in his lap.

Emilie chanced a glance over at Colin, and although he hadn't changed his position at all, his face had a satisfied grin on it. He probably knew that she was looking at him, but he just stared intently at the screen, ignoring her.

She was glad. She didn't want him to see the disappointment in her eyes. She didn't know what kind of game these three were playing, but she would have appreciated an explanation of the rules before they had begun.

Emilie sat through the movie with an uncomfortable feeling in the pit of her stomach. She didn't want to be a prop in someone else's drama. Dante shouldn't be sending out such confusing messages. If they were friends, then he needed to keep things within the boundaries of that friendship. With the way she already felt about him, she didn't want to nurture any false hopes about their friendship developing into something more.

She looked over at Dante a few times during the movie. He paid attention to the screen and kept his hands to himself, but Emilie had come to a decision. Immediately following the movie, she would make her feelings clear to Dante. If he wasn't going to commit himself to dating her, then he wasn't allowed any boyfriend privileges. She was familiar with bad boys and wasn't going to be anybody's play thing. She wanted more for herself.

After the movie, they filed out of the theatre together, talking pleasantly about the story. They stood inside the theatre lobby and shifted uncomfortably. This whole situation had been poorly planned and no one seemed to know what should happen next.

This was as good a time as any to have a discussion with Dante. Emilie's face became serious, almost angry as she stared straight at Jude and Colin. She said, "Listen, guys, I would really appreciate a minute to talk to Dante about something. In private."

They both appeared surprised and even intimidated, but they both turned to Dante at the same time. He just laughed and declared, "I think she means business, guys. Excuse us for a minute."

Colin and Jude stood blinking in confusion as Emilie dragged Dante off by the arm. "Do you mind explaining what kind of game the three of you were playing back there before the movie started?" she asked point blank.

Dante's smile faded slightly and he looked a little uncomfortable. "I wanted to come here on my own, but they insisted on accompanying me. They're curious about our growing friendship and wanted to chaperone me."

Well, at least he's making an effort to be honest, she thought. *But I've had enough games.* "Listen, are we friends? Or what?"

Dante's jaw hung open for a second then he blinked his brown eyes and replied, "We're friends."

"Just friends?" Emilie clarified.

He nodded. "Just friends."

"Okay, remember when we had lunch? We talked about the rules of our friendship," she began and waited as he nodded again. "Now wipe that defensive look off your face because I'm not finished." She paused for emphasis. "You didn't do anything wrong. I just need you to understand something. If you want boyfriend privileges with me, like putting your arm around me, then you have to be prepared to be my boyfriend. Otherwise there is to be no inappropriate touching between us. Am I making myself clear?"

By the time her rant was finished, Emilie had a big smile on her face even though she was wagging her finger at him in complete seriousness. His expression had gone from smiling mischievously to curiously serious, then defensive to downright shocked. She got the impression he was unaccustomed to being spoken to in this way. Hopefully she had impressed him with her stand on this issue rather than making him angry with her.

Dante smiled crookedly and said, "I'm sorry I crossed the line. I'll watch myself more carefully in the future. Thank you for being candid."

It was Emilie's turn to be surprised. She had expected him to get huffy and try to put the blame on her somehow. He was gorgeous, and beautiful men were probably used to being able to do whatever they wanted, without question or consequence. Most of the men Emilie had dealt with didn't take well to being scolded in public places. Dante was a real gentleman. He had listened to what she said and accepted responsibility for his behavior without getting petty or nasty. Emilie liked this guy way too much for her own good. "Thank you. You're a good listener," she replied, a silly grin creeping across her face.

She glanced over at Jude and Colin. They stood transfixed, their mouths hanging open slightly. They couldn't possibly have heard the conversation from so far away and with so many people walking between them, but they seemed to have some kind of appreciation for the seriousness of the lecture their friend had endured.

Emilie had to laugh. Dante followed her line of sight and joined her. "I told you I spend too much time with my friends," he grumbled, shaking his head. "What can I say?"

Emilie gathered every ounce of determination in her heart. "Listen, thank you very much for the movie. It was very...interesting. But I have a pile of studying to do so I think I'll say good-bye and leave the three of you alone. Okay?" She really didn't want to leave him but figured that she would be in a stronger position in their friendship if she did.

"I understand completely," he replied politely, holding his hand out for her to shake.

Emilie took his hand in hers, pulled him over, and kissed him on both cheeks. "I said no inappropriate touching," she explained. "This is okay. We're in Montreal after all."

She stepped away from him and reluctantly let go of his hand. She wasn't going to give up the opportunity to have his lips on her body for anything. She wondered if Dante suspected as much. She hoped so. She didn't want to close any doors; she just didn't want to get anything painfully caught in there.

He studied her carefully with a mysterious smile on his face. "I'll call you," he said.

"Good," she replied as she turned around and walked away. She waved to Jude and Colin, who were trying not to be so obvious about their staring. They both waved back.

Emilie had made up her mind not to look back at Dante, but her willpower broke when she got to the door and she glanced back. Jude and Colin had rushed over to him, but he was still watching her leave with that mysterious smile on his face. *Well now,* she thought. *Have I intrigued him?* Time would tell. She wasn't prepared to hold her breath. Not just yet anyway.

ᘜ

Dante watched Emilie's body strut away from him. Her long dark hair swayed rhythmically across her back. Her hips rocked back and forth seductively. He had to close his eyes and blink hard to get the vision of her hips rocking in a different way out of his mind. She moved hypnotically, every gesture fluid and graceful. He would love to see her dance.

He thought of how much her heart rate had increased when he had touched her hair and when he had put his arm around her. He was just curious and hadn't meant any harm. He needed to see if she was thinking about him in the same way that he was thinking about her. Finding out didn't make things any easier though.

She had to be one of the most intriguing people he had ever met. He remembered the fire in her bewitching aqua eyes as she had scolded him. Not to mention the poutiness of her full lips. Humans never spoke to him in that manner. He might not have found it so amusing if he wasn't so interested in her.

He should be offended, but instead he found her energy exciting. Her high-spirited personality suited him. Her intelligence challenged him. She was very aware—for a human. She picked up on things most humans wouldn't notice or, if they did, would dismiss without a thought. She would do well in forensics, a definite asset in any investigation.

"What just happened?" Jude asked when he reached his friend through the crowd.

"She was putting me in my place," Dante answered. He was smiling crookedly, still focused on Emilie.

"Really?" Jude asked, whistling quietly. "Your little human is bold."

Jude's comment immediately snapped Dante out of his reverie. "She isn't mine."

"Oh really?" Jude sneered. "In that case, I think I like her too."

Dante swatted his friend roughly. "She may not be mine, but I have dibs. I saw her first."

"No, my friend, you had your back to her. I believe I saw her first," Jude corrected.

Dante felt a rush of possessiveness wash over him and was taken off guard. "I'm not going to argue with you about this," he replied. He hadn't intended his tone to be threatening, yet somehow he managed to punctuate his statement with a growl.

"I believe we already are," Jude responded, eyeing Dante carefully. "You'll just have to march over to the council office and buy a permit for her so you can keep her all to yourself."

Dante took a deep breath to calm himself. Only the purest and bloodiest demons bought permits for human civilians. "I can't believe you would say something like that to me, and in front of Colin."

Colin had remained silent thus far but he could no longer contain his anger. "What do you mean?" he demanded. "In front of Colin...What exactly do the two of you discuss in my absence?"

The situation was escalating out of control. "Nothing," Dante snapped.

"Really?" Colin snarled. "Somehow I remain unconvinced."

"Jude is just deliberately provoking me, as usual," Dante grumbled and instantly felt like a petulant child.

"Hey, if you're going to drag me out here for your delusional fantasies, then I get to ride you, and you should say nothing but 'Heehaw.'"

"Drag you!" Dante hissed. "I didn't ask you to come, so I should expect you to be on your best behavior," he added far more defensively than he'd wished. He sighed heavily. "Listen, let's just forget about all of this. I've reached the limits of my patience."

Jude laughed softly. "You have to stop seeing her. You're only going to get frustrated, and I mean...*frustrated*." Jude sniggered crudely to himself, slapping Dante on the back.

"I know. I know. You know what they say about curiosity," Dante replied, sighing miserably.

"If you need to get your hands on a human girl then we can always go to the council office tonight. All you have to do is call and make a reservation. They'll be more than happy to accommodate your every need," Jude suggested.

Dante laughed devilishly. "I have a no-humans policy with all the offices. I would have to put in a special request. They likely don't have anybody who fits my requirements on such short notice."

Colin had been seething for long enough and finally erupted, "Hey, guys! Let's be serious for a minute. Sex with humans, or anything with humans for that matter, is strictly off-limits, civilian or not. You'll have to find something else to play with to satisfy your urges." Colin looked back and forth between his friends as though he wondered if they were even listening. "I will never understand your attraction to humans in the first place. In my eyes they aren't worth much."

"Oh, I can think of quite a few uses for them," Jude said, then stage-whispered to Dante, "But having sex with them is the most fun."

"Jude, you're nothing but a half-blooded animal!" Colin snarled, looking ill. "All of this talk is making me hungry. Let's go and get some decent food. I can't believe you ate all of that garbage. You'll be picking it out of your teeth for days."

Jude and Dante started laughing quietly to themselves but followed Colin out of the theatre without another word.

۞

Dante, Jude, and Colin had agreed to skip making reservations at the council office and had decided to go clubbing instead. Dante wanted to play a more active role in his choice of sexual partner this evening. Reds was one of the best spots in Montreal for his kind. No humans were allowed. It wasn't safe for humans.

Colin had gone in earlier, and now Dante and Jude were waiting to go through the security check. Jude always had to strip off so much metal before he could go through the detector. Dante made a conscious effort not to wear too much jewelry and accessories when he came. Otherwise going through the metal detector was a nightmare.

They were both thoroughly frisked and then allowed to go to the coat check to sign in for the evening. Dante scanned the sign-in sheet to see if anyone interesting was in Montreal today. He was never impressed with the regular crowd. He wanted to see someone different, someone special.

What he really wanted was to see Emilie, but it wasn't going to happen, especially not here. He still couldn't figure out what exactly it was about the little human girl that made him so crazy. It didn't matter because he couldn't have her. At least in this place he could find a substitute. He needed to focus his attention on the here and now. He could fantasize when he was alone at home.

"Let's get a drink and see what's going on," Jude suggested, heading for the bar.

Dante knew better than to try to keep pace with Jude regarding alcohol or drugs. Jude could handle about twice what Dante could and still work an eight-hour day without faltering. Dante's metabolism was excellent, but he needed to be careful. He had gotten himself into too many fights doing cocaine with Jude. Dante considered himself an aggressive person to begin with, and adding stimulants was not always the best mix. Heroin was better for his personality. He would still have to watch himself, as Jude seemed to take particular pleasure in seeing Dante get sick, trying to keep up with him. Dante was beginning to find the club scene so much less amusing. Maybe he needed to settle down. If anything, it would improve his life expectancy.

He sat at the bar next to Jude and took a look around. It was already quite late on a Sunday night and many people had work in the morning. He wondered if anybody worthwhile would bother to show up at this point.

The bartender came over. She was a handsome, six-foot-tall redhead built like a professional athlete. Dante leaned across the bar and kissed her on the lips. "Hello, Norma. How are you tonight?"

She leaned over and kissed Jude on the lips before answering. "Fine, and you?"

"I'm okay," he replied without enthusiasm.

"Why are you dressed all in black, Dante?" she asked.

People came to Reds to hook up, and wearing red signalled availability. There wasn't much point in coming to Reds if you weren't available. Dante stood up and turned around. An enormous red phoenix was rising out of a fiery pyre on the back of his shirt. The phoenix's wings spread out across Dante's shoulder blades, making him look even broader and better built than he already was.

"You always wear the most interesting clothes," Norma stated, impressed.

"I'm feeling picky tonight so I only put on a bit of red," Dante replied, smiling as he sat down.

Jude was starting to feel neglected so he added, "Dante has a thing for a human girl. Colin and I are trying to save him from making any big mistakes."

Dante glared at Jude resentfully as Norma began lecturing. "Come on now...A man in your position shouldn't be wasting time with human girls. You'll only get yourself in big trouble."

"I know. I know. I'm here, aren't I?" he grouched, still glaring at Jude. It irritated him to see his friend laughing at his expense.

"Well, you better find a bit more enthusiasm or you may end up alone at the bar doing lines of coke and drinking rum with no one but me to keep you company," she warned with a warm smile.

"I know, but I do enjoy your company," Dante said graciously, batting his big brown eyes at her flirtatiously.

"Dante, you're incorrigible," Norma giggled, obviously pleased with his attention. "Just remember that you're here for a much different kind of *enjoyment*."

"I'll be fine, Norma. Thanks for looking out for me," Dante said affectionately. "Can you bring us a bottle of rum, two shot glasses, and some Coke, please?"

"What kind of coke do you boys want tonight?" Norma asked, winking.

"Both," Dante answered, smiling broadly. "Just put it on my tab."

"Coming right up," Norma said as she walked away.

"I hope somebody interesting turns up. I'm already bored," Dante complained to Jude.

"You're just sulking because you can't have that human girl."

Dante shot Jude an irritated look and sighed deeply to himself. He wasn't going to bother trying to deny it.

A tiny, thin, blond-haired girl skipped up to them with two friends in tow. "Hello, guys. Fancy meeting you here." She put her hand on Dante's chest as she leaned in to kiss him on the lips. If he hadn't been sitting down, he would have towered over her. She kissed Jude as well.

"You know Martha and Tracy from work," she said, motioning to her friends, each of whom came forward and kissed both Dante and Jude.

"Yes, Melanie. I remember them," Dante replied politely, flashing them all a dazzling smile.

"Well, have fun," Melanie said as she and her friends giggled and started walking toward the dance floor.

"You too," Jude answered cheerfully, running his eyes up and down the back of them as they went. One of them turned and waved, throwing him a provocative glance. He waved back but then turned back to his shot glass.

"Do you really know who those girls are?" Jude asked incredulously.

"One of them definitely works in the lab. Melanie is the receptionist at the main entrance to the council office. The other girl...I've seen somewhere. It doesn't matter," Dante grumbled disdainfully.

"Melanie is cute, but I'd be afraid to break her," Jude joked crudely and laughed to himself as though he were imagining it.

"You would. I'm sure of it," Dante replied, looking at Jude as though he was crazy to even consider her.

"Let's go and dance for a while. Maybe we'll see Colin. If we can even get close to him. He's always popular." Jude got up and stretched out. He was wearing black pants with a red, long-sleeved button-up shirt.

"He's at the top of the food chain, for this place anyway. He can have his pick, and it helps that he isn't picky," Dante commented, waiting for Jude to get moving.

"You're falling behind, Dante. You need to drink more to catch up," Jude teased.

"Forget it, pal. I have to work tomorrow." They made their way to the dance floor at the back of the club.

"Well, if you're working then I'm working too," Jude pointed out.

Dante spotted Colin dancing with a group of people, most of whom he recognized. They made their way over. After a few introductions and a lot of kissing, everyone was dancing again.

৬৩

Dante sat at the bar talking to a couple of guys he knew from work. They were busy making crude jokes about some the women in the club they had taken upstairs to the playrooms. Dante found it all very interesting because he had a strict policy of not getting intimate with people he knew from work. He didn't need those complications in his life. He'd had to deal with a couple of girls who had gotten too attached to him before he'd learned his lesson. It wasn't worth the trouble.

Dante felt a hand run up the back of his shirt and into his hair. He turned around quickly and looked into the most beautiful brown eyes he'd seen all night. It was Tasia. Dante had always had a bit of a crush on her, but socially she was out of his league. He had still taken her to bed before. Just not anywhere near as often as he would have liked.

"Hello, gorgeous," he said quickly, leaning over to give her a kiss.

She was feeling generous and let his lips linger on hers longer than would normally be considered polite for a greeting. "Hello, yourself," she replied sensually. She seemed rather pleased with the reception she was getting from him.

"What are you doing in Montreal?" Dante asked, anxious to keep her with him for a while longer.

She ran her fingers through her long chestnut hair and then twirled a strand around her finger, glancing casually around the room. "Just visiting."

"Are you shopping for a husband?" Dante asked mischievously, trying not to sound interested.

"Just browsing. I'm not shopping…yet. Is Colin here?"

Dante could sense the maliciousness of her tone but decided to let it slide. Colin outranked Dante socially, but if Tasia had wanted Colin, then she would have had him by now. "Yes, he was dancing with a bunch of people last time I saw him." Dante gestured to the back of the club, trying to make it look as if he was ready to go and join them if she was in the mood.

"What about Jude?" she asked with significantly less enthusiasm.

A woman of Tasia's social standing would never consider Jude as a potential partner. "He found somebody to take upstairs," he answered, running his eyes over Tasia's body. She had on a spectacular red dress that left very little to the imagination. She looked great. "So can I get you anything?"

"I think I've already had too much." Tasia leaned in closer to him and whispered, "I'm wondering if I should risk taking you upstairs."

Dante was definitely interested, but he knew better than to take her too seriously. She was a notorious tease, and she could afford to be. "I wouldn't argue with you, but I know how your father feels about me. He wouldn't appreciate you lowering yourself to my level."

"When have I ever let that stop me?" she asked, smiling suggestively.

When? he asked himself. *When you refused my marriage proposal, that's when.* He had taken it seriously, even if she hadn't. But then again, her father was one of the most notorious demons of the noble class, and would never agree to have his princess married to a Dark Angel. Plus Dante was considered tainted because his father was a changeling and not a nobleman. No matter how pure his mother's bloodline had been, she had disgraced herself with her choice of husband.

Dante didn't want to argue with Tasia. He had something else in mind. If he could get her pregnant then her father would have to agree to the marriage. It never hurt to try. Well, in her case, it probably would. But that was part of the fun. "Oh, I haven't gotten nearly enough of your attention, my dear," he purred.

"How much cocaine have you had tonight?" she asked.

"Not very much. I have to work tomorrow." He watched her reaction curiously. He wasn't sure what answer would be most advantageous.

Tasia leaned over and whispered into his ear, deliberately brushing him with her tantalizing lips. "You have a reputation for being quite an animal when you've had too much cocaine. I don't know if I'm in the mood for that tonight. I can't get too bloody and bruised because I'm here with my father on business."

Dante sniggered quietly, trying not to show how much her closeness was affecting him. "I can make an effort not to leave too many noticeable marks on you, if you want." He dragged his bar stool over a bit closer to hers. He looked her right in the eyes as he ran his fingers along the side of her face, tucking a few stray hairs behind her ear. He leaned in closer and whispered in her ear. "I seem to remember having to work pretty hard to make you scream."

"You're a good boy," she murmured as he pulled away from her and sat smugly in his seat. "I think I might have to refresh my memory." She ran her index finger down the front of his shirt and hooked it into his belt, tugging gently on his pants as though she might want him to follow her.

Dante smiled wickedly and asked, "Do you want me to have Norma send some cocaine up to our room?"

"Definitely," Tasia responded, mirroring his grin.

Chapter 6

Emilie stood staring out of her living room window. It was a beautiful fall day, and on top of that it was Saturday. In Montreal, the beginning of October could have some of the best fall days. Cool and crisp in the morning, warm in the afternoon, and then cool and crisp again in the evening. The best part of all was the leaves. Maple trees made the best fall colors. During this time of year it looked as though the city was on fire. Yellow, orange, and red were everywhere, but Emilie knew it wouldn't last for long. A good couple of days of wind and rain and the trees would be bare until May.

She had spent many hours jogging around the Mount Royal Park area, admiring the changing colors. The exercise helped clear her mind and stimulate her senses. She savored the crisp scent of fall, the sound of the wind in the leaves, and the feeling of the cool breeze on her warm skin.

Emilie had injured her knee in a ski race as a child. Jogging was perhaps not the best choice considering the severity of the injury she had sustained, but her leg never gave her any trouble. Plus she loved to run. The accident had soured her taste for skiing, much to her parents' dismay. Emilie still enjoyed being on the slopes, but she hadn't embraced the sport with the same fervor as had her late parents.

Today's weather was perfect for a run, and she was suffering from a serious case of cabin fever. If only Caroline enjoyed to run as much as Emilie did. The company and conversation would be a welcomed change of pace. Caroline loved to dance, but that was about the full extent of her physical activities. Caroline was far too embroiled in the university party scene for Emilie's taste. Caroline had been out late last night and would be sleeping in this morning. Emilie took her studies very seriously. She had opted to stay in to catch up on her reading. This morning, she felt she deserved a break.

Her thoughts strayed to her angel. She hadn't seen or heard from him since she had walked away at the movie theatre. But only a week had gone by since then. He was often out of town during the week anyway. *Maybe I was too bold with him*, she wondered. He had looked intrigued, but maybe he liked his women more compliant and insipid. *Oh well, you can't change the past and we're only friends.*

On their drive to the restaurant, Dante had said that he liked the fall leaves. She needed some excuse to see him again. Perhaps he was a jogger. He obviously took very good care of his body and was also conveniently located since he lived somewhere in the downtown area. He might enjoy a little exercise on a Saturday morning. What was the harm in asking? He could say no. *So what.*

Emilie had always considered herself impulsive, a trait she had inherited from her father. He had always wanted to jump into the car and race off on some adventure. Her mother had been far more cautious and would plan out everything in exacting detail. They had made an excellent team, and their personality differences had complemented each other nicely.

One thing Emilie had inherited from her mother was her appetite and metabolism. Emilie had already been awake for hours and was getting hungry. Lunch was an option for an outing. She probably had a better chance of luring Dante out with food than with fitness anyway. She decided to call him. *No*, she thought unhappily. *I'm not brave enough to call. Speaking of exercise...*She would be heartbroken if she found out he was cuddled up in bed with some bimbo. She would send him a text message instead. *You can't get any more impersonal and noncommittal.*

She walked into the hall, took her phone out of her purse, and fished his card out of her wallet. She just stood there for a few seconds, running her fingers over his business card. She was trying to figure out what to write. She remembered what he had said to her on the day she had run into him in his father's office and sent:

R u hungry?

Now she would have to wait and see. She put the phone on her desk and sat back down to her school work. Midterm exams were coming and she couldn't afford to take any time from her studies. But it was such a beautiful day. Perhaps Caroline would be free for lunch if Dante was busy. Nothing cured a hangover better than a greasy breakfast. Emilie had been neglecting her social life these days and should be spending more time getting to know all of Caroline's new friends. *You know what they say about too much work and not enough play*, she thought sadly to herself.

Her phone buzzed and she snatched it up. There was a message from an unknown number that read:

Always!

Emilie was surprised by the rush of excitement that flowed through her. One word from Dante sent her heart racing. She knew she was setting herself up for disappointment. Even if she did get to see him, it would only make her want to see him more often, and more of him. Her imagination grabbed her and took off running. She shook her head to redirect her thoughts. Emilie wasn't sure what she was feeling for Dante. It could be nothing more than a heart-stopping infatuation. Whatever it was, it had the distinct possibility of getting out of her control fast.

She would have to burn that bridge when she got to it though. Today she was going to do everything in her power to see him. She found herself in the mood for a taste of her old life in Vancouver. There was a great sushi place not far from the university library, close to a Metro station. She didn't know where Dante's condo was, but he could probably meet her there fairly easily. They could get take-out from the restaurant, go to St. Helen's Island by Metro, and have a picnic in the leaves. It would be fun, fast, and even a bit romantic. She typed:

Sushi?

Emilie was smiling ear to ear. She couldn't wait to see his reply. She tried to review some class notes while she waited, but she couldn't keep her eyes off the phone. Finally it rang. This time the unknown number had called. *Good sign,* she thought and answered, "Hello."

"Hello," Dante's magical voice rang cheerfully in her ear. "Sushi sounds good."

Emilie shivered. Just the sound of his voice gave her so much pleasure, and it was completely disconcerting. *I'm in big trouble with this guy,* she scolded. *At least I'm not in denial of my feelings and I know the risks involved. I'm walking into this with my eyes open and my wits about me. I'd love for something to happen between us, but I know where I stand with him, so I'm not unrealistic about my chances.*

"I remember you saying that you loved the fall colors. Do you want to have a picnic with me?" she asked hopefully.

"A picnic?" Dante choked. "I don't think I've ever been on a picnic in my entire life."

The tone of his voice hinted of his interest, but Emilie was still discouraged and scrambled to convince him. "I could pick us up some great sushi from a place I know and we could meet at a Metro station. We could go to St. Helen's Island for a nice picnic in the leaves."

"I don't like being out in the sun much," Dante replied.

His voice contained enough encouragement to make Emilie add, "We can sit in the shade. It's such a beautiful day." She was trying desperately to hang on to the tattered shreds of her hope but was already preparing herself for his refusal.

"Okay, it's a deal," he announced. "When's this thing going down?"

Emilie had much to prepare. "How about an hour from now?"

"Do you want me to drive?" he asked.

She didn't want to inconvenience him. This outing was her idea. "No. I think it's faster and easier by Metro."

"Do you want me to bring anything?"

"Nothing and *nobody*." Dante couldn't seem to go anywhere without his friends. Emilie wasn't in the mood to deal with a crowd. "Just yourself," she clarified.

"Sounds like a good deal for me. What's the catch?" he asked, a suspicious harshness to his words.

Emilie chose to believe that he was just joking around with her. "No catch, just company," she answered cheerfully.

"Hmmm. Okay, then. Where are we meeting?"

She still found his tone rather suspicious, but she chose to dismiss her negative thoughts. She and Dante made their arrangements and Emilie sprang into action. She had a nice bottle of wine in her fridge that she had brought from the Okanagan Valley, not too far from Vancouver. She had been saving it for a rainy day. There was something special about Dante, and she decided to share it with him. She had a thermos and some Styrofoam cups. Not too environmentally friendly or romantic, but when drinking in a public place, discretion was the better part of valor.

Emilie put a ratty but clean blanket with all of her other supplies into her sports bag. She also called the restaurant and ordered a mix of sushi and sashimi for pick-up. Then she had to work on herself. She needed to get changed and make an effort to look presentable, even for a picnic with a friend. She had a bit of a walk ahead of her so she rushed to get ready.

అ

Colin was away at the Angel Temple in Thailand and Dante couldn't be more relieved. At least he wouldn't have to endure any lectures about this crazy picnic. Colin was trying to be a supportive friend, but Dante was fully aware of his opinion of the Emilie situation and understood to soundness of his arguments.

Dante was about to leave Jude and go off to some open-air outdoor location with a human girl he barely knew. Being in the black market venom business and such a trusted employee of the council was dangerous enough. Many of his own kind wanted his high paying job. The humans wanted more transportation rights, and to see more shipments fall off the truck, so to speak. If his enemies caught wind of the fact that he was so enchanted with this girl, then God only knows the trouble he could find himself in. This meeting could already be a trap, and he was going to blunder head first into it, with a big stupid grin on his face to make matters worse.

Dante had no idea how he was going to break this news to Jude. He normally didn't care about the women in Dante's life. But Emilie put him at risk on so many levels. Jude was trying to hold his tongue, but it wouldn't take long before even he lost his patience.

Dante walked into Jude's room and leaned on the door frame. Jude looked up from his computer desk curiously and asked, "What's up?"

"I'm going out," Dante explained, bracing himself.

Jude jumped up from his chair and reached for his wallet and phone.

Jude had been Dante's bodyguard since Dante had entered manhood, and it had been a very challenging job from the beginning. All people of noble blood had bodyguards. In a world filled with unscrupulous demons, wealthy families needed to know that their precious heirs were protected. But some members needed more protection than others. Dante had always been vulnerable because his mother was dead and his changeling father was not a rich and powerful man.

"No, Jude," Dante explained. "I'm going alone…"

Jude shot him a stern glance. "What's the matter with you?" he demanded.

"I know what you're going to say," Dante replied with a growl.

"If anything happens to you, then I'll be blamed. If you're going to get yourself killed, could you at least do me the favor of letting me die with you?"

"Don't be so melodramatic," Dante grumbled.

"Where are you going?"

"I don't want to say."

"You can't possibly be serious," Jude snapped.

Dante sighed heavily. "You're only going to lecture me."

"If I have reason to lecture then you shouldn't be going."

"I know…Don't you think I know!"

Jude could surely sense Dante's agitation. Instead of going off on a rant, Jude's expression softened and his tone became more soothing. "Why are you doing this?"

"I don't know," Dante answered and threw his hands in the air to express his utter frustration. "I'm just so drawn to this woman. I can't help myself. Every time I see her, I hope that I'll finally see her for what she is… human. But she's like an addiction. The more I get, the more I want."

"You've gotta stop this. She can never be anything to you, and one way or another you're going to get her killed."

The truth of Jude's words cut Dante deeply. Putting himself at risk was bad enough, but his life wasn't the only one on the line. He was willingly tempting fate, but Emilie was ignorant of the danger.

"I've gotta get changed," Dante said.

"You should be in New York, visiting Tasia," Jude argued. "She's better for you. Marrying her would be a good thing."

"I tried," Dante grumbled.

"She wants you."

"Maybe, but Daddy doesn't," Dante countered. "And she would be a naughty little princess if she went against her father."

"She's old enough to make her own choices."

"She made her choice, and it wasn't me. I have to respect that."

"Do you have the same feelings for Emilie as you have for Tasia?" Jude asked.

"No," Dante answered with confidence. "Tasia was a challenge. She's everything I should aspire to attain. I've always liked her and we have great chemistry, but Emilie is different. She's got me so knotted up. I've never felt like this before, and I don't think I like it."

"So just leave her alone," Jude pleaded.

"I can't," Dante replied. "I've gotta go."

ῶ

Emilie picked up her order at the restaurant then practically ran to the Metro. Thankfully Dante wasn't there yet. She took the opportunity to adjust the contents of her bag so she could carry everything conveniently, without making a mess. While she was zipping up the bag, she glanced up and saw him striding toward her.

Dante was even more handsome than she remembered. He had on his dark sunglasses, jet black cargo pants, and a black long-sleeved shirt with a large red Japanese symbol on the front. His longish wavy hair bounced around the sides of his face with every step he took. He looked like a rock star again.

"Hello," Dante said, smiling magnificently. He pushed his dark glasses up into his hair.

"Are you ready to go?" Emilie asked, trying to disguise the fact that she had been practically drooling on her shoes.

He took her bag from her, put it carefully over his shoulder, and started walking down the stairs. "Let's go," he commanded.

They rode together on the Metro, making as much small talk as possible. She asked him about work and he answered vaguely as usual, but he had a lot to say about his trip to China. He asked her about school, and she rambled on about papers and exams. Luckily it wasn't too long a ride.

They left the Metro and walked up the stairs into the light. Dante quickly put back on his sunglasses but still had to shade his eyes with his hand. "Do you have somewhere special in mind?" he asked.

"Let's just walk along the path for a while and see if a specific spot calls to us," Emilie answered.

They found one of the biggest, most colorful trees under which to spread their blanket and stretched out in the shade of its boughs. Although Emilie was amazed by the spectacular view around her, she couldn't seem to tear her eyes away from Dante for long. She hoped he wouldn't notice and felt that she had better ask him something intelligent before he grew suspicious. "I like your shirt," she said conversationally. "What does it mean?"

He sat cross-legged on their blanket, staring peacefully out at the scenery. He looked down at the symbol on his shirt. "I think it's Japanese for 'fortune,' but it probably means 'tourist.'"

Emilie had to laugh. His light-hearted humor had eased the uncomfortable knot developing in the pit of her stomach. "Did you buy it in Japan?"

"I don't remember where I got it. It's old." He ran his hands absently down the front of the shirt as he spoke. Emilie was having trouble reading Dante's face with his eyes masked behind his dark glasses.

As they began setting up their lunch, she wondered why, on a beautiful day like this, he wouldn't want to be basking in what was left of the sun before things froze solid. *Maybe I just want to see him without his shirt,* she thought to herself. "So why don't you like the sun?" she asked as she examined the rich golden color of his skin. "You look like you get a decent amount of it."

Dante lay down on his back, folded his hands behind his head, and stared up at the sky. He seemed very relaxed. Emilie was beginning to wonder if he was even going to answer her when he said, "I have sensitive eyes and skin, and I burn easily. Maybe I'm just getting neurotic about cancer."

Emilie took out the thermos and poured him a cup of wine. Dante sat up again and took the cup from her, sniffing it suspiciously. "Very elegant," he declared, his voice dripping with sarcasm.

"It's from the Okanagan Valley and reminds me of home. It's one of my favorites, though I don't know much about wine."

"I know a bit, but I'm picky," he said, sniffing again. He didn't look as if he wanted to drink it, but he didn't seem to want to be rude either.

"Don't be such a baby!" she teased, smiling at him. "Just try it. If you don't like it, you don't have to drink it."

He shot her a tentative glance, but took a sip, obviously struggling with a distasteful grimace. He swished it around in his mouth and swallowed. "Better than I expected," he said backhandedly. "Sauvignon Blanc?"

"I don't remember. I left the bottle at home. I think it's a Pinot Gris." *Just how much can a twenty-six-year-old messenger actually know about wine anyway?* she wondered.

Dante took another sip. "Not too bad at all," he announced authoritatively. It appeared as though he was going to drink it after all. She handed him some wooden chopsticks and some soy sauce and made herself comfortable for lunch.

After they ate, they sat making small talk together, enjoying the fine day. Dante drank his one cup of wine while Emilie finished the rest herself. Much to her embarrassment, the alcohol affected her more than she anticipated.

"Let go for a walk," she suggested. She was feeling too relaxed lying there so close to him. She was afraid that she was either going to lose her inhibitions and cuddle up to him or just fall asleep.

Dante was lying on his back, focused on the rustling leaves and breathing deeply as if savoring every nuance of the breeze. "Oh yeah!" he announced, turning toward her.

In her tipsiness, Emilie had been openly admiring him and was startled out of her fantasies by his sudden attention. He seemed unaware of her leering, much to her relief. He stood up and pulled something out of one of the many pockets in his cargo pants. He tossed a small package to her. "I bought you something in China. I haven't had a chance to give it to you until now."

It was a gold-colored satin bag pulled closed at one end with beaded draw strings. Emilie stood up and opened it, feeling a bit self-conscious. She hadn't expected him to bring her a gift. Inside was a large round bracelet of solid green jade with dragons carved around the outside. It was a tight fit, but she could get it on and off easily enough. Emilie found it very pretty and was touched by his thoughtfulness. It was incredibly sweet of him, and she wasn't sure what to think of the gesture.

She felt herself blushing as she said, "Thank you. It's so nice, but you didn't have to."

She was having trouble meeting his gaze because she didn't know what kind of response to give him. She was confused about the significance of the gift. Dante seemed pleased with her reaction. He was smiling broadly. Then it dawned on her that he must have planned on seeing her again, upon his return from China.

Dante waited for Emilie to precede him as they started down the path, leaving everything but her wallet behind them. "I was in a market one day and thought of you," he explained. "So I just picked up a little something. I don't really know what friends buy for each other. I thought maybe a silk robe would be…inappropriate."

"I think you made an excellent choice. Thank you again," Emilie said, twirling the bracelet around her wrist as they walked together. He was trying to make it clear that she should not read too much into his gift. *A wise move on his part*, she thought, though she couldn't help feeling a bit disappointed.

They were just friends. She needed to remind herself. But she'd had boyfriends who were less fun to be with and far less refined and considerate. For that matter, she had been more aroused innocently lying fully clothed with Dante on their picnic blanket than she had been with some other guys in much more intimate situations.

They walked around for a while making more small talk and admiring the spectacular colors. He asked her a lot of questions about her life and her interests. He was evasive as usual, but she did discover one interesting fact. Every single dog they passed either barked at or cowered from them. *Very strange*, she thought. Dante didn't even notice.

On the island was a large, round geodesic metal building built as part of the Expo '67 World's Fair, but it had caught fire many years ago and was now just an interesting metal skeleton. As they passed by, Emilie decided to head in. It would be fun to explore all of the tunnels and steps inside.

"This place reminds me of a cheap sci fi horror movie," she explained.

"How so?" Dante asked, looking curiously around.

"It's just all empty, echo-y, and creepy, like something from one of those suspenseful chase scenes in the movies."

"Do you want me to chase you around?" he suggested playfully, a devilish grin decorating his face.

Emilie couldn't help but laugh. He was so mysterious and unpredictable. She had never met anyone like him and was getting increasingly worried about her feelings for him. "I guess we could act out some kind of scene, but I get to be the innocent heroine."

"What does that make me?" he asked, narrowing his eyes.

"If you're doing the chasing, then you have to be the bad guy," Emilie explained, punching him in the arm.

Dante looked her up and down strangely, rubbing his arm. She hadn't hit him very hard, but perhaps he was delicate. He had certainly felt well muscled in Emilie's opinion.

"Okay. Give me a minute to get into character," he said as he started breathing deeply and repeating, "I'm a bad guy."

"What's my motivation?" he asked, furrowing his brows in concentration.

"I guess you're trying to catch me or kill me or something. Whatever...use your imagination," Emilie suggested, watching him give her what she suspected was a bit of a suggestive glance, but it was difficult to know for sure through his dark glasses. Luckily he took them off and stuffed them into one of his many pants pockets.

"You go and hide or something," Dante ordered. He smiled broadly, turned, and walked out of sight through a tunnel. Emilie could hear him mumbling to himself, "I'm a bad guy and I'm going to kill Emilie."

She walked up some stairs and found a corner in which to hide. She wondered if he had taken some acting classes. He was just so silly. She didn't think he could pull this off. She was laughing to herself when she heard a very dark voice calling from close by.

"Emilie, are you in here? You can't hide from me."

He had an excellent dark and scary voice, but she couldn't help cracking up with laughter.

Dante's regular voice scolded, "Hey! You're ruining my focus."

"Sorry!" she yelled then covered her mouth quickly with her hand in a useless attempt at getting a grip on her giggling.

The dark and scary voice was back. "I know where you are now, silly girl. And I'm coming to get you."

Emilie couldn't tell where he was, but he sounded fairly close. She decided to move from her spot. She crept out and started walking away from where she thought she'd heard his voice.

"Emilie," he called eerily.

"Leave me alone!" she screeched, trying not to laugh.

"Oh, I wish I could," Dante growled. He sounded very close, but she still couldn't see him. She kept moving but tried hard to keep quiet. She was hoping to spot him before he found her.

"You're making me angry, and I'm not very nice when I'm angry."

The depth and resonance of his voice were extremely impressive. There was an almost animalistic rumble to his words. He must have taken classes. Emilie heard a menacing laugh echo from around a corner so she decided to run the other way as fast as she could. She headed back to her initial hiding place.

"Emilie, I can see you," Dante's dark voice called.

"What do you want from me!" she yelled. She had to cover her mouth again to keep from laughing out loud. She really didn't want to ruin his focus. He was doing so well.

There was a long pause and then his voice came from a completely different direction. "I want to hurt you."

Emilie was getting more and more impressed with his abilities by the minute. He was giving her the chills. She couldn't figure out how he was getting around so fast. She couldn't hear his footsteps anywhere.

"What did I ever do to you?" she cried, trying to use her best weepy hysterical heroine's voice. There was another pause and she tried desperately to locate him. She jumped when she heard his voice again.

"I'm a monster…and monsters hurt people."

He sounded really close again so she had to move fast. She started walking in a different direction, casting about desperately for any sign of him. "Please don't hurt me!" she begged.

His voice came from farther away now. "Don't worry. It won't last…forever."

He was creeping her out now. She walked through a tunnel and started to feel slightly disoriented.

"I can see you again, Emilie." His voice was coming from right behind her. She bolted into a run. All of the hair on the back of her neck was standing up. "It will all be over soon, my dear," he soothed.

Emilie glanced back and saw Dante emerging from a dark tunnel. She was amazed at how magnificently frightening he looked all dressed in black, striding toward her with such grace and confidence. It almost appeared as if there was a slight red glow to his eyes in the darkness. But she was sure it was only a trick of her imagination.

"Dante, you're scaring me now!" she cried over her shoulder in her real panicked voice as she fled. She ran up some stairs and heard his foot land on the bottom step behind her.

"Good!" he growled.

His voice had come from immediately behind her, and Emilie squealed in fright. She turned quickly, her hands coming up defensively, expecting him to be right there. She was shocked to find that he wasn't. She could have sworn he had been right behind her.

As she ran down some other steps, Dante jumped out of the shadows and grabbed her. He was incredibly strong. She screamed at the top of her lungs. He clamped his hand hard over her mouth and brought his beautiful yet terrifying face down to her ear. "Shhhhhhh," he whispered.

Emilie felt his lips gently brush her ear, and the sensation sent shivers down her spine. Then he suddenly released her and headed for the exit, leaving her staring wide-eyed at him. He turned around and called to her with a calm, smiling face and his normal magical voice, "I win! I'm hungry again. Let's go get something to eat."

Emilie was frozen in place, swallowing hard and trying to get her heart to stop pounding. He was much better at the game than she had originally given him credit for. He was almost out of the building when she finally started following him. She had to shake her head in wonder. He was one of the most fascinating men she had ever met, and she was becoming increasingly enamored with him. At that moment in time, she could have sworn she smelled the smoke of bridges burning.

ꙮ

Dante had to force himself to slow down. Emilie was falling behind. He just couldn't be near her any longer. He remembered the look of wonder and excitement on her face as he had chased her. She so easily gave in to her emotions. She was so free. She knew how to experience life to its fullest. She was…instinctive. She had almost enjoyed it as much as he had. Not a very human response. Humans got scared easily. They couldn't let themselves go and still manage their fear.

But she had been afraid in the end. Her fear had only made it more exciting for him. It had taken every ounce of control he possessed to walk away from her when he

finally had her trembling and panting in his arms. He
shivered, remembering how much he had wanted her at
that moment. But she had already screamed at the top
of her lungs. It would have been suicide to try anything
stupid.

All human civilians were protected by the council.
Demons, changelings, and humans unavoidably led to a
violent mix, and the council's relationship with human
governments was precarious. Therefore the council
needed to assure the humans that their citizens were
protected from the abusive appetites of vampires and
demons alike.

Council spies were everywhere, watching for potential problems. Council employees, in particular, were
under strict scrutiny. If anything happened to Emilie,
Dante would be held responsible, and the repercussions would be most severe. He was an Angel and if
he got caught out with her, it could ruin his reputation. The Dark Angels believed that one of the reasons
the originals had been cast from Heaven in the first
place was because they had chosen to seduce humans.
Consequently Angels were forbidden from having any
type of relationship with humans, especially romantic
ones. Dante was already stretching the grey areas of his
religion with his involvement in the venom trade and
the human criminals therein.

He glanced back to see if Emilie was still following.
She was. She had a mysterious expression on her face.
He could sense her fear as well as her desire. He should
really dash behind the nearest tree, disappear into

space, and head home, but he couldn't bring himself to
leave her. He wanted to slow down and let her catch up
to him. He could pull her behind a tree and kiss her.
Just one kiss. What was the harm?

Dante shook his head, trying to get the image out
of his mind. He couldn't risk it. He would only end up
wanting more, and that crossed lines he wasn't prepared
to cross. He saw an ice cream vendor and quickened his
pace. His teeth were too sensitive to eat such things, but
he was absolutely desperate. He would pick something
with a high fat content and hope he could choke it down
without drawing too much attention to his discomfort.
He needed a distraction from the direction his thoughts
were leading him.

પ્છ

As they lay back down on their picnic blanket, Emilie
saw Dante's friends coming up the path. Somehow she
wasn't surprised to see them.

Colin and Jude stopped and sat on a bench about
one hundred feet from them on the opposite side of the
path. Colin had brought a book to read as if he planned
to stay for a while. Jude just sat quietly, trying to look as
if he was minding his own business.

Emilie waved to them. Jude waved back, smiling
broadly. Colin peeked out from behind his book for
a second, but that was all. "Your friends have come to
chaperone you again," she mentioned to Dante, who was
staring up at the sky again.

"I spend far too much time with them," he mumbled, groaning in irritation. He just raised his head up off the blanket and peered over at Jude and Colin, then resumed his original position. "I didn't invite them. They're here on their own."

"Why are they here?" Emilie asked. *What kind of strange relationship do these three men have with each other anyway?* she wondered.

"We all have our issues," Dante began. "Jude doesn't like me to be out in public, and Colin doesn't like me to be out with..." He paused suddenly as if he had stopped himself from saying something important, then he continued more guardedly, "...Women."

Emilie glanced at him curiously. "Are they going to sit there the whole time we're here?" She was uncomfortable with the idea of being supervised.

"I'm sorry, but probably," he answered in a disinterested tone. "I told you that I have trouble getting away from them. I obviously wasn't just kidding."

"Can I ask you a favor?" Emilie asked mischievously.

"What?" he replied, lifting his head.

"Can I violate our no inappropriate touching rule and give you a back rub?"

"What?" he choked, sitting up.

"You know. A back rub." She opened and closed her hands in demonstration.

"Out here? In public?" he muttered incredulously.

"You can keep your shirt on," Emilie assured him. "This is going to be clean, so don't get any ideas." *What kind of massages are you used to receiving?* she wondered. "I just want to give your friends something to watch," she added out loud.

He smiled a crooked, dirty grin. "Where do you want me?"

"Just lay down on your stomach over here." She shifted and showed him where on the blanket she wanted him to lay. "Then you can watch them watching you." He obediently laid where she had indicated, crossing his arms out in front of him and resting his chin on his fists. His shoulder muscles were bunched up nicely under his shirt. *I'm going to have fun with this*, Emilie thought. "Are you comfy?" she asked.

"Ready."

She got up and stood over him with one foot on either side of his hips, facing Jude who was looking at her strangely. Then she knelt down on top of Dante, sitting on his behind.

Dante seemed as surprised as Jude. "You're going to get me into so much trouble with them."

She couldn't see his face, but he sounded amused. Emilie ran her hands slowly up his back and started kneading his shoulders. He groaned happily and stretched his arms out in front of him, laying his face down on his right cheek. His eyes closed and he smiled peacefully.

Emilie had rubbed many a man's back in her day and knew exactly what to do. She started at his neck and worked outward with both hands, then down his arms and back up to his neck. In the process she was practically lying down completely on top of him. Once she had worked her way back up to his neck, she glanced over at Jude and Colin. Jude was staring as though he had never seen anything like it before. Colin's mouth was hanging open, still holding his book out in front of him. *They weren't expecting a show like this one,* she thought, but was still curious why it mattered so much to them.

Dante propped his chin back on his hands and laughed to himself as he watched Jude and Colin's reactions. "You really complicate my life, you know, Emilie. I hope you aren't planning on seeing me again this weekend. I think I'll be away on a religious retreat."

Emilie had no idea what he was talking about, but his laughter was tightening the muscles she had worked so hard to loosen. "Hey, cut that out. You're getting all tense again. I'll have to start all over."

She felt him deliberately clench up all of the muscles in his arms and shoulders. He was very well put together indeed. He laughed and relaxed again then laid his head back down and closed his eyes. Emilie continued kneading down either side of his spine between her thumbs. Dante groaned and sighed happily. Her hands gentled as his muscles became more relaxed. Emilie's legs were starting to fall asleep, and she thought Dante was too, so she decided to stop. She stood up and stretched, trying to get the circulation flowing again.

She sat back down cross-legged on the blanket next to Dante. He barely seemed to notice her. She lay down on her stomach as well, crossing her arms and propping her chin on her hands. Jude laughed quietly to himself and Colin went back to reading, but he occasionally peeked out at them suspiciously. Emilie just closed her eyes and enjoyed the feel of the wind and the smell of the leaves. It was a glorious day, probably the last of the season. The air was already cooling. It was getting late in the afternoon.

"Hand me my phone. I seem to be unable to move at the moment," Dante teased. "You have a real talent and I need to schedule a regular appointment with you. How's every Thursday at four o'clock?"

"I have class Thursdays at four, sorry. We'll have to see. It might not be as much fun without our audience," she answered with a chuckle.

He snorted. "It'll be fun for me, I assure you," he insisted. He sat up and looked at her mysteriously. Then he yawned and stretched his arms up over his head with his fingers knitted together. Yawning is contagious of course, so Emilie yawned as well. Looking up, she saw Jude yawning too. *What a strange day,* she thought.

Dante pulled out his phone and dialled. Jude answered his phone over on the bench.

Dante ordered gruffly, "Go home!"

Jude covered his mouth and phone with his hand, whispering.

Dante listened carefully on his end. He grinned and looked briefly over at Emilie. "Don't be ridiculous," he hissed. He covered the phone and whispered to her, "He wants to know if we're planning on doing anything under the blanket." He rolled his eyes as though it was the most outrageous thing he'd ever heard.

Emilie just smiled back at him. *I'd be perfectly willing to crawl under the blanket with you, mister,* she thought. *Even out here in public.* They could always pretend they were all alone.

Dante was listening again. "We'll be leaving soon too. It's getting late. Emilie has work to do, I'm sure." He looked over at her again as though seeking confirmation.

Reluctantly she nodded her agreement. She wasn't ready to leave him just yet. Though she had to admit that she was unlikely to ever want to leave him. Especially with thoughts of what she would like to be doing with him under the blanket tumbling around in her imagination.

After a pause Dante said, "Listen, I came here with her alone, and I'm going to leave here with her alone. Go home." He was looking increasingly annoyed as he listened. Emilie wished she could hear what was being said. "I'm going to walk her home and then I'll be right back," Dante grumbled and rolled his eyes in frustration. "Yes. Right back. Good-bye, Jude."

He put his phone away, shaking his head. "Sorry about that. They don't get out much. They have quite vivid imaginations, I'm afraid," he explained.

"Don't worry about it. It's all good." She could relate to vivid imaginings a bit better than she was prepared to admit.

Jude and Colin got up and left. Jude waved to Emilie as he walked away.

"Next time I'm sneaking out and not telling anyone what I'm doing. No matter how risky it is," Dante grumbled to himself.

What an odd thing to say, Emilie thought. "What's risky about you being out without them, Dante?"

His mouth dropped open as if he had just realized that he'd actually spoken the words out loud. "It's nothing. I was just kidding," he mumbled. He put his sun glasses on and started helping her pack up their stuff. Emilie ran her eyes appreciatively over his body while he was facing away from her. *He's a very mysterious guy*, she thought. *I'm in big trouble now.*

ॐ

They rode back on the Metro, talking about all sorts of little nothings. Instead of finding it awkward, Emilie found it comfortable. She felt more at ease with Dante now that they had spent some time together. She tried hard not to think about how long it would be before she could manufacture an excuse to see him again. It would have to be after exams anyway. She had wasted far too much time today, but it had been worth every minute. She would have to knuckle down to work as soon as she got home.

Dante was true to his word and walked her home, carrying her bag over his shoulder. She was surprised that he actually followed her into her building and up the stairs, without saying a word about it.

Emilie unlocked her apartment door and opened it. "Do you want to come in?" she asked. Maybe he had changed his mind about what he had said to Jude earlier.

Dante poked his head in without stepping inside. He looked around carefully as though he was searching for something in particular. "I was just curious," he explained, handing her back her sports bag. Then he started backing away down the hall. "Good-bye, and thanks for the picnic. It was really fun," he added.

Emilie was disappointed to see him leave. "Good-bye, Dante. See you soon," she replied. She watched him turn around and walk out of sight, obviously heading for the stairs rather than waiting for the elevator. She already felt empty without him. This was going to be an excruciating couple of weeks.

She closed the door and stood in the entrance, running the day's events through her mind. Emilie had anticipated this very situation. Now she was even more attached to Dante. She had always been physically attracted to him, but now her desire had intensified. Being held so tightly in his arms and having his lips brush her ear had been one the most sensual experiences of her life.

She would be able to dismiss these shallow sentiments if they were alone. Unfortunately they were in very good company. Spending time with Dante had allowed her to get to know him better as a person, and what she had learned had only made her respect him more. *What am I going to do?* she demanded of herself.

Emilie had to admit that she wasn't simply infatuated with Dante. She was falling head over heels in love with him.

۵

Dante stepped into the stairwell of Emilie's building. He stopped, took a deep breath, and rubbed his hand across his face. She was all alone in her apartment, and she had been telling him, in many ways, all day long, what she wanted from him.

He should never have let her touch him. *What a big mistake,* he thought angrily. He closed his eyes and remembered the feel of her skillful hands. Even fully clothed it had been too exciting. It was a good thing that Jude and Colin were right there watching or he might have made a terrible mess of things. It would have been easy.

When you can travel inter-dimensionally through space, you can go anywhere. Well, not anywhere, and each individual had their own skill level. It was greatly facilitated by having a visual picture of where you were going. This was the reason for his little peek into Emilie's apartment. He would never dream of entering her place uninvited, but just in case.

Dante wanted to go back to her right here and now. No one would have to know. He indulged his fantasies for a minute, fully accepting that he couldn't risk it. It went against everything he believed.

What did he believe? No humans…Why? *I'm not going to hurt her. Why did this have to happen to me?* he thought miserably.

Emilie wouldn't be his first human girl, but his past transgressions didn't justify what he was currently contemplating. She would be his first human civilian. Big trouble. It was one thing to indulge your fantasies through the safety of the council. It was quite a different thing to risk something like this.

Dante felt ill. He couldn't figure out why he always felt so sick to his stomach whenever he was away from Emilie—or with her, for that matter. Why did he spend so much of his time, waking and non-waking, thinking about her? It was affecting everything in his life. He couldn't eat. He couldn't rest. He was distracted at work and at play. Jude had almost broken his skull open the other day in training because he had been distracted even then.

What's wrong with me? he thought angrily. Maybe he needed to go to the hospital. Perhaps there was some medication he could take for this problem. *Who am I kidding? I know exactly what the cure to my problem is: Leave her alone!*

It made his chest ache to think about not seeing Emilie again. He must be ill. This had never happened to him before in his life. Dante gasped. He realized for the first time what his problem was. He was love sick. How could this have happened? He was falling in love with her. *This is love,* he thought resentfully. *This can't be love. This is Hell!* He was supposed to be getting bored with her, not falling in love. He was so confused.

He listened to see if anyone was coming. No one. He opened an inter-dimensional doorway and walked through to the entrance of his condo.

Colin ran out of the kitchen and stared at Dante as though waiting for a confession.

"I didn't do anything!" Dante yelled. "Don't look at me like that!" He wasn't in the mood for this. Being a nobleman had certain perks, but he was becoming increasingly envious of those who led simpler lives with less responsibility and more privacy.

Jude came out of his room in his track clothes, laughing. "Do you have any energy left?"

"Did you call Colin home from Thailand?" Dante accused. Colin had the same ability as Dante and could be beckoned at a moment's notice.

"Of course I did," Jude admitted unabashedly. "Did you really think I would leave you alone, out in public?"

Dante glared at him but had to smile. He marched into his room to change. He would run until he was too weak to stand, then he would shower and go to bed. Alone, in Hell. He wasn't in love. He just couldn't be.

Chapter 7

Emilie, locked up in her apartment to study for her exam tomorrow, was startled as her phone rang in the silence. She checked the number and picked up. "Hello."

"Howdy, stranger," Caroline said cheerfully. "'Sup."

"Oh, I have so much review to do. I'm never gonna get through it all."

"You're gonna ace that exam, chickita. You worry too much," Caroline soothed. "Sophie and Melissa want to meet for Tonkinese soup tonight. Are you in?"

Emilie sighed wistfully. Vietnamese soup was one of her favorite comfort foods. "You know how I feel about pho, but I can't. If I stop now, I'll never get through this."

"Come on, Emilie. It seems the only person who can get you out of your books these days is Dante Ashton."

"I know," Emilie muttered. "My life's messed up."

"Have you heard from him?" Caroline asked.

"We've texted back and forth a bit, but I haven't seen him since the picnic."

"He's an idiot, and a blind one at that," Caroline replied.

"No, he's been up-front with me from the beginning. I can't blame him for my problems."

"He bought you jewelry and he'd just met you. Don't you think there might be something going on?"

"I don't," Emilie answered. "Maybe he prefers blonds."

"He's an idiot," Caroline repeated. "You should come out with the girls. It would be good for you to meet some new people. I'm worried about you."

You should be. I'm falling for another emotionally unavailable bad boy, Emilie thought. Out loud she said, "I'm being realistic about this, Caroline. I'd rather be friends than nothing. I think he's a good guy, deep inside. Maybe we'll get along famously as long as I don't try to become something I'm not and make him run screaming."

"I don't agree," Caroline argued. "You're attached to him, and as long as he's in your life, you're going to keep yourself available for him. I don't want you to miss out because you're hanging on to something that isn't even there."

"You're such a good friend, you know," Emilie declared. "I know you care about me, but I'm fine. Really."

"Okay, but you have to eat. You know how you get when you don't?"

Emilie chuckled. Caroline knew her well. "I'll take care of myself. You go out with the girls and have some spring rolls for me with extra peanut sauce. Soon the exams will be over and I promise we'll celebrate."

"I'm gonna hold you to that, sister!"

"I promise you," Emilie insisted.

"Good," Caroline grumbled. "Good-bye for now."

"I'll see you tomorrow."

Emilie put away her phone and stood up to stretch. She walked to the fridge and took out her last can of Coke. Not a good sign. She would have to nurse this one carefully to get her through her study session. She cracked open the can and headed back to her desk.

A couple of hours later she was starving. She had no food worth eating in her fridge, and she didn't have the time or the energy to go get any groceries.

She was going to be up cramming half the night, but she needed food and a descent boost of caffeine to make it through these last chapters. Emilie regretted refusing Caroline's offer. The thought of soup was making her salivate.

Emilie sighed deeply. Maybe she could just have a bag of popcorn for supper. It was nine o'clock already. She would have to make a decision soon.

It wasn't very tempting to go out alone, and it didn't take long for her thoughts stray to a certain someone who also didn't like to eat alone. She wondered if Dante was even home. He was often out of town all week. Emilie decided to send him a text message. She smiled as she typed:

R u hungry?

These words had worked before, maybe they would again. She would have to wait and see if he would even get it. He could be somewhere where he didn't get any cell phone service. She wouldn't be able to wait for long because she was too hungry. Luckily her phone soon received a reply.

Always!

She sent:

R u @ home?

He could be away on business. Her phone beeped.

Yes.

Emilie felt especially lucky because Dante had a car. She didn't have much time to waste. She sent:

Studying. Starving. Need caffeine. Please come save me!

He was smart and had an adventurous sense of humor. He would understand. Her phone beeped.

15 mins.

Dante was on his way, and Emilie was a complete disaster. She dashed into her bedroom to find something to wear. She couldn't be seen with the most gorgeous man in the world looking the way she was. She needed to think of a good place to go as well. She had one idea in particular, an excellent little coffee shop not too far from her apartment that had the most fantastic sandwiches. They were always busy, but they were open late. It was a Wednesday night, in the middle of exams. It shouldn't be too bad.

Emilie's phone rang, and Dante's magical voice said, "I'm here, let's go!"

"I'll be right down," she answered, already turning off the lights and locking up.

As she stepped off the elevator, she eagerly looked for Dante to be standing on the other side of the door. She couldn't wait to get her eyes on him again, and was curious to see what outfit he would be wearing this time.

But he wasn't there. She saw a red car with its hazard lights flashing, double parked in front of the door. She ran to it.

As Emilie closed the car door, Dante smiled broadly and said, "Where to?" She gave him directions to the coffee shop and then they were off. Parking was going to be a nightmare. At least it wasn't cold and raining.

"Thank you for saving me," she said.

"Anytime," he answered cheerfully.

"I was surprised you were in town in the middle of the week like this."

"Last week I worked nine days in a row so I'm taking it a bit easy this week."

"Sounds like you earned it."

"I wish my employers were as sympathetic," he joked. "I'm glad you called tonight because tomorrow I'm going to London and I'll probably be gone for a while."

"Then I'm glad too." Emilie didn't want to mention that she would call him every day if she could.

Dante's eyes kept darting in her direction. "You smell really good tonight," he purred in a bewildered tone. "What's different about you?"

Emilie didn't know whether he was complimenting her or insulting her. "How do I normally smell?" she asked, giggling self-consciously.

He may have realized his error and started back-pedaling. "I'm sorry," he began. "That didn't come out right at all. Let me try again. You always smell good. Tonight you smell better than usual. Did you do some-thing different?"

Dante's eyes were running over her very intently, almost intimately. Emilie felt awkward and uncomfortable so she just answered, "I have no idea. I haven't been paying attention."

He just smiled mysteriously and mumbled, "I have."

After a relatively easy search for parking, they walked together toward the coffee shop.

"This place has the best sandwiches," she commented hungrily.

"Sounds good," Dante said less enthusiastically.

Emilie remembered something. "I'm sure you'll find something raw on the menu," she teased.

He threw her a tentative glance. "I don't have to eat everything raw," he replied defensively.

She shot him a dazzling grin and added, "You could always have a nice salad."

Dante made a sickened face. "Sounds great," he replied sarcastically. "Actually, I've already eaten. I just needed to get out for a bit."

"Oh…I thought you were hungry."

"I am. I just don't need to eat a whole meal."

Once seated at a table, they browsed quietly through their menus.

"So what tempts you?" Emilie asked.

Dante looked at her over the top of his menu and smiled mysteriously. "Nothing on this menu," he muttered somewhat resentfully.

Emilie's heart sank. "Do you want to go somewhere else?" she asked. She hoped they wouldn't have to leave because she really didn't have time to waste. She was also beginning to feel a bit desperate for food.

"No, that wouldn't help," he answered, sticking his face back behind his menu.

"I don't mind going somewhere else if you can't find anything good here," she urged, suddenly feeling guilty for her selfishness.

"I'm fine. Tell me what you're having," he said, obviously trying to put her at ease.

Emilie scanned the menu and made a final choice. "I'll probably have a sandwich and a milk shake."

"I don't like cold things. I have sensitive teeth."

The waitress came and took their order. Dante had decided on a bagel with smoked salmon and some green tea.

"Boy, you must be jet-lagged or something. You seem really cranky tonight," Emilie said, not quite joking. She had grown accustomed to his light-hearted sense of humor and was unprepared for this change of attitude.

"I know, I know. I'm sorry," Dante grumbled but gave her his sad-puppy look for good measure. "I'm feeling a bit stressed tonight. Maybe I won't be very good company."

Emilie smiled. "You're *always* good company."

He smiled back and said, "So what's new with you?"

"Not much. Just studying for exams." She felt embarrassed that she had such a boring life, especially compared to his. "It must be wonderful, jetting off to faraway lands. Where have you been lately?"

He smiled at her strangely. "I've been mostly in Asia, Bangkok, Beijing, Tokyo, and other places."

Emilie couldn't imagine what that must be like. "What's your favorite city?"

"Now that's a tough question," Dante answered, leaning back in his seat. "Thailand is my favorite country, but I've been to some fantastic cities over the years. To pick just one is impossible."

The way Dante had spoken those words sounded like an old man reminiscing about decades of work.

"How many years have you been working?"

Dante paused, thinking carefully. "It feels like forever. Why don't you tell me what exam you have tomorrow?"

Emilie hadn't missed how he had switched the focus back on her. "Comparative religious mythology."

The waitress interrupted them with Emilie's double espresso and milk shake as well as Dante's pot of green tea. He thanked her sweetly and watched her go then quickly turned back to Emilie. "Do you find anything interesting about it?"

"I find people's definitions of Heaven and Hell interesting," she answered. She noticed a gold necklace around Dante's neck with a cute little angel charm on it. "Are you religious?"

He seemed taken aback by her question. "I am. Why do you ask?"

"I was curious about your angel charm. Does it mean anything special?"

He reached for the charm. "It's just a religious symbol. Nothing special. Are you religious?" he asked, looking at her with interest.

"No...I consider myself an atheist," Emilie replied. *He's doing it again*, she thought. "What's your definition of Heaven?"

"That's a hard one." He took a deep breath and let it out slowly. "I don't know. Somewhere you can be with the people you love. What's yours?"

"Not being religious, I find the idea of Heaven rather disturbing. What do people do in Heaven anyway?"

"I have no clue. Spend time with loved ones, I suppose. What are your thoughts on Hell?"

"Now there's some imagery. Cultural perspectives of Heaven can be described as vaguely inspirational, but there are some very detailed depictions of what Hell is like. It's supposed to be a place of absolute suffering. In my opinion, life can be Hell sometimes. Maybe Heaven is just not having to slog through life anymore. What's your definition of Hell?"

Dante froze, eyebrows raised speculatively. Then he shook his head and laughed. "I may be cranky, but you're feeling rather dark tonight."

Emilie didn't know what to say. "Sorry..."

"No, it's okay," he interrupted. "My definition of Hell is being trapped between this world and another and being unable to be a part of either. Why do you think life's Hell? You always seem so happy."

Emilie thought carefully. "Life is really hard sometimes. There can be a lot of unnecessary pain and suffering." She was beginning to relate to his need to change the subject. This line of thought was leading down a dark path. "Do you want to spend time with any loved ones in particular when you're in Heaven?"

"I'll be lucky if I get to go to Heaven," Dante answered. "I believe my mother is there and I would like to see her one day. So tell me...Do you believe any pain and suffering is necessary?"

Emilie felt for Dante. She had lost both of her parents. "Sometimes pain and suffering help us to learn and grow. We can gain a better appreciation for the things we have in our lives. How old were you when your mother died?"

He looked sadly into his cup. "I was very young. Are your parents still alive?"

"No...My parents died almost two years ago in a car accident. They had a head-on collision and...there was a fire." For some reason Emilie couldn't understand, her memories overwhelmed her and her emotions clamped her throat shut, preventing her from speaking.

Dante looked across the table with concern etched into his lovely features. "I'm sorry. I didn't mean to upset you," he whispered. He seemed uncertain about what course of action to take in order to comfort her.

His sincerity in itself did make her feel a bit better. Emilie took a drink of coffee to try to loosen her throat. She refused to embarrass herself in front of Dante by blubbering in a public place. "I'm sorry about that," she muttered with a dismissive wave of her hand. "I don't know what got into me. I've had lots of time to come to grips with my loss, and I'm surprised I got upset about it now for no apparent reason."

"There's always a reason to be upset about losing people we love," he soothed.

"I guess you're right. Everybody dies. It's part of life, and there's never a good way to lose somebody."

Dante snorted. "Okay, now I'm cranky and depressed. Can we talk about something else? How about something more cheerful…like global warming?"

Emilie wondered what had been going through her head. Religion and death, great topics of conversation for friends and food. A change of subject was definitely in order.

They were both chuckling when the waitress finally brought their food. As the woman set down Dante's plate, Emilie noticed that he was particularly well dressed. He had on an emerald green sweater with an elegant button-up shirt underneath. The shade of green brought out the gold in his brown eyes.

"That color suits you," Emilie commented, trying not to drool as she spoke.

Dante looked down at his sweater curiously. "I like green, but mostly I wear black and red."

"I like purple and black myself." She appreciated his rock star style, but this runway model look really worked for him. She would never get tired of looking at him, no matter what he was wearing. *Or not wearing*, she thought longingly.

"What's so funny?" he asked resentfully, glaring at her as though she was hiding something of interest from him.

Emilie felt herself blushing from head to foot. She hadn't realized that she'd been smiling so broadly. He'd caught her fantasizing about him and now she didn't know what to say. "I was just thinking, that's all. Nothing interesting."

Dante narrowed his eyes suspiciously. Emilie knew he was too smart to believe her, but she wasn't about to tell him the truth.

They finished eating without any other embarrassing incidents or controversial topics of discussion. Unfortunately Emilie could hear her school work calling from home. *Time really does fly*, she thought angrily.

When the bill came, she tried to take it before Dante, but he wouldn't cooperate. She glared at him in mock anger. "Going out tonight was my idea. You don't always have to pay for me. I have money too, you know?"

"I know, but if you want to pay then you'll have to beat me in a fight," he challenged. He puffed himself up and put an aggressive snarl on his face.

"What kind of fight?" Emilie asked, slightly distracted by his broad shoulders.

"Martial arts," he answered with the kind of confidence that only came from experience.

"Sorry, I'm a ballerina, or at least I was when I was younger," she conceded.

"I'm not surprised," he murmured as he stuffed some money into the folder. "Too bad then. I'm paying."

"Okay...Thank you again," Emilie said. She didn't like feeling as though she owed a man anything. But in his case she would have been more than happy to make it worth his while. Even if he had let her pay for their food.

"Are you ready?" he asked. "You seem anxious to leave."

"It's not the company," she soothed. "It's my exam."

"Don't worry, I understand."

They walked quickly back to the car. It was getting colder at night these days. The ride back to her apartment went too fast. She hardly had any time to admire him, but at least there was less time for her to fumble around incompetently, trying to think of something interesting or intelligent to say.

As Dante pulled up to her building, Emilie said, "I would invite you in, but I've got to get back to work if I'm going to be ready for tomorrow." On any other day, she would have loved to get him alone for a while.

"I'd love to come in, but I leave early tomorrow morning."

Emilie leaned over to kiss him on the cheek, but they got confused over which cheek to offer and ended up brushing their lips together. She felt the color rush up her face, but she didn't regret the accident. She was more than happy to have her lips on his, even for a fleeting instant. "I'm sorry. I'm usually more coordinated than that," she mumbled in embarrassment, trying not to meet his gaze.

"Me too. Don't worry about it," he replied reassuringly, punctuated with an uncomfortable chuckle.

"Thanks again and good night." She sighed as she slid out of the car and smiled sheepishly as she closed the door. He waved to her as he drove off, smiling devilishly.

Emilie stood and watched him go, cursing her luck. Now she was going to have an impossible time studying. She would be spending too much time thinking about their lips touching. Even if it wasn't a real kiss, it was close enough for her.

❦

Dante had to pull the car over to collect himself. He couldn't catch his breath. He stabbed at the window buttons beside him. He had to get Emilie's scent out of the car before he lost his mind completely.

His sense of smell was delicate, and he could tell exactly what time of the month it was for her. She was fertile. His nasal passages had the pheromone receptors necessary to detect these subtle nuances in body chemistry. He rumbled a long, ragged growl from deep within his chest. He found her desirable on an average day, but today he was lucky he had managed to resist her.

What's wrong with me? he growled. *She's just a human.* He prided himself on his self-control. He wasn't a complete animal. His losing control signified that something was at its most extreme. He closed his eyes and let the cold, clean air wash over him.

He had to smile to himself. He had set Emilie up to "accidently" kiss him. He had wanted to grab her and kiss her long and hard, but it would have required an explanation. He wasn't prepared to go down that road. He was just curious and wanted a little taste. No harm done.

He thanked God in Heaven that she hadn't asked him to come in because he probably would have gone with her. Jude and Colin could have yelled at him in the morning until they were blue in the face but he would have smirked all the way through their lecture.

Dante had been around fertile human girls before and none of them had ever affected him to this level. He had never felt so compelled by any woman before. Emilie had been almost mystically alluring, like something out of the legends.

Having sufficiently regained his composure, he closed the windows and pulled back out into traffic. He had to stop seeing this girl. It was getting too tempting. She was trouble in capital letters, and he was obviously enchanted by her, body and soul.

Dante was almost painfully aroused and decided to head to the council office. He had an undeniable craving for the warmth and comfort of a woman's body, and the office guaranteed him an easy solution to his problem.

He arrived at the office and headed down into the underground parking lot. He had to stop and riffle through his wallet for his employee parking permit. Travelling inter-dimensionally meant that he didn't often bring his car. He was waved through and drove off in search of a good spot.

He popped from the garage right to the reception entrance. The office had a system of sensors that detected anyone travelling in this way. There were only two places that people of his ability could arrive without setting off the alarm system. One was the main reception area and the other was the hospital emergency entrance.

He headed directly to Roberta Pitrya's department to speak to the receptionist. He didn't have an appointment and this might throw an inconvenient wrench in his plans. As he passed the main locker room, he heard a great many female voices and the running of water. *Must be a busy night*, Dante thought. Maybe there wouldn't be anyone available on such short notice.

"Hi!" he said to the receptionist, whose name eluded him at the moment. She was a changeling, and he didn't bother to keep as careful track of them.

"Hello, Dante," the girl replied, smiling cheerfully.

"I need to see someone tonight," he declared. She glanced at her appointment book in confusion, but he quickly added, "I don't have an appointment."

She looked surprised and uncertain. "I don't know..." she began. "Roberta has gone for the day, as have most of the people in the building. I don't know if we have anyone for you."

Dante didn't normally touch human girls and he didn't particularly enjoy having women who were only entertaining him because they were being paid to do so. The council offices had a system where all of his kind could volunteer themselves to be on the fantasy lists of any individuals they found attractive. Dante had always found it more fun to be with someone who had agreed to warm his bed. On the other hand, many people were encouraged to volunteer because they could earn generous "performance bonuses" from the office for offering such services.

Because of the social class system, this policy gave many individuals the opportunity to experience someone below them or above them, whatever the case may be, in a safe and controlled environment. Everybody won. Plus having easy access to sex made it less likely that his kind would be driven out into the human population to satisfy their cravings.

"What about a nice human girl?" the receptionist asked. "We've recently received a new batch."

Dante shuddered. "Humans are off limits."

"Oh, right," she corrected herself, smiling sheepishly. "I forgot."

"Isn't there anyone?" he asked with a hint of desperation in his voice.

She ran her eyes over him speculatively. "Well, I could call around and see if anyone on your list is available. How long are you prepared to wait?"

"I'm in a bit of a hurry," he grumbled. Maybe he would have to go home and get dressed to go out to Reds. But it would take so much time and energy, and he was feeling lazy. He just needed an itch scratched.

"Are you looking for something special tonight?"

Dante knew exactly what he was looking for, but it wasn't within the realm of possibility. "How about someone with long dark hair and aqua eyes?"

The receptionist laughed. "Are you really going to be that picky?"

"You know me," Dante purred and batted his eyelashes at her.

"Yes, you're extremely picky," she replied with some irritation. "Unless you want to come back later."

Dante sighed heavily. "Fine," he conceded. "See what you can do."

"Okay," she said. "Do you want to have a seat or do you want to wait in a room?"

"I'll wait here," Dante answered.

"Sounds good," she stated. "Hopefully this won't take long."

Dante finally noticed that the receptionist had long dark hair and blue eyes. She might serve his purposes quite nicely. "When do you get a break?" he asked with a mischievous grin.

She laughed again, but this time more uncomfortably. "I don't think I'm brave enough to take you on."

"Oh, I'm harmless," he purred.

"That's not what I've heard."

"I can be tame," he replied in a smooth and silky voice.

She shook her head with confidence, and Dante sighed in defeat. It was probably for the best. He didn't want to feel awkward every time he came here during her shift.

"Okay, let me know if you change your mind," he said and sat in a seat close to her desk so he could eavesdrop on her calls.

She smiled sweetly, nodded her head, and picked up the phone.

Who was put on your lists was usually kept secret. This way if anyone changed their minds or refused an opportunity, the matter could be handled with delicacy. Even in his cold world, people could be easily offended.

While Dante waited, he sent Jude a text to let him know what was going on. If Jude thought Dante had just snuck out of the condo for a little immediate gratification then he might not be so furious.

Dante noticed a small collection of human girls of various races being ushered toward the locker room by armed guards. Many of the girls looked very young, and some were openly weeping.

Dante felt bad for them. Human traffickers sold many girls to council offices around the world. Most of them ended up milked of their blood and used as sex slaves. Demons and Angels alike tended to enjoy rather aggressive behavior with each other between the sheets, but a human's body didn't have the same pain resistance and healing capabilities. In order to keep his kind from seeking sexual satisfaction in the civilian population the council had to offer services which would satisfy even the most twisted and bloody cravings.

Dante had felt so badly for some of these unfortunate girls over the years that he'd actually bought a few and set them free. Regrettably many of those he had saved had ended up right back in the office. There were just too many unfortunate people in the world. It was common for desperate humans to sign contracts with the council, virtually selling themselves into slavery. His species referred to it as "selling your soul to the Devil."

Maybe one of those girls was destined to be another nobleman's mistress. Many of his fellows tried to father illegitimate children of mixed blood called "nephilim." The council encouraged this behavior and offered girls for sale to keep men out of the human population. Pregnancy was a death sentence for a human, so it was imperative that nobody had any "accidents" with civilians. It was technically against the law to have sex with a civilian, and the penalty was harsh enough to discourage most people from taking their chances. Both men and women could buy any services they desired from the council. Secrecy was imperative, and nothing drew attention more quickly than bloody rapes and murders.

His species had such a undeniable instinct to breed, and yet had a terribly low birth rate. Infertility had plagued his people since the Fall. Also the ratio of men to women was extremely skewed, leaving far more males with few available mates. Women of his kind were highly prized and picked only the strongest, richest, and most powerful men with whom to have a child. Competition was fierce, which left a great deal of frustrated individuals who required easy access to an alternative source of satisfaction.

A human girl dressed in a silk robe came in to collect the key to her room. Dante's eyes flicked up to hers but went right back to his phone.

The girl leaned over the receptionist's desk and whispered, "Sabrina, is this who I'm seeing tonight?"

Dante's eyes flicked up again, but only because he wanted to see if she was referring to him. Sabrina looked appropriately embarrassed. "No," she answered quickly. "He's waiting for someone else."

"Well, how about I take him, and his girl can take my client?" the girl suggested.

Dante flashed his irritation to the receptionist. He wasn't interested in any exceptions tonight.

The red glow in his eyes had allowed the human girl to identify him as someone special, but instead of realizing her place and showing more respect, she only became bolder. "Oh..." the girl murmured, obviously impressed. "He's born, not made."

Sabrina was looking more uncomfortable by the second. She leaned in closer and put her hand in front of her mouth, but Dante could still hear her say, "He's not just born, he's a nobleman. So leave him alone!"

"I have always wanted to try a real v—" the girl began, but Sabrina actually leapt out of her chair and clamped her hand over the girl's mouth, silencing her. Sabrina shot Dante a concerned glance as if she expected him to bolt out of his chair and tear the human girl to shreds.

"You're just lucky he's an Angel, you stupid girl. Now go to your room and wait there," Sabrina snarled, all friendliness gone from her voice. She released the girl's mouth and stuffed a key in her hand. Sabrina pointed toward the playrooms and shot the girl a look as if to suggest that if she continued to humiliate herself, she would be left to face the consequences on her own.

Dante was beyond irritated at this point and glared angrily at the girl, allowing his eyes to glow bright red. The girl finally realized her mistake and walked quickly away without another word.

Sabrina leaned over toward him and said, "I'm sorry, Dante. We have so many new girls, and some of them just haven't been paying attention."

"It's not your fault, Sabrina," he soothed. He stood up and put his phone away. "But I think I've lost my appetite."

"Oh, Dante," Sabrina said with a sigh. "I'm so sorry."

"Don't worry about it," Dante added, an artificially cheerful grin plastered to his face. "Next time I'll know better than to come here without an appointment."

She smiled warmly to him as he left. He headed toward the parking garage. It was better this way. He would have been thinking of Emilie the whole time anyway.

Chapter 8

Dante rushed down the hall toward his father's office. As he walked along, his skin crawled with so many desirous eyes wandering over his body. His nose was filled with a disturbing combination of pheromones and the smell of blood. He was already feeling agitated because his schedule had been disrupted and also because he hadn't had enough to eat. His instincts were sending him confusing messages about his appetites and he had to concentrate harder than usual to keep himself relaxed. He really hated meeting his father at the university. He leaned on the door frame of his father's office door and knocked.

Graham Ashton looked up from his desk and motioned Dante in. "Close the door behind you please," he asked.

Dante complied with his orders and sat in a chair in front of the desk. "So what's so important that you had to call me away from work?"

"I want to talk to you about this," his father answered, holding up a manila envelope.

Dante growled his irritation. He had received a copy of the envelope as well. "You can't be serious," he grumbled. Now he knew exactly what this was about—marriage. "Couldn't this have waited until the weekend?

I had to go to the condo to change, and now I'll have to go back before I can head to work again."

His father looked slightly sheepish. "This was the only way I knew to get your attention."

"You shouldn't cry wolf, Dad," Dante scolded. "There might come a time when you really need me and I'll be afraid to come."

"Don't be ridiculous. You're my son. You'll always come," his father replied with confidence.

Dante rolled his eyes impatiently. "So?"

"Annapurra Enasvant has sent you a very nice letter, suggesting her illegitimate daughter as a possible bride."

"Forget it!" Dante growled.

"Anna is the chairman of the Beijing Council. She's from the top-ranking family and she's venomous. Plus she was your grandfather's favorite wife and has known you your whole life. This is quite an honor and an excellent opportunity."

"Really?" Dante sneered.

"Yes, really. You carry a venom gene and so does Asura. You could get lucky and have a venomous child together," his father explained in a tone that suggested Dante was a simpleton if he hadn't figured it out on his own.

"She isn't even sexually mature yet," Dante complained.

"She will be in the next four years or so. I think it's an advantageous match for you."

"I'm too young to get married," Dante argued.

His father snorted disdainfully and slammed the envelope on his desk to stress his annoyance. "Most men your age have been married at least three times."

"Okay, then. I don't want to get married."

"Dante, this marriage would be good for you."

"I know...But I don't want to marry an illegitimate girl," Dante grumbled. "No matter how high ranking she may be," he added for good measure.

"How many times do I have to apologize to you for my genes," his father snapped defensively.

"That's not what I meant, Dad. It's not your fault," Dante soothed.

"Yes it is. Don't try to pretend otherwise," his father muttered. "If I wasn't a changeling then you would be able to marry much better. I blame myself."

Dante always felt bad when his father started down this line of argument. "My mother loved you and you gave up being human to marry her. She chose you as my father. I'm proud of that fact."

"Not much to be proud of."

"It could have been worse," Dante argued. "You could have remained human, and then I would have been born illegitimate. Then Anna wouldn't be making me this offer at all. Because of your sacrifice, I was born a nobleman."

"I thank God everyday for giving me the strength to have myself transformed. I don't know what we would have done if you were illegitimate. Your being born a man of noble blood has made all the difference in your life...and mine."

"I still don't want to marry this girl."

"Will you at least consider it?" his father pleaded.

"If it will make you happy," Dante conceded. "But what am I going to do with a pubescent fiancée?"

"You'll be given her virginity," his father purred.

Dante made a disinterested face. "Whatever..."

"Most noblemen are willing to go to great lengths to be a well-blooded young lady's first husband."

"I'm not like most noblemen, Dad," Dante argued. "I don't bed my servants. I'm not trying to father any illegitimate children, and I don't feel the need to collect virginities."

"Still," his father began, "you need an heir, and you're running out of time."

"Give me a break!" Dante roared. "Running out of time...I still have at least a hundred years, probably two!"

"You're just cocky because you have such a high sperm count," his father corrected with a dirty grin. "If you'll excuse the pun."

Dante sniggered. "I'm lucky, I know. There are a great many noblemen who die without an heir, and not for a lack of trying."

"What are you waiting for?"

"I don't know," Dante admitted, letting his own frustration show.

"You're not still hoping to enchant Tasia, are you?"

Dante sighed heavily. Everyone knew that he'd asked and been refused. Now everyone thought he was unmarried because he was still pining after this girl. How ridiculous! "I gave up on her a long time ago. Now we see each other once in a while and it works fine for us."

"You may yet get her pregnant." His father's hope was coming through loud and clear. "Speaking of a fortuitous marriage."

"Her father will have me killed first. Not to mention Gavin. He's hoping Tasia will bear him an heir. He would be extremely vexed if I was to father her child." Dante chuckled to himself, thinking of the look on his old friend's face when he got that piece of news. Dante would love to be a fly on the wall to witness it. He laughed even harder as he realized that Gavin, being a shape-shifter, would just turn himself into a lizard and pluck him off the wall.

"Oh well," Dante sighed. "I have to get back to work. If you don't have any other pressing matters to discuss." He shot his father a stern glance so he would be sure to understand that this type of discussion didn't warrant an interruption in his work schedule.

"Okay," his father agreed. "I'll drop this if you'll promise to consider Asura Enasvant as a potential wife."

"Fine," Dante conceded. "I'll consider her, but I won't make a decision until she's sexually mature. Deal?"

"Fine," his father replied. "As a changeling, I don't have as long as you left in my life, and I would like to hold my grandchild before I die."

"I hope you will." Dante quickly rapped his knuckles on the desk so as not to jinx himself. Breeding was serious business, and he couldn't afford to get cocky no matter how humorous it seemed at the time.

જી

Midterm exams were finally over, and Emilie was ready to unwind. She was honoring her promise to her best friend by planning to go out dancing with Caroline and some of the girls. Dancing was always a great form of stress release. Emilie could think of a better way, but she was single.

Seeing that her mind was already in the gutter, she allowed herself to imagine what it would be like to relieve a little stress in bed with Dante. She knew she would be better off if she didn't think about him beyond the boundaries of their friendship. What she needed was to find a real boyfriend. Someone other than Dante, but that thought didn't hold as much appeal as the ones preceding it.

Emilie wasn't the type of person to brag about her abilities, but she was a good dancer. It would be great if she was able to show off for him. Maybe he would see her in a different light. With the right dress and a little liquid courage she might persuade him to add some extra benefits to their friendship. The very thought sent shivers down her spine. Emilie decided call him. At this point she had nothing to lose and everything to gain.

As the phone rang she sat holding her breath, hoping Dante would pick up. She hadn't thought this plan of hers through all the way because she didn't even know what she was going to say. She was thankful for her impulsive nature. If she thought things through, she would talk herself out of so many potentially beneficial situations. Sure, she might save herself some pain, but she would miss out on some fantastic adventures.

"Hello," a magical voice answered.

Another shiver run down her spine just hearing his voice in her ear. "Hello, it's Emilie."

"I know," he replied mischievously. "It's the only reason I bothered to pick up."

"Oh...Are you busy?" she asked, suddenly embarrassed.

"Nothing important. What's up?"

"My midterms are done and I'm going out dancing tonight with a bunch of friends. I was wondering if you guys wanted to join us." She couldn't believe how lame she sounded.

Silence. Emilie wasn't sure if he had even heard her. Maybe he was busier than he had let on. "Sounds tempting," he finally answered.

Emilie's excitement seized up her throat. She wanted to squeal with glee, but his voice had sounded undecided. "Great!" she cheered before he had a chance to change his mind. "Do you think Jude and Colin will want to tag along?"

"What do you think?" he answered with a laugh.

Jude and Colin almost never left Dante alone, for any reason. They would show up whether or not they were invited. Those three were definitely going to attract attention tonight.

They worked out the details, and Emilie scrambled desperately to get herself out the door. She had to undertake the daunting task of finding the perfect dress.

She picked up her phone to call Caroline but quickly put it away, deciding not to mention anything about the boys to Caroline. Emilie owed her friend a special surprise and wanted to see the look on Caroline's face when she saw Dante and his friends for the first time.

ॐ

The girls met for a late dinner before heading to the club. It was advisable to have a good meal before you went out drinking and dancing. Fortunately everyone lived downtown and no one had to drive. The girls walked together to the club, chatting casually. Emilie was anxious to meet Dante. Hopefully he wouldn't bail at the last minute.

As the four girls were walking uphill toward the club, Emilie noticed something interesting. Dante and his friends were walking downhill at the same time. Her eyes flew open and a huge grin spread across her face. Caroline looked at her suspiciously. Emilie pointed up the hill and announced, "Caroline, I have a surprise for you. I invited a few friends to meet us tonight." Emilie laughed out loud when she heard Caroline's sharp intake of breath. Caroline's face said it all.

Dante was walking between his friends, wearing black on black. He had on his long, dark trench coat, which was open and blowing out behind him. Jude and Colin were looking sharp on either side of him as well. The three of them were talking and laughing with each other, looking relaxed and spectacular.

Caroline exclaimed, "Oh...my...God...You should have warned me! I would have worn something different." She was smiling from ear to ear, and Emilie knew she was impressed. "Dante's the one in the middle right?"

"Yes. Isn't he breathtaking?" Emilie sighed wistfully.

"Wow..." Caroline replied almost incoherently.

The two girls behind them were asking all sorts of questions about the three gorgeous guys waiting outside the club.

Emilie felt the need to make something crystal clear before the men were within hearing range, "The tall, dark, and handsome one in the middle, dressed all in black, is mine. The rest of you can fight over the other two."

Dante and his friends smiled broadly as the four girls approached. Emilie smiled up at them proudly. She felt it was her responsibility to make all of the introductions, so she did.

ψ

Emilie had wanted to meet at the club early enough in the evening to secure a good table near the dance floor. Unfortunately this also gave everyone enough time to buy many rounds of drinks, and she was starting to feel she should take it easy. She had inherited her mother's tolerance for alcohol, which had served Emilie well over the years. Not that either parent was a heavy drinker, but her father had definitely been the cheap date between the two. If they shared a bottle of wine with dinner, her father would be slurring by the end of the meal, and her mother would just smile affectionately and pretend she didn't notice.

Emilie surveyed the relaxed faces of everyone in their blended group. They all seemed to be having a good time. But the one thing she found extremely disappointing was the fact that Dante refused to dance. He had assumed the responsibility of guarding the table, making Emilie feel obligated to keep him company. Jude and Colin looked as though they were having fun being the center of attention for the other three girls.

Dante leaned over and yelled in Emilie's ear over the thumping noise of the music. "Why don't you go and dance with your friends?"

Meeting people in a dance club was not a great idea if you wanted to have a meaningful conversation. She leaned toward him and answered, "I don't want you to be lonely here by yourself."

"Don't worry about me. You came here to dance, remember?"

If the expression on his face was any indicator, he was fighting off a migraine. "You should have told me that you don't like to dance," she scolded.

"I like to dance," Dante corrected. "What I don't like is loud music. I have sensitive hearing. Or at least I used to before tonight," he joked, looking at her with a hint of something mysterious in his eyes.

The song finished, and one of Emilie's favorites started playing. This might just be her opportunity to show off. *Okay, mister, you want to see me dance,* she thought.

"If you're okay here by yourself, then I'll dance to this song," she yelled, getting up off of her stool.

"By all means," he replied graciously.

Emilie had managed to find a cute, simple black dress. It wasn't too fancy to be out of place in a dance club, but it also wasn't too sexy to betray her intentions. She felt it was appropriate for seducing a friend without looking too conspicuous about it. The fabric flowed wonderfully, and when dancing, sometimes having the right fabric made all the difference.

As a woman, Emilie knew how to watch a man without being too obvious about it. Men, on the other hand, were completely apparent when they watched women. She found Caroline and the others in the crowd and started to dance. She wasn't planning to go all out, but she did want to be less than subtle.

Emilie and Caroline had been dancing together for years, and Caroline knew exactly what Emilie was up to. Caroline smiled knowingly and winked. Emilie chanced a glance over at their table and wasn't disappointed to see that Dante was definitely a typical man. He was watching, but with a bewilderingly serious expression. He seemed to be frozen in his seat.

She didn't know if that was good or bad. She figured that she would have to do something to gauge his reaction. She performed a few of her more alluring dance moves from her repertoire to see if she could get a better mark from the judge. When she checked back, Dante was casting about as if searching for the nearest

emergency exit. Not a good sign. Maybe he was bored
and had a headache after all.

Emilie assessed Dante's two companions. They
were both watching her carefully and glancing over in
Dante's direction with concern on their faces. Jude, in
particular, had on a very dirty grin and was looking over
at Dante with quite a bit of mischief in his eyes. Dante
appeared most uncomfortable. Their eyes met, and
Emilie felt embarrassed at being caught watching him.
She compensated by shooting him a dazzling smile so it
would appear as if she was the one who had caught him.
He seemed to recognize that he had been staring with
his mouth practically hanging open and smiled sheepishly, trying to pretend nothing had happened.

When the song ended the whole group went back
to the table. Emilie tried to snuggle her seat closer to
Dante's but he was quicker and deliberately moved over
to sit closer to Colin, who had become sandwiched
between Dante and Caroline. Caroline was flirting
shamelessly with Colin, and he barely noticed Dante.
Jude was also sandwiched and seemed to be enjoying
the attention of both Melissa and Sophie, although
Emilie didn't miss the looks that passed between him
and Dante. She didn't miss them, but she certainly
didn't understand them.

Emilie enjoyed talking to Dante in the club. It forced
them to sit very close together regardless. Plus they had
to put their cheeks together and speak directly into
each other's ears simply to be heard. Emilie wondered if
Dante was deliberately trying to excite her by brushing

his lips so tantalizingly on her ear as he spoke. She, of course, was retaliating by doing the same thing to him.

Being so close to him made her heart palpitate. He smelled so enticing and his eyes were so much more hypnotic up close, blinking seductively under long lashes. Emilie had an irresistible urge to kiss him. His lips were just so close and tempting. *Tempting...Isn't that the word Dante used on the phone?* Was it just a coincidence or was there something more to it? One thing was for certain: she needed to try and keep her hormones in check.

Not surprisingly, another round of drinks arrived. Emilie wasn't sure if it was just her imagination, but she didn't think they normally received such good service. She assumed the change was due to the fact that the waitress enjoyed flirting with the men at their table, who were also generous tippers. At this point in the evening everyone had consumed quite a bit of alcohol, but obviously the waitress had seized her opportunity to flirt with Dante while he had been alone at the table.

Caroline was definitely reaching her limit, and even Emilie was beginning to get more light-headed than she preferred. "You're going to have to stop buying drinks, or you'll find yourself going home without Colin. I think Caroline's going to eat him alive," Emilie teased.

Dante burst out laughing. She was confused by his reaction. What she had said wasn't all that funny, but Dante was having trouble getting himself under control. Maybe he had reached his drinking limit as well. Jude looked curiously at him. Dante motioned for Jude to lean over and tried to yell as privately as possible, under

the circumstances, into Jude's ear. Emilie smiled in confusion, watching the two men. Perhaps Jude and Colin
were a couple and Dante was enjoying the fact that
Caroline was truly wasting her time. Jude laughed even
harder than Dante. Emilie thought he might actually
fall over. Colin was glaring at them both, obviously
miffed at being excluded.

She leaned over and asked Dante, "I'm sorry, I didn't
quite get the joke. Can you explain it to me?"

He suddenly got very serious, but quickly recovered
with a silly smile and answered, "It's nothing. Colin isn't
very experienced with this…type of situation."

Emilie raised her eyebrows at him and tried to yell
as discreetly as possible into his ear, "I think Caroline
might like to teach him a thing or two." Colin did look
young, but being so gorgeous should have given him a
lot of experience flirting with women. Maybe he was
very shy or very picky.

Dante smiled at Emilie, knowing exactly what she
meant. "Caroline isn't going to have much luck with
Colin, I'm sorry to say. She isn't his type."

Emilie felt sorry for her Caroline. She was obviously
pulling out all of the stops and making every effort possible with Colin. He did look a bit uncomfortable, but
he seemed to be enjoying himself. "What's his type?"
Emilie asked, looking dreamily into Dante's big brown
eyes again.

Dante paused as if confused by her question then
shrugged his shoulders helplessly. "I wouldn't really
know. I've never met anybody Colin's type."

Emilie's inhibitions were blurring and she was feeling a bit naughty so she asked, "What's your type?"

Dante grinned devilishly and glanced almost imperceptibly over her body. "I don't really have a type. I like variety."

Obviously Dante was feeling naughty as well. She punched him hard in the arm, and the big grin instantly disappeared from his face. His eyes darted across the table to Jude, who was staring at Emilie in wide-eyed surprise. Dante shrugged his shoulders at Jude, looking very innocent, and pointed over in Emilie's direction with his thumb as though denying any responsibility for her behavior. Jude burst out laughing again and shot Emilie a look that implied that she was asking for trouble. Colin had missed everything because Caroline was still monopolizing his attention.

When Emilie turned her attention back to Dante, she found his brown eyes smoldering at her in a most exciting way. He stretched and casually slipped one arm behind her. Then he yanked her stool closer to him. She was impressed by his strength because it was no small feat to accomplish that task one-handed. She wobbled unsteadily on the stool and looked at him wide-eyed but smiling. He leaned in close and said, "Where I come from, when a woman hits a man like that, it means something entirely different. It would be better if you didn't do it to me, and please don't ever do it to Jude because I don't want to end up in the hospital."

Emilie glared at him as if he had spoken a different language. "What are you talking about?" she demanded.

Dante shot her another smoldering look and leaned in even closer than before. "In your culture, when a woman hits a man, it means 'cut that out, you silly guy,' but where I come from, it means she's initiating something sexual with him."

Emilie didn't believe him for a second. He must really be feeling naughty. She leaned back in her seat and nodded her head disdainfully. He rolled his eyes, smiling broadly. Then she thought, *If Dante's making it up, why would Jude react, with no prompting, the way he did?* Obviously there had been something inappropriate about what she had done.

Hadn't Dante looked at her strangely when she had punched him in the arm during their picnic? She wasn't sure where exactly he came from, but she resolved to consider herself warned. Although if they weren't in such a public place, she might have hit him again, a little harder this time so there would be no misunderstanding.

Jude had gone back to flirting with his admirers, but he kept flicking his eyes over in Dante's direction to check up on his friend.

Emilie leaned back to Dante and said, "Sorry, I'll try to keep my hands to myself."

He just smiled and nodded.

All of the girls decided to get back on the dance floor, leaving the three guys sitting together at the table. Emilie definitely needed to burn off some energy. She had become far too excited, sitting and flirting with Dante.

She lost herself in the music the way she always did when dancing. She tried not to think about Dante. He just made everything complicated—exciting but complicated. She tried not to look over at the guys very often, but whenever she did, she still caught Dante watching. He wasn't leering or anything and he was making every effort to appear disinterested. He was legitimately enjoying himself, talking and laughing with his friends and wasn't paying much attention to the girls.

It was getting late, and Emilie was still feeling quite tipsy. She would have to cut herself off from any more alcoholic drinks. The club was going to close soon anyway. The evening hadn't gone entirely according to plan, but Dante had always made it clear that he just wanted to be friends. It was her own problem if she couldn't keep her mind out of the gutter.

Emilie decided to go to the bar and get a Coke. The bartender saw her coming and smiled. She thought he might recognize her, which was flattering because he must see a lot of girls in a place like this. Plus he was very cute and probably didn't lack for feminine attention. He came over and shot her a flirtatious look before asking, "What can I do for you, pretty lady?"

Emilie smiled and responded with a flirty look of her own. "I've had too much to drink and I need a Coke, if you please."

He winked at her and took a couple more orders before getting busy. While Emilie waited, she noticed that Dante was staring in her direction with some concern. Much to her surprise, he actually got up and came over to stand very close to her. If Emilie didn't know better, she would have thought he was acting possessive with her.

"What are you doing over here?" he asked casually.

"Applying for a job," she replied playfully.

Dante made a sour face and was about to go off on a rant when Emilie laughed and said, "I'm getting a drink, you silly man. What did you think I was doing? The real question is: what are *you* doing here?" She batted her eyelashes at him expectantly.

Dante looked a bit sheepish and didn't quite know what to say. The bartender came back with her Coke and glared at Dante. Dante tried to act casual and relaxed, but his body language was uncomfortable and tense. Emilie took her drink and paid, thanking the bartender politely. He smiled and winked at her while looking over at Dante to be sure he had seen. Something strange was going on between them.

She pointed at Dante in an accusatory manner. "You didn't answer my question."

He was obviously flustered but surprised her by saying, "I wanted to dance with you."

Now that was music to Emilie's ears. He hadn't danced all evening and now he wanted to dance with her. She took a big sip of her drink and started walking back to their table. She put her glass down, took Dante by the hand, and pulled him toward the dance floor. He seemed nervous, and Jude laughed as she led his friend away with a determined look on her face.

Dante was actually a pretty good dancer for someone who had spent the evening avoiding it. Colin and Jude could hold their own as well. The problem was that Dante kept a safe distance from Emilie, which she found most frustrating. She had hoped to get her hands on him. *Oh well. Another time maybe,* she thought.

After a couple of less interesting songs, a very familiar one began playing, with a much sexier rhythm. Emilie smiled evilly to herself. She glanced over at Caroline, who gave her the thumbs up as discreetly as possible. Caroline knew what Emilie was thinking. She was going to get her hands on Dante after all. She moved closer to him and put more effort into her moves. He looked her up and down nervously but didn't try to escape. She let the music wash over her and inched closer to him as the song played on.

Emilie put her arms around his neck and looked him in the eyes. There wasn't a hint of a smile on his face, but she could feel the electricity passing between them. He ran his long, elegant fingers lightly up the bare skin of her arms, sending shivers throughout her body. Unfortunately he took her hands from around his neck. But he didn't let them go. He turned her around in front of him, and she thought for a second that he was going to release her at a safer distance from him, but somehow the electricity flowing between them brought her back up against him even closer than before. Then Emilie shut out everything except the sensual pulse of the music and the feel of Dante's hands on her body.

༃

This was one of the biggest mistakes of Dante's life, and he knew it. He wasn't allowed in places like this so he never should have come. He was putting himself and his friends in danger. But most of all he was putting Emilie at risk. *Emilie...*He stood there breathing hard and holding her tightly. The electricity charging between them was almost making him tremble. He was just moments from kissing her. He could almost taste her lips.

She looked up at him expectantly, passion sparkling in her bewitching aqua eyes. Why did she have to be so tempting? It was already difficult enough trying to keep away from her in the first place without her making her desire so apparent.

He held her closer, if that was even possible. Their bodies were already touching far too intimately for a public place. His self-control was eroding fast. She felt too good in his arms. He was going to give in to her. Then he took a deep breath and thought of the consequences.

It would be one thing to kiss her in private, but to do it here, in public, in front of all of these witnesses. He could get himself into the worst trouble of his life. He had to get out of here fast. It was way too dangerous in here...with her.

༃

A new song started up. Dante's face was so close to Emilie's. She thought he was going to kiss her. The look in his eyes suggested that he wanted to kiss her. She wanted more than anything for him to do it. *What's he waiting for?* she wondered.

The dance floor was getting crowded again and people were pushing and shoving for a spot to dance. Emilie was just about to reach up and kiss Dante herself when somebody shouted, "You two love birds need to get a room!"

Dante shook his head for a second, blinking his beautiful brown eyes. Then he let go of Emilie and quickly backed away, dragging her off the dance floor by the hand. He hauled her over to the wall between the men's and women's washrooms. It was a quieter and less crowded spot in which to talk.

"What the hell was that?" Dante demanded angrily, staring at her as if she had just slapped his face.

"I don't know. I was just dancing," Emilie responded. She felt defensive and even a bit intimidated by the intensity of his voice.

Dante gaped at her as though he thought she was absolutely out of her mind. Everything about his body language told her that he was extremely agitated. He ran his hand through his hair, shaking his head. Then he said, "Just dancing...I need a cold shower." He added, "What happened to the no inappropriate touching rule? That was your idea, remember? I got chewed out for putting my arm around you." He punctuated his statement with a noise that sounded like he thought he had been treated most unfairly given their current situation.

"Hey! You were touching me too," Emilie retorted. His ardor had been translated through his hands and she was surprised by this sudden change. She had been hoping for more affection and less attitude.

"Listen, missy...I may be your friend, but I'm still a man. If you rub yourself all over any male with a pulse, like you just did to me, then you'll definitely have his complete and total attention. I can assure you! Just dancing?"

"Maybe I want to be more than your friend," Emilie declared before she had a chance to stop herself.

Dante's facial expression changed instantly. He went from angry and indignant to sad and uncomfortable in a heartbeat. He sighed heavily and said as gently as he could, "Trust me, Emilie. You shouldn't get romantically involved with me. You'll only get hurt."

"I'm more than willing to take my chances," she replied without meeting his gaze.

"Listen, you've had a lot to drink, and after that *dance*, as you call it, I would really like to take you home with me tonight. But...we would both regret it in the morning." He paused and looked directly in her eyes. "We're friends. That's all. I value our friendship and don't want to ruin what we have with any...inappropriate touching. Am I making myself clear?"

Dante was trying to be firm yet still considerate of her feelings. Although what Emilie saw in his eyes didn't quite match what she heard from his lips. "Crystal clear," was all she could reply. *After the way we moved together on the dance floor, I doubt either of us would regret anything in the morning,* she thought bitterly to herself. She was willing to put his theory to the test and face the consequences later, but she was too humiliated to argue her point. As it stood, she feared she may have just ruined everything that had been gradually building between the two of them.

"Listen, I think it would be better if I left now. Are you going to be okay?" Dante asked, casting about for someone, probably Caroline.

"Yeah, peachy," Emilie muttered. She tried not to sound too cranky, but she did want to express her disappointment.

"I'll call you tomorrow to see how you're doing," he said, backing away. Then he turned and went to collect his friends.

Emilie went immediately into the ladies' washroom and locked herself in a stall. Tears were building up fast. She sat on the toilet, crying dejectedly to herself. *What an idiot I am!* What did she honestly think would happen? She was absolutely miserable. Somehow she had convinced herself that Dante had feelings for her that went beyond friendship.

Well, he doesn't. It's perfectly clear. Now what am I supposed to do? Just stop loving him? No problem... Emilie wondered if she would ever be able to look him in the eyes again. A groan of agony almost escaped her lips as she thought of those big beautiful brown eyes of his. *That is if I ever get to see him again.*

"Emilie, are you in here?" Caroline's voice came from the other side of the stall door.

Emilie was instantly snapped out of her wallowing. "Yes," she growled.

"Dante and his friends just left," Caroline explained, her own disappointment evident in her tone.

Emilie sighed, the biggest sigh of her life. She might never see Dante again. "I know," she choked. The painful lump in her throat prevented her from saying much else.

"He was really worried about you. He said you guys had some kind of argument."

Caroline's tone was delicate and concerned. Emilie opened the stall door to let Caroline in. Their conversation was too personal to share with everyone in the washroom. Caroline's eyes were filled with empathy. She knew how Emilie felt about Dante.

"It wasn't an argument," Emilie corrected. "He gave me a lecture and then left." She was too embarrassed about her complete lapse in judgment to get into any details. Once she'd recovered from this humiliation she would explain everything to Caroline.

"It's blatantly obvious that Dante cares about you," Caroline soothed. "He could barely take his eyes off of you all night long. You should have seen the way the two of you looked together on the dance floor. I've never seen anything like it. You were made for each other."

Caroline's words only made Emilie's pain worse. "He cares about me, but not in the way I care about him," she argued. Her tears had returned. She wanted to retain what was left of her dignity, but obviously she needed to admit to herself that she had been horribly wrong, have a good cry, and get on with her life…without Dante.

Caroline wrapped Emilie up in her comforting arms. Emilie felt completely ridiculous. Two grown women holding each other in the public washroom of a crowded bar. *Could my life get any worse?* she grumbled under her breath. She wiped her face with her hand and tried to straighten herself out. "Let's get out of here. I need a drink."

"I don't know if it's a good idea for you to have anything else to drink," Caroline suggested delicately.

"The man I love just told me that he only wants to be friends. I think I need a drink," Emilie argued. "I've had enough lectures for one night."

"Okay, one drink. Let's go to the bar and flirt with the good-looking bartender."

"You flirt and I'll drink," Emilie replied, sighing in defeat.

ॐ

Dante looked back to see if he could spot Emilie one last time before he left. She had disappeared and he was worried about her. He hadn't meant to hurt her. It was one thing for him to torture himself, but she was suffering too. More than he had realized.

He had been so wrapped up in his own personal struggle that he hadn't thought much about how she was handling this *friendship* of theirs. He knew she was attracted to him, but he hadn't realized it was serious—until now.

"Are you okay?" Jude asked as they started walking uphill toward the condo.

"Man, what a bad idea!" Dante answered, running his hand through his hair.

"Ya think?" Jude replied with a chuckle.

"Hey, I was only flirting with one human girl. You had two."

"Yeah, but I was only flirting. What you were doing was more like…foreplay."

Dante took a deep breath and shook his head. "I know. I know. Bad idea."

"You did the right thing by leaving," Colin stated, trying to show his support.

Dante snorted disdainfully. He didn't want to tell Colin about Emilie admitting that she wanted to be more than friends. *It's all out in the open now…no more flirting.*

Despite his level of agitation, Dante smiled. Emilie had set a trap for him tonight. He was almost angry with himself for stumbling head first into it. She knew what she wanted and how to get it. She was a smart and creative opponent, which only made her all the more attractive. He had underestimated her—and his feelings for her.

What made it more painful was the knowledge that she was in the club, quite seriously intoxicated, with all of those slobbering men and the dirty vampire bartender. Dante knew the man was a fairly recent changeling. He worked as a scout for the council and was planted in human clubs in order to keep an eye out for trouble-makers of his species as well as to enlist humans to serve the council in various different capacities.

Those were the only reasons a changeling's presence would be tolerated in a human club. The scout was sure to report the fact that Dante and his friends had been caught out of bounds. This stunt made it look like they were a bunch of horny devils out trying to sneak a little something nasty in the civilian population. The council had eyes and ears all over the place. It was an essential part of everyday operations. Dante should have known better.

Unfortunately this changeling also had a reputa-tion for craving human blood. It was one of the perks of being a council scout. They were given leniency as long as they were discreet about their dealings. It was also one of the main reasons so many changelings were called vampires. The very thought made Dante shudder. Dark Angels didn't drink human blood.

He felt irresponsible for leaving Emilie there to her fate. *But what am I supposed to do about it? Take her home? Great!* He would already be in enough trouble with the council for getting caught in a human club. To be seen leaving with a human girl would suggest that he was flaunting his illegal activities and challenging the coun-cil to punish him for it. Plus Jude and Colin would never have allowed it. They had reputations to protect as well. The last thing they needed was to appear as though the three of them were out hunting humans together. It wasn't uncommon for men of his kind to hunt in packs and share a prize amongst themselves, working together to cover-up their tracks.

Maybe I could just escort Emilie back to her apartment? he thought. *No...Out of the frying pan and into the fire.* Dante would have to give her the impression that something inappropriate was going to happen between them in order to convince her to leave. At least at his condo, Jude and Colin would keep him out of trouble. Once alone with Emilie at her place, he would never be able to just say goodnight and leave.

One thing was certain: he would have to find a way to slip away from his friends at some point to check up on her. Dante really hadn't appreciated the way that vampire had been looking at Emilie. Dante was worried she may have been marked as a target. Hopefully she would be smart enough to stay away from the bartender, but changelings could be very charming and persuasive. He was unlikely to make a scene or pursue her if she showed no signs of interest, but if she gave him an opportunity, then who knew?

Dante was determined to hide in a mesay doorway and watch. He wouldn't approach her; he would just make sure she was safe from the vampire. If she chose to go home with a human, then he would have to respect her decision. He had no right to feel as possessive as he did. He didn't have any claim on her. He had asked Caroline to make sure Emilie didn't do anything stupid. Caroline was a good friend. She would watch out for Emilie. He certainly hoped so, for all of their sakes.

Chapter 9

The handsome bartender's name was Ethan, but Caroline had given up flirting with him and had gone back to dance with the others. Melissa and Sophie were both quite annoyed with Emilie for chasing Jude and Colin away. Emilie didn't know if Jude had been interested in any of the girls, but from what Dante had told her, she was sure that Colin hadn't been.

Dancing had lost its appeal for Emilie, so she had decided to sit alone and sulk instead. This was also to be her last drink. She was starting to feel a little too out of control for her comfort.

A couple of guys tried to chat Emilie up and buy her drinks. She told them she already had a boyfriend, but they persisted. It was Ethan who came to her rescue. He started paying particular attention to her, and the two guys suddenly felt outclassed and left, maybe even assuming that Ethan was her boyfriend.

One way or another, Emilie was grateful for Ethan's help and quite enjoyed his company. It was flattering to have such a good-looking and obviously popular man paying so much attention to her. She was full of alcohol and pent-up sexual energy, and Ethan presented too good an opportunity to let slip away.

He was making his interest in her clear without being too obvious or pushy. Ethan was a bartender and could surely recognize when someone was drowning their sorrows. He was also smart enough to know that Emilie's sadness had to do with Dante. Ethan simply worked on lifting her spirits. Emilie found him sweet and funny. He made her feel good about herself, and most of all, he made her laugh. At the moment, laughter was the best medicine.

He was very busy, of course. He couldn't just hang around and chat. But he kept a watchful eye on her while he was serving the other customers, which caused many of the other girls to abandon flirting with him and go off to find other prey.

Emilie got lost in her thoughts while Ethan was off on a particularly long stretch of bartending, and she was startled by his friendly voice. "So is your boyfriend coming back to pick you up later?"

She looked up into his compelling hazel eyes and frowned. She didn't want to think about Dante any more than she already was. "He's not *really* my boyfriend. We have a complicated relationship."

"I'm sure..." Ethan said, smiling at her suggestively.

Emilie couldn't help but smile back. He really was very charming.

"You didn't answer my question," he insisted.

"No, he's not coming back. As a matter of fact, I don't know if I'm ever going to see him again," Emilie replied sadly. Suddenly her chest felt very tight and she looked away from Ethan so he wouldn't see her tears.

"His loss," Ethan responded. "I asked the DJ to play some better music. I'm hoping to convince you to dance some more. You are very sexy." He leaned in more closely, and she wondered if his intention was to kiss her. But he simply added, "It's also good for business."

The alcohol and his compliments had made Emilie feel quite bold. He definitely knew how to sweet talk a girl. "I might dance if your DJ plays something interesting."

She smirked at him, and he nodded confidently as he went off to serve the other customers. Right on cue a familiar song with a fantastic rhythm started playing. If Ethan had picked this song then he had good taste in dance music. From across the bar, he checked to see if she recognized it. He smiled suggestively and winked, gesturing for her to join her friends.

Emilie searched the dance floor for Caroline. She waved to Emilie, encouraging her to come and dance. They could be quite a pair when they danced together. Ethan wouldn't be disappointed.

As it turned out, he did have particularly good taste in music and impressed Emilie with the play list he had chosen. Even though her heart wasn't entirely in it, she still felt obliged to show off for his sake.

Caroline leaned over and asked, "So what's going on with you and Ethan?"

Emilie shrugged her shoulders and answered, "I think he likes me, but I'm not sure. He's cute and funny, but I really can't get Dante out of my head."

"If Dante just wants to be friends, then maybe you should pursue other avenues. You don't owe him any loyalty," Caroline declared, giving Emilie a nudge and a wink. Caroline really should have been born a man. She was always thinking with her hormones. But perhaps she had a point. The idea of being in bed with anyone other than Dante made Emilie's heart ache, but perhaps if her body was otherwise occupied, she might not notice her heart.

Emilie decided to return to the bar. Ethan brought her a Coke, leaned over, and said, "On the house."

She smiled at him. "Thanks. But you didn't have to."

He winked at her and replied, "Yes, I did. You earned it."

Emilie felt herself blushing. Ethan had shifted his flirting into a higher gear. She assumed it was because the bar was going to close soon.

She was thirsty and quickly finished the drink. As Emilie watched Caroline and the girls dancing, she found that she had trouble focusing her attention. She had definitely had too much to drink.

Ethan came back and leaned in again as though he intended to kiss her. She suddenly had the chills. She hadn't kissed a man in a long time, but she was feeling guilty about her body's reaction to Ethan. Emilie may not owe Dante any loyalty, but somehow he still seemed to have it.

Ethan didn't try to kiss her. Instead he spoke into her ear. "What are you doing after we close?"

Emilie wasn't sure what to say. Part of her wanted to take him home and part of her wanted to tell him to go to Hell. "The four of us girls will probably get something to eat before heading home."

"Can I join you?" he asked, looking a bit nervous.

Emilie figured it couldn't hurt. It would give her some more time to think about whether or not she wanted to do anything else with him. She needed to sober up a bit. She probably shouldn't make any important decisions in her current condition.

"Sure, sounds good," she answered, though she was still uncertain.

"You can stay here and keep me company while I close up, and then we can meet up with your friends," he suggested.

"We'll see," Emilie replied with hesitation. She would feel better talking to him in the safety of her circle of friends. Being alone with him might not be the best plan in her current state.

Ethan chose that moment to kiss her. He caught her off guard, but somehow her lips parted and she returned his kiss. Her heart might be against it, but her body was ready and willing. It felt nice to be kissed again, Emilie was ashamed to admit to herself.

Ethan was neglecting his other customers, so luckily he didn't let his lips linger for long. He winked at her again as he went quickly back to work. He might have been trying to gauge her level of interest in him. Emilie felt a little dirty inside, and not in a good way. She hadn't meant to lead him on. She liked him, but she was hurt and confused and shouldn't be trying to transfer her affection for one man onto another. Fortunately she doubted that Ethan was thinking long term.

※

"Emilie is going to stay here with me and rest while I finish closing up," Ethan explained to Caroline. "Then we'll meet you at the restaurant. Okay?"

"I don't know, Ethan. She's had a lot to drink. Maybe I should just take her home," Caroline argued.

"I'm okay," Emilie slurred, flapping a dismissive hand at Caroline.

"She'll be fine. Just leave her here with me. There are lots of people here closing up. You don't have to worry." Ethan smiled and patted Emilie on the shoulder. "Listen, I have to ask you guys to leave now. We'll only be about twenty minutes."

"Are you sure about this?" Caroline whispered into Emilie's ear.

"Yeah. Yeah. It's fine," Emilie replied, feeling a bit sick to her stomach. "I'd rather not walk anywhere right now."

"We could get a taxi."

"At this time of night?" Emilie muttered incredulously. "There won't be a taxi to be found. Plus I would die of embarrassment if I barfed in some guy's cab. I'll be okay. It's just for a few minutes. If you're really worried then you guys can wait outside."

Caroline shook her head. "It's too cold. We'll meet you there, if you're sure you're okay."

Caroline didn't look happy about the situation, but Emilie felt safe with Ethan. It wasn't like they would be all alone. "I'll be fine," Emilie soothed, motioning toward the door with her hand, not so subtly gesturing toward the exit.

"Okay...See you at the restaurant in twenty minutes or so. Call me if there's anything. We'll be back here in a flash. Promise."

"Okay. I'll be fine," Emilie urged, hugging Caroline. "Good-bye."

Emilie waved to her friends as they left then went back to sit at the bar. Ethan brought her a glass of water then busied himself tidying up. There were lots of people wandering around. She heard someone ask Ethan who she was and what she was doing there. He explained that Emilie was just a friend who wasn't feeling very well and that he was going to take her out to get some air as soon as he was done closing up.

Her thoughts and feelings were jumbled. She longed to be with Dante, yet he had made his feelings clear. She had crossed the line tonight, and maybe he would decide against continuing with this friendship. It might be too awkward for him. As much as it pained her to admit, it might be better if they stopped seeing each other. She had become too emotionally attached to him. She had thought it was all under control, but it had become painfully obvious how much she had been deceiving herself.

Emilie felt the fog in her mind thickening. She had to concentrate for a second just to remember where she was.

"Let's go out back and get you some fresh air for a minute," Ethan suggested, taking Emilie's arm and encouraging her to follow him. "We'll just sit on the fire escape stairs right outside the back door. Then we can get going. Okay?"

"Okay," she said and grabbed her purse off the bar. Her stomach was beginning to churn. As they walked toward the back door, Emilie watched the bathroom door pass by. *I might be returning here very soon*, she thought uncomfortably. *What am I doing?* Suddenly Emilie wanted nothing more than to be home in bed. Alone.

Ethan opened the bar's back door. He had their coats. Emilie was too disoriented at this point to care about how he had gotten her coat, but she obediently put it on when Ethan handed it to her. It was surprisingly cold outside. They sat down together on the fire escape stairs.

"How are you doing?" Ethan asked, smiling broadly.

"I'm okay," Emilie replied, admiring him. He really was very good looking. He had such a nice smile and he seemed genuinely concerned. "The cold air feels nice, but it doesn't smell very good up here." The garbage dumpster was right underneath them, tucked under the fire escape. She wasn't feeling well enough to stomach the smell for long.

"Then let's go down. There are stairs leading into the storeroom so we can go in through there and leave out the front of the building when you're feeling better. You'll also be upwind of the garbage."

He started pulling her down the fire escape stairs before she could protest. Despite her drunken nausea, Emilie was feeling strangely relaxed and drowsy. She had to struggle to focus her thoughts. Her vision was beginning to blur so she just followed Ethan blindly. She had to concentrate on every step so as not to trip. Emilie could see the stairwell into the storeroom on the other side of the dumpster. It wasn't far. She didn't want to fall onto poor Ethan and put them both in the hospital. *What a great impression,* she thought unhappily.

As they came around the dumpster and headed toward the stairs, Ethan dropped back behind Emilie, allowing her to lead the way. She was relieved to see the end in sight. Suddenly he grabbed her from behind. He pinned her hard up against himself, clamping his hand over her mouth and picking her right up off the ground.

Emilie was shocked. He was incredibly strong, stronger than she would have thought possible. He had one hand over her mouth and his other arm locked across the front her body, pressing her back into his chest. Emilie could barely breathe he was squeezing her ribs so tightly. She also felt as if her neck was about to snap.

She tried feebly to escape him, but she could hardly move her limbs. She clawed at his arms with her hands, but he was holding her like a steel trap. She couldn't get a grip on his short hair either. She tried to scream, but she was struggling for breath. She kicked at him with her legs, trying to knock him off balance, but all of her efforts had little effect.

He was taller and broader built than she was, but he was in no way a huge man. She would have thought it physically impossible for a man of his size to carry a struggling woman in this way. Emilie was seized by panic and could do nothing but melt weakly into tears.

Ethan laughed in her ear and taunted her. "Go ahead and fight with me, baby. It just makes it better for me."

He carried her into the space between the dumpster and the railing of the stairwell down to the storeroom. It was dark despite a light shining above the storeroom door. Emilie doubted anyone would be able to spot them, even from above. The fire escape landings on the first and second floors would block anyone's view. He shook her in his grip, adjusting her position slightly. He squeezed her breast hard with one hand, and Emilie fought him with all of her quickly fading strength.

Ethan's voice was in her ear again. "Feeling sleepy yet, baby? I put a little something special in your water glass." He sniggered wickedly. "Somehow I didn't get the feeling you would have come home with me willingly. I don't usually have to do it like this, but I felt I should make an exception in your case."

Ethan's hand was excessively rough, and Emilie whimpered in pain. Ethan purred out his arousal and put his lips back into her ear. "I've noticed you before, but I have to say I was shocked to see you arrive with that little prince tonight. I couldn't believe my luck when he and his guards left without you."

Ethan bent Emilie's head hard over onto her shoulder, stretching her neck out into the cold night air. She felt him run his face along her throat, breathing deeply. "You smell delicious. I'm really going to enjoy finding out what makes you special enough to draw the little prince out of his tower. I could tell by the way he watched you that you were something very special indeed. I've heard he has extremely particular taste in women." Ethan laughed softly. "You know, no matter what happens to you, they'll probably assume it was all his fault. I can enjoy you thoroughly, and everything will be taken care of for me quickly and quietly."

Emilie had no idea what Ethan was talking about or to whom he was referring. She hadn't noticed anyone watching her other than Dante. Mind you, she hadn't been looking at anyone else. What guards was he talking about and who was the prince?

The questions swirled through her mind as her body grew more and more relaxed. She wouldn't be conscious for much longer, and she knew Ethan was counting on it.

Suddenly something stung her neck. Then she heard footsteps pounding down the fire escape stairs. Ethan heard them too and stopped whatever he was doing. He clamped his hand over Emilie's nose and mouth, completely taking her breath away and making it impossible for her to utter a sound.

"Ethan, I can see you. Put her down and back out of there fast and no one has to get hurt."

Through the fog in her mind, Emilie recognized that magical voice. Ethan released her and she crumpled to the ground facing the wall between the railing and the dumpster, gasping for air. Ethan walked out to meet Dante, leaving her alone on the ground.

"Didn't anyone teach you how to share your toys?" Ethan asked in a facetious tone.

"I don't want to fight you, but if you don't get out of my sight, this could get ugly."

"I wasn't going to kill her," Ethan responded, his voice almost cheerful. "But I might just have to take my time with her now and have a little fun."

"You'll have to do it over my dead body," Dante replied with icy calm.

"I might really enjoy that. This situation keeps getting better and better."

Emilie managed to drag herself around to look into the alley. Her eyes were blurry and she was having a hard time focusing. Ethan was between her and Dante, and she could barely differentiate them. Dante stood only a few paces away from Ethan with his hands up and out in front of him. As Ethan walked farther, Dante backed away and Emilie could no longer see him past the dumpster.

"I think I can take you on your own," Ethan declared. "What are you doing out without your bodyguard, you naughty boy? This plaything of yours must be very special indeed."

Emilie couldn't get herself up off the ground. She tried with all her might but only managed to pull herself up on all fours, bracing herself against the dumpster for extra support. She could hear Ethan and Dante arguing but couldn't understand what they were saying anymore. It took all of her concentration just to keep her balance. Slowly she started crawling forward on her hands and knees.

She lost her balance and toppled over as she heard Dante say, "Ethan, I haven't got all night. Are you going to attack me or are you planning to bore me to death with your ranting?"

There was growling. There was fighting. Then the night closed in around Emilie, and there was nothing.

అ

The next thing Emilie knew, Dante's concerned voice was in her ear whispering, "Emilie? Emilie? Are you all right?"

He was stroking her hair gently as he scanned her body for injuries. "Where's Ethan?" she croaked.

"He must not have known that I grew up in Thailand. I could kick-box with the best of them before I hit puberty," Dante announced triumphantly. "Listen, he's not going to be out for long. We have to leave. Now."

He started to pick her up off of the ground. There was a loud bang and Dante grunted. He mumbled something through clenched teeth that sounded very much like, "Not again…"

He gently put Emilie back down and stood up. She looked weakly up at him. He stood very still, facing her with his hands up and out again. He was waiting for something.

Then she heard Ethan's voice. "Not too bad for a spoiled brat. I have to give you credit. But I don't need to fight fair. I think I'll just shoot you somewhere that you won't easily recover from, just to keep you out of my way for the rest of the evening."

Ethan's voice was getting closer, but Emilie couldn't see him past Dante's body. In a sudden blur of movement, Dante reached behind himself with his right hand. Another shot echoed through the still night air. Emilie watched as Dante yanked something forward under his arm. It was Ethan's hand, holding tightly to a gun. Dante struggled to get the weapon away from Ethan. He brought Ethan's arm up and sank his teeth into it with a growl. The gun finally fell to the ground.

Ethan snarled, "What have you done to me?"

Dante spun around to face Ethan, and through Dante's legs, Emilie saw Ethan drop to the ground, clenching his forearm. He howled like an animal, but Emilie was temporarily blinded by a cloud of dust. She wiped it from her face and eyes, coughing all the while. When her vision finally cleared, Ethan was gone. *Where'd he go?*

She hadn't seen or heard him get up and leave, though in her state she could easily have missed it. Where he had been lying was nothing but a pile of grey dust blowing quickly away in the autumn wind. Emilie thought she saw fabric from Ethan's clothes hidden in the pile, but she was having trouble seeing anything clearly because she was downwind and dust blew into her face with every gust.

She heard Dante running around, pausing here and there. After a few seconds he came back to her. He crouched down quickly to pick her up. "We've got to get out of here fast."

She heard voices and footsteps coming from above. Dante cradled Emilie in his strong arms, and she cuddled against him, burying her face in his coat.

Everything suddenly went pitch black and silent as the grave. They were walking down a narrow corridor. The walls seemed to be made of sheets of softly glowing, multi-colored paper that stood floor to ceiling and faced the corridor edge-on. The sheets ruffled silently as they passed as one ruffles a ream of paper before putting it in the printer.

She must have blacked out and been dreaming because the next thing she knew, they were in the entrance of her apartment. Dante carried her quickly into the bedroom and laid her out on the bed. He reached over and switched on her reading lamp.

He bent over her, asking, "Are you all right? Are you hurt?"

Emilie lay weakly as Dante examined her body. "You came back," she mumbled. "You saved me. I love you. I've always loved you..." Then she started to cry.

Dante stopped his probing and sat beside her on the bed. He smiled sweetly and wiped the tears off her cheeks with his long fingers. Then he bent down and hugged her gently to him. Emilie managed to wrap her arms weakly around his waist. He ran his lips along her cheek, then brushed them lightly against her ear as he whispered in his soothing, magical voice, "You foolish little girl. What am I going to do with you? You scared me half to death." He hugged her harder and kissed her cheek, breathing raggedly. "I don't think I could survive losing you. I think I'm finally going to have to admit that I love you too much for my own good."

Dante kissed her cheek one last time, pulled away, and sat looking down at her dusty, tear-streaked face. He reached out, cupped her face in his hands, and bent down closer. He stopped, his lips hovering so close to hers, almost touching. He stared intently into her eyes as though he was thinking about what to do next.

Emilie tried to wrap her arms around him again. She parted her lips. She wanted to kiss him, but she was afraid he would pull away if she moved. Then Dante slowly brought his lips down and brushed them against hers ever so softly. She gathered what little strength she had left and pressed her lips more firmly to his.

Emilie could barely draw a breath. Had she lost consciousness again? She had to be dreaming. Or maybe she had died, because she was definitely in Heaven. She was finally kissing her angel.

Dante pulled away slowly, breathing hard and wincing. He shifted slightly so that he could sit on the bed with both feet on the floor. Emilie tried to focus on him but was still recovering from the kiss. Something strange drew her attention. Something had moved down the back of Dante's coat. She tried to clear her vision then realized what she had seen. It was blood, and it was dripping down the back of his coat onto her bed from the top of his right shoulder. Ethan, the coward, had shot him in the back.

ﷲ

Dante winced in pain as he took his phone out of his pocket and dialled. He cleared his throat as a voice answered, "Hello."

"Colin, come over to Emilie's right away. She's been drugged and attacked," Dante explained. He hoped the urgency in his voice would make Colin spring into action instead of going off on a rant.

Colin gasped in horror. "What have you done?" he accused.

"You've gotta be kidding me!" Dante hissed. "When have I...*ever*...in all the years you've known me, drugged and attacked a woman?"

"Okay! You're right," Colin soothed. "But you've been acting out of character these days. You have to admit."

Dante sighed heavily. "I'm not going to deny that Emilie affects my better judgment, but she was attacked by the bartender from the club. You idiot! I can't believe you would think—"

"I can't believe you snuck out of here on us. And now look at the trouble you've gotten yourself—"

The pain in his shoulder made Dante bark, "Colin, shut up! I've been shot. I have to go to the hospital. Just get over here and make sure Emilie's all right. Have Jude meet me at the hospital. Okay?"

"I'll just get a few things together and I'll be right over," Colin muttered.

"Bye," Dante said and put his phone away. He turned back toward Emilie. She was still conscious, the tough little thing. She was staring up at him with such a love-struck expression on her face. He tucked a strand of her dishevelled hair behind her ear. "I have to go," he whispered to her. "Colin will take care of you."

"Don't leave me," she begged and clung to the sleeve of his coat.

He ran the backs of his fingers against her cheek. "I'll see you soon," he soothed. Then he found himself running his thumb over her lips. They were so delicious. He already regretted kissing her once, but it had felt so fantastic, and despite the searing pain of his gunshot wound, he wanted to kiss her again. He wasn't going to, but then Emilie parted her succulent lips and closed her eyes with a sigh. Before he even knew what he was doing, his lips were on hers again.

Emilie kissed him eagerly, and it took all of Dante's self-control to keep from growling enthusiastically. She felt amazing, tasted wonderful, and he wanted her with such a passion that he was glad Colin was about to arrive at any moment. Otherwise…

He knew this would happen if he was left alone with her. He was injured and in serious trouble with the council for being caught in a human club with civilian girls, and then for causing the death of the scout who had undoubtedly reported him. Yet he was still enjoying himself far too much. He gave Emilie a long, lingering kiss, savoring her because he knew it had to be the last one ever. Then he stood up and went to unlock the front door. Colin knew where she lived, but he wouldn't be able to get into an unfamiliar, locked apartment.

Inter-dimensional travel was complicated, and individuals had different capabilities. Colin used his ability to get from point A to point B. He hadn't spent his life exploring the boundaries of his ability in the same way Dante had.

He poked his head back into Emilie's bedroom and found her unconscious. She had finally succumbed to the drugs. Colin would take good care of her. He was a perfect Angel and a superb friend. Dante was deep in his debt.

Colin opened the front door and stuck his face nervously inside. Dante gestured him in. "I'm glad you're here. I'm worried about what that stupid vampire gave Emilie. Please make sure she's okay." Dante heard his voice crack and stopped.

Colin was looking at him rather harshly. Dante needed a distraction so he took off his coat and showed Colin his shoulder. "How bad is it?" Dante asked with a hiss. He needed Colin to think that the emotion he had heard in his voice had been from the pain of his injury rather than his attachment to Emilie.

Colin sucked in his breath and put a tentative hand on Dante's shoulder, examining the wound more closely. "It looks pretty bad." He glanced around and added, "And you're making a mess everywhere with your blood."

Dante hadn't thought about the mess. How would he explain all of this to Emilie? Colin raised the plastic bag he held in his hand and winked. "Good thing I brought all of this stuff with me. Now off you go and take care of yourself. Okay?"

Dante nodded. He didn't know how to put his feelings into words. He was so grateful to Colin. He had been so patient and understanding through all of this, and now Colin was putting himself at risk to literally clean up Dante's mess. Colin shouldn't be getting involved. He should distance himself from Dante and deny any responsibility for the evenings events. "Thanks, man," Dante said, eyes downcast.

Colin nodded and headed into Emilie's bedroom. Dante gathered up all of Ethan's personal effects, which had been set aside, opened a mesay doorway, and headed for the hospital. He arrived at the emergency entrance and leaned against the nurses' work station.

"Hello, Dante. What are you doing here?" one girl asked, glancing up at the clock on the wall. "Are you on Beijing time?" she added as if it was a common occurrence.

Which it was. In his line of work it never paid to get your body accustomed to functioning exclusively in one time zone. "I've been shot...again," he announced.

The girl continued to sit at the desk, smiling up at him in confusion. So he turned around. Once she saw his injury, she leapt to her feet and declared, "I thought you were kidding. I'm so sorry, Dante."

She came running around the desk and ushered him into an examination room, barking orders as she went. She took everything he had been carrying and asked, "Can you take off your shirt?"

"I will if you will," he replied as he gingerly began peeling the fabric over his wound.

The nurse tittered behind her hand. "You are incorrigible."

Dante shot her as dazzling a smile as he could muster through gritted teeth. Then he got more serious as he saw the sleeve of Ethan's shirt dangling down the chair on which she had placed everything. He had to take responsibility for his actions and hope to be treated with leniency. "Listen, I'm going to need to file an incident report."

She nodded. "Okay. I'll let someone know to come see you before you leave."

"Thanks," he said, and in walked the doctor.

ॐ

Jude ran into the hospital room and looked Dante over carefully, assessing the damage. Satisfied with the insignificance of the injury, Jude barked, "If you weren't already in the hospital, I would put you in here myself! What on Earth were you thinking, you slobbering moron?"

"I was worried, that's all. And obviously with good reason too, I might add. Anyway, let's not talk about it here." Dante glanced around anxiously to see if anybody was listening to their conversation.

"I'm going to beat the crap out of you as soon as you've healed," Jude continued, obviously too wound up to be discreet. "I'm so angry with you. Why do you pay me if you're just going to sneak off and get yourself shot behind my back?"

"Let's talk about this later," Dante hissed, pleading with his eyes.

"Fine!" Jude conceded.

The doctor had given Dante a shot of pain medication. He smiled happily to himself. Morphine was wonderful stuff. Now he wouldn't feel a thing.

While he was drifting happily in a drug-induced stupor, Dante thought about Emilie. He replayed her dancing in his mind. Her body moved like nothing he had ever seen, and he had watched many women dance in his long life. He savored the memory of what it had felt like to have her body rubbing so sensuously against his. It was a small taste of what it would be like to be all naked and twined together in bed. "Hmmm," Dante purred happily. Followed quickly by, "Ouch!" The doctor's digging had ripped him from his fantasy.

"Sorry," the doctor apologized. "The bullet is more deeply embedded in your shoulder blade then I suspected."

Dante groaned uncomfortably.

"Are you okay?" Jude's concerned voice penetrated Dante's haze.

"Peachy," Dante replied, returning his thoughts to Emilie. Admitting his feelings to her had been a serious mistake, but she had been completely intoxicated. She was unlikely to remember anything in the morning. What was done couldn't be undone. He would have to worry about the consequences later.

Right now he wanted to enjoy the morphine and think of Emilie. That woman could distract him from almost anything, and this was an excellent time to be distracted. It had felt wonderful to have finally gotten his lips on hers. Even with the searing pain in his shoulder, he had still enjoyed kissing her. He shouldn't have done it, but he couldn't resist. He had just needed a little taste. No harm done.

But this had to be the last time. The situation was getting out of control. She was just too tempting. He would have to wrap this up with her later, once and for all. He would have his phone number temporarily disconnected and use another for a while. Then they both could get back to their regular lives.

Hopefully Emilie wouldn't have too many questions about what had happened. She would be confused, if she remembered anything at all. He could use that to his advantage. He knew it would be easy to pick a fight with her. Then, no matter how strongly he felt about her, he could walk away guilt free.

Chapter 10

Emilie heard her phone ringing somewhere on the floor. At first she was so disoriented that she couldn't even remember where she was, but she quickly recognized her own bedroom. *What time is it?* she wondered and checked her clock. *Late...Wow, I slept like a baby.*

Mercifully, her phone stopped ringing. She got up in search of her purse, which she found over in the corner. Emilie couldn't remember how it had gotten there. For that matter, she couldn't remember how she had gotten home. She tried to figure out what had happened, but everything about last night was a confusing blur. She was drawn out of her musing by the furious pounding of her head. It was too painful to ignore so she went to get a glass of water and some Advil. Then she planned to return to bed for a few more hours.

Her phone rang again. She fished it out of her purse. "Hello," Emilie answered weakly.

"Oh my God! I'm going to kill you!" Caroline's voice bellowed into her ear. "I've been worried sick about you. I almost called the police."

Emilie winced and held the phone away from her head until Caroline finished yelling. When things seemed quiet she brought the phone tentatively back to her ear. "Caroline, I'm not feeling very well. Do we have to talk about this right now?"

"You have got to be kidding me! You never showed up last night and we were worried sick. We went back to the club and you and Ethan were nowhere to be found. I overheard some talk about a fight and gunshots. I was freaking out of my mind. You should have called me. What the hell happened to you anyway?"

Blurry images flashed through Emilie's mind. She saw herself at the club and Dante's angry face. She remembered hearing Ethan's voice whispering in her ear and gunshots, then Dante urgently calling her name. "Caroline, what happened last night?" Emilie asked, feeling panic rising in her chest.

"What? I just asked you what happened. How am I supposed to know when I wasn't there?"

"I don't…I don't remember," Emilie stammered. "You have to help me. I'm forgetting something important."

"You drank too much and you have a hangover. What *do* you remember?" Caroline asked more sympathetically.

"I remember dancing with Dante. He was angry with me," Emilie said, trying to keep her voice from cracking as tears started filling her eyes. "He said we're just friends."

"He probably didn't want to take advantage of you when you were so obviously drunk. Give him some time. I'm sure he's going to change his mind soon enough."

"I remember talking to Ethan," Emilie added, shaking her head in a vain attempt at clearing her mind. "I remember you leaving the club with our friends."

"Hey...I really didn't feel comfortable about leaving you there with him, but you insisted you'd be fine," Caroline argued defensively. "Did you bring him home with you?"

Emilie knew in her heart that something important had happened. "I can't remember!" she growled in frustration.

"Are you naked? Are you sore? Do you feel like you did something you shouldn't have?" Caroline asked gently.

Emilie hadn't even thought to check herself. Much to her relief, she was still in all of her clothes from the night before, including her coat. Her ribs were sore and her neck was stiff, but except for the hangover, she didn't feel too bad. "I'm still in all of my clothes. I don't think anything happened," she explained, though she still had a nagging doubt in the back of her mind.

"Maybe Ethan brought you home because you passed out at the bar. Maybe that's why you didn't call me. He must have gotten your address from your purse. Your house key was in there too. Maybe he just brought you home and nothing happened. He did seem like a nice enough guy."

"Perhaps you're right. It does make sense. I must need more sleep. I'm really not feeling very well."

"I'll let you go then. Call me when you're feeling better. We can talk later and maybe everything will come back to you."

"Okay. Thanks for calling, and I'll talk to you later. Bye." Emilie hung up and put her phone back in her purse. She staggered to the bathroom and looked in the mirror. Her reflection wasn't so bad. She cleaned herself up a bit then swallowed some Advils with a glass of water.

She dragged herself back to bed. Her best bet would be to sleep this off. Hopefully she would remember more when she woke up. Emilie closed her eyes, fell asleep, and dreamed.

She was afraid. She was in pain. She was struggling. She could hear a voice in her ear whispering about a prince. It was Ethan's voice. He was going to hurt her. The sound of Dante desperately calling her name echoed in the background. Then there was the sharp sound of gunshots and a dark tunnel. She could hear Dante's magical voice soothing her. She could see pain in his beautiful brown eyes—and blood. No!

Emilie bolted upright in her bed. She just sat there breathing heavily and blinking her eyes to wash the memory of Dante's blood out of her mind. She had to call him. She threw off the covers and rushed to the phone. She could barely get her shaking fingers to dial. Emilie was desperate to hear his voice. The phone rang and rang, but he didn't pick up. It was going to go to voice mail on the next ring. She was trying to figure out what she was going to say to him when finally he answered.

"Hello," he said in his magical voice.

Emilie couldn't believe how wonderful the sound of his voice could be. She was breathing hard and her heart was pounding, but at least he was still alive.

"Hello? Emilie, are you there?" he asked.

"Dante, I was so worried about you," Emilie choked, her throat tight with emotion.

"Why?"

"Because you got shot, you idiot, that's why!" she shrieked. All of her fear and anxiety had suddenly turned into irritation.

"What are you talking about? I'm fine," he muttered. He didn't sound as if he found her sense of humor amusing.

Emilie was feeling unbelievably confused. "I saw you get shot. I saw you bleeding. Where are you?" she demanded.

"I'm at home. What the hell are you talking about?"

"Last night…In my dream," she mumbled. The pit of her stomach was filling quickly with doubt. Emilie began trembling. She had seen Dante injured. The images in her mind had been too detailed to be figments of her imagination.

"You were dreaming, Emilie. I'm okay. How are you doing?" he soothed as if speaking to a small child.

"I'm not doing very well," she admitted reluctantly. "I'm having trouble remembering what happened last night." She had already embarrassed herself enough in front of Dante. She didn't want him thinking any worse of her.

"Emilie, Ethan drugged you and tried to attack you last night. I took you home. Do you remember?"

"No…I mean yes. I remember some of it…I think," she stammered as tears began leaking from her eyes.

Dante paused and sighed deeply. "Why don't I come over and talk to you about this. Would that make you feel any better?"

"Yes…" was all she could say through her sniffling.

"Okay. Give me about an hour," he said. He sounded distracted.

"Thank you…" Emilie mumbled meekly.

"Bye."

"Good-bye."

She put her phone away, shaking her head miserably. She was having a difficult time trying to sort out what was real and what wasn't. Had she seen him injured or had she been hallucinating? She went back to her bed and carefully examined the blankets and sheets. There was no blood to be found. There was nothing on her clothes either. She couldn't understand.

Emilie spent the time waiting for Dante sorting through her memories. She thought in the shower. She thought while she got dressed and while she ate a bowl of cereal. She had to unearth what was buried in her mind. She had to piece together every word, every sound, and every feeling. She replayed the night over and over, and by the time Dante arrived, she was beginning to feel more confident. Nothing made any sense, but at least she had some idea of what had happened.

The phone rang. It was Dante. Emilie buzzed him up and stood by the door, waiting for him to arrive. She was so wound up that, even though she had been expecting it, she still jumped at his knock. She opened the door to find him standing there looking perfectly normal, except for the worry etched into his features. There didn't seem to be anything wrong with him at all, which only served to make Emilie doubt herself all over again.

"Come in," she said, showing him where to put his coat. She walked away from him into the living room and sat on the couch. He followed her as soon as he was done with his things.

"You don't look so good. How are you?" he asked gently, sitting down and glancing around her apartment curiously. He had never been in her apartment before, except last night.

"I'm not doing very well," she admitted, but she couldn't refrain from giving him a thorough examination with her eyes. He was wearing a charcoal grey, light cotton v-neck sweater with a black t-shirt under it. He looked good—and strong. There was absolutely nothing to indicate that he was recovering from a recent gunshot wound. "I was sure you got hurt last night," she said, feeling totally ridiculous.

Dante smirked as if he found her confusion amusing. "Where did you see me get hurt?" he asked, brushing his hands down the front of himself.

Emilie concentrated for a moment, trying to call up the image of where he had been shot. "You were shot in your right shoulder from behind."

Dante's expression changed, as though he found her confusion somewhat less amusing than before. He stood up and faced her, stretching up his arm. He swung it up and down and back and forth. He turned away from her and repeated the exercise from the other side. He seemed perfectly fit and healthy.

"You were drugged, Emilie. I don't think you can differentiate between what was real and what wasn't. Between the alcohol and the drugs, I'm surprised you can remember anything at all," he soothed. "Do you want to call the police? You might want to report this incident even if you can't remember everything. I can take you there myself and help you as much as I can." He sounded as if he was ready to jump up and go right away.

"I don't know," was all Emilie could reply. So many things were criss-crossing through her mind at the moment. She really needed to sort through all of her memories before she made any decisions about what action to take.

"Why don't you tell me what you remember," Dante suggested helpfully.

"I remember our little…argument…and then you left with your friends."

"Yes," he replied with a disapproving snort, but kept further comment to himself. "What do you remember *after* I left?"

"I was at the bar with Caroline and Ethan," she mentioned, trying to focus her mind.

"You really shouldn't have had more to drink. You were already pretty wasted," he scolded.

"I was upset!" Emilie snapped defensively. She didn't want any more lectures. She needed to figure out the truth. He looked away, obviously trying to bite his tongue.

"I stayed with Ethan when the bar closed. I was feeling sick."

"What were you thinking?"

"I obviously wasn't thinking, okay?" she snapped again. "I don't need any lectures from you right now."

"I'm sorry. Go on." Dante made every effort to wipe the disapproving look off of his face.

"I was feeling funny and we went out for some air," she mentioned, getting lost in her memories. "Ethan grabbed me from behind. He was so unbelievably strong. He said all sorts of strange things to me. I think he was talking about you, Dante."

"What exactly did he say about me?"

"He called you a little prince with particular taste in women. He wanted to find out what made me so special," Emilie whispered, trying to avoid eye contact. She knew what she remembered sounded like some sort of twisted fairy tale. Dante wasn't a prince. He was the son of her anthropology professor. The sneer she had heard in Ethan's voice had implied that she and Dante were more than friends, much more.

Dante just sat quietly. Emilie couldn't bring herself to look at him. *Is he waiting for me to continue?* she wondered. Then he stood up and started walking away. He turned and came back over to sit down again, looking deeply concerned.

"What else did he say?" he asked gently.

Emilie was distracted by the intensity she saw in his beautiful eyes. She wanted to reach out and touch him. She was forgetting something important, something about Dante. He was beginning to look impatient, so she returned her focus to his question. "He said that whatever happened to me, you would be blamed, and he wouldn't get into any trouble."

Dante was off the couch and pacing again. Her revelations were obviously upsetting him. He seemed to be having a hard time listening to her story. He wasn't saying much, but his body language sure was.

"Do you know him, Dante?" Emilie asked, watching him pace back and forth. "Do you know what he was talking about?"

"I only know *of* him. I don't know him personally, and I don't have a clue what he was talking about. It all sounds unbelievably strange to me. Are you sure you understood him correctly? How do you know he was even talking about me? Did he use my name?"

"I didn't know what he was talking about, until he said how lucky he was that my guards had left me alone," she answered, beginning to find Dante's intensity worrisome. "He must have meant you and your friends. Then everything else just fell into place."

Why is Dante so interested in what Ethan said about him? Wasn't it all just some kind of drug-induced hallucination? It all sounded like nonsense to Emilie. *I must be out of my mind*, she thought miserably.

Dante stood with his back to her. Then she noticed something odd. He reached up with his left hand and rubbed his right shoulder. It was just a quick, unconscious motion. Did it mean anything? She couldn't tell.

He turned around and came back to sit on the couch. He looked deeply into her eyes and said, "Did Ethan say anything else?"

"I don't think so," Emilie answered quickly, but she was flustered by Dante's closeness. Then she remembered something. "Wait...Didn't he tell you to share your toys? You were there. You remember, don't you?"

"I don't remember him saying anything of the sort."

Dante had a very strange, smooth, unreadable expression plastered on his face. Emilie couldn't tell what he was thinking or feeling. It was as if he was deliberately trying to hide something from her. "Dante, what's going on?" she asked, watching his reaction carefully. "You're acting a bit weird."

His eyes flew open for a second and then he looked away. "This is all very upsetting. That's all," he answered. "I'm worried about you. I wish I knew what drugs Ethan gave you. It must be awful to be so confused."

Emilie wasn't satisfied with his answer. *Why would Dante want to draw attention to my confusion and make me feel worse in the process?* He couldn't have meant to be deliberately hurtful. *I'm probably just over-sensitive because I'm exhausted and hung over.* She decided to dismiss his comments and move on to some of the more interesting questions she needed his help answering.

"What happened to Ethan?" Emilie asked.

Dante's unreadable expression wavered for a second, but he quickly composed himself and answered, "Ethan ran away after I got the gun away from him." Dante had avoided making eye contact with her while he spoke. His body language was getting more and more agitated. He seemed almost surprised that she could remember anything at all and was acting as if he was losing patience with the turn of the conversation.

Did Dante come here with the intention of feeding me some kind of story? Emilie thought suspiciously. *It's as though he hadn't expected me to have any memories at all or any significant questions about what happened.*

Here goes nothing. "I could have sworn Ethan turned into a pile of dust right in front of my eyes," Emilie reluctantly explained. She deliberately avoided Dante's gaze because she realized how crazy her words sounded. But she couldn't resist taking a peek.

Dante was staring at her with pity in his eyes and was slowly shaking his head in disbelief. "I don't know what that guy put in your drink, but it must have been really nasty."

He was right of course. Emilie had to be absolutely certifiable if she thought someone could magically turn to dust. But she just couldn't remember anything about Ethan running away. She had listened for his footsteps and had heard nothing but the wind. Also, Caroline hadn't mentioned anything about the police finding a gun or talking to Ethan.

Emilie's resolve wavered as her doubts compounded her confusion. *I know I'm forgetting something important. I just wish I could remember.*

Dante continued his restless pacing around the living room.

"Dante, how did you get me home?" she asked.

He stopped and stood with his back to her. His hand came up and rubbed his right shoulder again.

What's going on? she asked herself, her brows furrowing. He didn't look injured, but he seemed to be tender or something. Could it be coincidental?

"We took a cab back here," he answered. He briefly turned toward her then paced across to the other side of the room without looking in her direction.

Emilie didn't appreciate his answer in the slightest. She didn't remember walking back through the club out to the street or down the alley to the street. Plus it was virtually impossible to get a cab on a Saturday night right after the bars closed. She would have remembered waiting for one or at least riding in one. "Dante, are you lying to me?" she blurted.

He stopped dead in his tracks. He turned and glared at her, his anger pouring off of him in tangible waves. "Why would I do that?" he snapped.

"I don't know. I'm getting a bad feeling about all of this. The holes in my memory and your answers aren't a very good fit. I'm just having so much trouble piecing everything together cohesively."

"How do you think I got you home?" he sneered. By the tone of his voice, he anticipated an unbelievable answer.

"I can't explain it," Emilie began hesitantly. "It was as though one minute we were there and the next... we were here. Almost instantly." She knew it sounded insane.

"Emilie, are you listening to yourself?" He looked very upset, and she couldn't blame him. "You can't just jump through time and space on a whim. You were drugged...You have to expect some discontinuities in your memory. That doesn't mean you accuse your friends of lying. I thought I was here to help you. Maybe I should just leave."

Dante stood in front of Emilie, glancing longingly at the door. She didn't want him to leave. She had already done enough damage to their relationship. She didn't want to ruin everything. She was actually surprised to see him at all, after the way he had left the club. Visions of his face kept flashing through her mind, but she couldn't get a clear picture. There was some memory trying to surface, but Emilie had damage control to deal with. "I'm sorry, Dante. You're right. I just don't know what to think. I feel like I'm going crazy here."

Her apology seemed to appease him, and he sat with her on the couch again. *Does he want to leave?* she wondered. *He's acting incredibly uncomfortable for someone with nothing to hide.*

While they sat quietly together, his left hand came up and rubbed his right shoulder again. *That's it!* Emilie had reached a conclusion. *If I can prove he's injured, then I can prove he's lying.*

She looked him hard in the eyes. "Dante, I want you to take off your shirt."

His smooth, unreadable expression didn't waver for a second. "What?"

He tried to look confused, but he had heard correctly.

"I want you to take off your sweater and your t-shirt. I need to see the skin of your right shoulder." Emilie had spoken slowly and clearly to express her determination as she glared at him in all seriousness.

"Are you out of your mind?" he snarled. "Why should I?"

"You said you weren't hurt, but you've been rubbing your shoulder over and over," she explained, watching his reaction carefully.

"I don't need this…I'm leaving!" He got up and headed for the closet to get his coat.

"Oh no you don't! We're not finished here." Emilie dashed to the front door and stood in front of it, blocking his escape. "If you have nothing to hide then show me your shoulder!"

Dante glowered down at her. She had never fully appreciated just how large and intimidating he could be.

"Emilie, I don't think we should see each other anymore. Now please get out of my way."

She felt a surge of panic. Perhaps she had overplayed her hand. Dante was really angry, and she was about to lose everything. For some inexplicable reason, as she looked into his hard, angry face, something in her mind flashed to the previous night. Her visions suddenly began to crystallize. Emilie remembered his beautiful face hovering over hers. She remembered the ardor of his kiss and the sound of his magical voice in her ear, whispering words of love.

What was happening now was wrong somehow. Something didn't fit. The way he had acted with her last night and the way he was acting with her today didn't match. Then it finally hit her.

"What's the matter with you?" Dante demanded, staring angrily as she tried to clear her mind and focus back on the present.

"I know you love me, Dante," Emilie insisted.

His eyes flew open, as if her words had frightened him.

Before he could respond she continued. "You're trying to protect me from something. Aren't you? Something really bad. I appreciate your concern, but I would rather deal with whatever it is and have you in my life, because I love you too." She had spoken with conviction, standing her ground in front of the door.

Dante stared at her restlessly, torn between anger and fear and...something else. Her words had caught him off guard, but there had to be some truth to them. He hadn't shoved her out of the way and bolted out the door, so he must be considering telling her the truth.

She needed to make it easier for him somehow. "Dante, I'm willing to do anything to get you to stay and talk to me," she pleaded as calmly and quietly as she could.

A diabolical grin stretched across his beautiful face and he snorted disdainfully. "Anything?"

"Anything," she repeated. She locked her eyes on his so he could see her resolve.

"I wish you could understand what an incredibly difficult thing you're asking of me." He rubbed his hand across his face in frustration.

"I want to understand, Dante. Please," Emilie begged.

She stepped a little closer to him. He watched her with guarded eyes but didn't retreat from her. She stepped closer still. She was almost touching him. Emilie took Dante's hand in hers and twined her fingers into his. She lifted her other hand slowly up to his face. He closed his eyes and let her stroke his cheek and run her fingers into his hair. When he opened his eyes again she could see his fear and pain. He knew what she was going to do. She was going to kiss him. Emilie stretched herself up on her tiptoes and pulled his face down to hers. At first she thought he wasn't going to let her do it, but she was wrong.

When their lips finally met, it felt so right. They were meant to be together.

Dante released her fingers and wrapped his arms around her waist, drawing her tighter against him. She slipped her arms around his neck and pressed her lips into his. He kissed her so deeply that she simply melted into his embrace.

He buried his face into her neck and hugged her even harder. "I can't do this to you," he whispered miserably into her ear, holding her tightly as though he couldn't bear letting her go. "I want to be with you more than anything, but it's impossible. You would have to give up too much for me. It isn't worth it."

"Dante, you have to let me decide for myself. I want to be with you too. I love you," Emilie whispered back. She slipped her arms around his shoulders and squeezed him tightly. He hissed into her neck and she immediately realized what she had done. She leapt away from him. "I'm so sorry. Are you okay?" she asked as she jumped up and down in place, wanting to comfort him somehow but not knowing what to do.

He rubbed his shoulder, a crooked grin on his face. "It's okay. It'll be almost completely healed by tomorrow," he declared, trying to make it sound unimportant.

"How can that be?" she asked incredulously.

"It's a long story." He stretched his injured arm up in the air, twisting it around and wincing.

"I have all the time in the world," Emilie insisted as she took him by his other hand and led him back to the couch. "So tell me this. You had Colin clean up all of the blood when he got here last night, right?"

She could tell by the shocked look on his face that she had hit the nail on the head. "You really complicate my life, you know," he answered evasively.

"I need to know how much of what I remember actually happened the way I think it did."

Dante seemed undecided, but then he sighed heavily and declared, "All of it."

"All of it?" Emilie repeated, suddenly realizing that this was going to be more serious than she had first imagined. Whatever he was trying to protect her from was going to be unbelievable.

"Emilie, I can't do this to you!" He jumped to his feet and headed for the door again. "You don't know what you'll be risking."

"Tell me!" she demanded, following close on his heels.

He spun around and looked her hard in the eyes. "Your life!" he snapped.

She rushed to get herself between him and the door again. "My life?" she repeated. "What are you talking about?"

He smiled. "Not worth it, is it?"

But Emilie could see the sorrow he was trying to disguise. "I didn't say that. I just don't understand what you mean." She wasn't prepared to give up, and she wanted him to know it. He was trying to protect her again. He wanted to scare her into allowing him to walk out of her life. She wasn't going to let him get away without a fight.

"Emilie, if I tell you the truth about what happened last night and especially the truth about *me*, then there will be no turning back for you. It'll be too late to change your mind. Your life will be in danger as soon as you know anything. Look at what happened to you last night. You don't even know anything at all, and just being my friend almost cost you your life. I live in a very dangerous world and I can't protect you. I couldn't survive you getting hurt because of me." He was breathing hard and balling his fists in agitation.

What am I getting myself into? Emilie thought as she looked into Dante's hesitant face. Did she really want all of this trouble? She could just let him leave. It would be easy. If she let him walk out the door, she would never see him again. The very thought made her heart ache. She had her answer. She was in too deep already. At this point, she had to jump into the situation with both feet.

"Are you part of some kind of organized crime ring like the Mafia or something?" she asked with trepidation.

"Something like that…But way worse than you could ever imagine. It's something out of your darkest nightmares," he answered, obviously trying to give her another chance to let him go.

"I can handle it. Now let's sit down and talk about this."

She tried to take his hand, but he stepped quickly away and brought his hands up in front of himself. "You can't be serious!" he hissed. "What am I going to have to do to get out of here before I say something I'll surely regret?"

"It's too late, Dante. We can only move forward from here. Now come and talk to me before I get angry," she teased, walking toward him with a smile on her face.

He couldn't help but smile at how ridiculous she was behaving. "I can't believe how much you complicate my life, woman!"

"I know…But you love me anyway." Emilie managed to wrap her arms around his waist and snuggle her cheek into his uninjured shoulder.

Dante sighed heavily in defeat, wrapped his own arms around her shoulders, and rubbed his face in her hair. "I never meant to fall in love with you so deeply," he declared. "And here I actually thought I had everything under control. Now look where I find myself. I'm going to get us both killed. What an idiot I am!" Dante released her from his embrace and led her by the hand back to the couch. "Remember, *when* this all blows up in your face that I tried to warn you."

"I will. Now where do you want to start?" Emilie asked a bit too enthusiastically for his taste.

"This is serious, Emilie. This is your last chance to change your mind."

"Too late. You're stuck with me now."

He rolled his eyes and sighed deeply. "It's absolutely imperative that you promise not to share any of this information with anyone, under any circumstances. Understand?" He wagged his finger in her face to stress his point.

"I promise," she replied, shoving his hand away from her nose.

"Okay. Where do *you* want to start?" he asked, closing his eyes and shaking his head in disbelief.

Emilie knew exactly what she wanted to know most of all. "How long have you loved me?"

He smiled and rolled his eyes with a chuckle. "Of all the questions you could have possibly asked, you would want to know about my feelings for you."

"You've done a good job of keeping them hidden until now," Emilie accused.

"I don't think so. I couldn't keep myself away from you no matter how dangerous it was for either of us. Do you know I actually waited for two and a half hours for you to come to my Dad's office that first Thursday morning?" he admitted sheepishly.

Emilie stared at him for a second before saying, "You're kidding me. I thought you were there to meet your father."

They went back and forth recounting how their feelings for each other had grown and developed from their first meeting until today.

"I can't believe it," Emilie declared once there was a convenient pause. "And all this time I thought you found me silly and annoying."

"Silly, yes. Annoying, no. Intriguing would be a better word. You're impulsive and unpredictable."

"Most guys find those qualities annoying." She certainly had experience to back her up.

Dante laughed. "I'm not like most guys." He spoke with eerie confidence.

"There you go again. You're always making these little comments that seem to have more than one meaning," Emilie scolded.

His big brown eyes sparkled with mischief. "You really are a clever girl, aren't you? I'm going to have to watch myself even more carefully."

"Why don't you just say what you mean in the first place?" she argued, rolling her eyes at him in frustration.

"Where's the fun in that?" he teased.

A silent tension was building between them on the couch. "You have no idea how badly I wanted to kiss you during our picnic," he admitted.

"Really?" Emilie asked. "You scared me half to death that day. You have a real talent, mister."

His smile disappeared and his face grew dark. "You have good instincts. I should terrify you." His words contained a threat, but his body language and his tone of voice really didn't. He looked rather pitiful over on his side of the couch.

Emilie needed a break from all of this talking. A kiss was a great idea. She wondered how obvious she was going to have to be in order to make it happen. "Why don't you kiss me right now," she whispered. She crooked her finger at him and sank down on the couch.

He laughed at her complete lack of subtlety but slid over to her side. "You really complicate my life, you know," he murmured as he climbed on top of her. "Now keep my injury in mind here. If you put me back in the hospital, Jude's gonna kill you."

Emilie held her breath as he brought his lips to hers. He was so beautiful. They were just getting comfortable together when Dante's phone started ringing. She wanted him to ignore it, but he didn't.

"I have to get this or they'll spaz out," he muttered apologetically, climbing off and sitting up.

"Hello," he said. "Yes." He looked at his watch. "I don't know. I didn't realize I had a curfew. Yes. Sort of," he smiled at Emilie and rolled his eyes. "I won't be too much longer, okay. Tell Colin to take a pill. You guys make more trouble and questions for me by calling all the time." He listened restlessly with his eyebrows furrowed. "Don't you dare! I have to draw the line somewhere," he grumbled. "Okay. I promise. Now can I go?" he snarled. "Bye."

Dante put his phone away and sighed heavily. "They're going to come over here themselves if I don't go back soon. They're worried about me, and they don't trust you alone with me. I've already gotten myself into serious trouble on your account, as far as they're concerned." He paused introspectively. "And obviously they have every reason to be worried."

He slid farther away from her and smiled sadly. "Okay. I have to go soon, and as much as I'd like to continue what we were doing before we were so rudely interrupted, there is something you might want to know before you get too physical with me." He was acting really serious now. "Are you sure about this? You still have time to change your mind."

Emilie was confused by the fear she saw in his eyes. This had to be a significant revelation for him to look at her as though he was bracing for something horrible. "I'm listening," she encouraged.

"Okay, you asked for it." Dante took a deep breath. "I'm...I'm not human." He stared at her, gauging her reaction to his declaration.

Emilie thought she must have misunderstood him. He looked perfectly human. *Maybe he is a delusional psychopath after all.* She suddenly felt even more afraid than she had been before. "What are you talking about?" she asked, her voice high and squeaky.

Dante just smiled. "You aren't going to believe me, so I'll just have to prove it to you."

"Okay..." she said, but she stared at him as if he was completely out of his mind.

"How old do you think I am?" he asked.

"Twenty-six, I thought."

Then he changed. For an instant his face shimmered as if she was looking at its reflection in a pool of water. Suddenly he appeared to be no older than twenty. Emilie gasped. Then he changed again. Another strange shimmer, and he looked almost fifty. He had crow's feet around his eyes, laugh lines on his brow, and even his hands had grown liver spots. His hair hadn't changed, and his body didn't seem to have altered. He had just aged.

Still looking fifty, he asked, "Do you like my eyes?"

As she watched, they changed quickly from brown through a spectacular rainbow of colors, stopping at an icy blue. Emilie couldn't believe it. *What is he?* He couldn't possibly be human!

Dante smiled uncomfortably at her bewildered expression. "This is our camouflage," he explained. He turned himself back to normal—or at least back to the Dante she recognized. "It allows us to blend in with you humans and change quickly if there's any trouble and we need to hide or make an escape. It works similar to an octopus's camouflage. It affects color and skin texture only, and only the living cells, meaning not my hair or nails. I'm also restricted by my skeletal structure and body mass. I can't make myself fat or short." He was looking at her apprehensively, as if she was going to scream or run away.

"Absolutely incredible," Emilie managed to squeak, reaching out a trembling hand to Dante's face. "Is this what you really look like or is this part of your camouflage as well?"

"This is me," he replied, brushing the front of himself with his hands. "Anything else takes effort and energy."

"Are you an...alien?"

"No, I'm a different species from you. We're different from you in many ways."

"What *are* you?" Emilie whispered, staring at him wide-eyed.

"It's complicated," he began. "I'm Beyowan. That's the word we use to define ourselves. It comes from the Hebrew word for 'enemy.' We were once considered enemies of God, enemies of Light and enemies of... humans."

"Sounds ominous. Why would you be considered my enemy?" Emilie asked, her fear returning as her astonishment faded.

"This is where it gets complicated. Remember you once asked me about this?" Dante touched the golden angel hanging on the chain around his neck. Emilie nodded. "I told you it's a symbol of my religion. Well, it's more than that. It's a symbol of what I consider myself to be. Beyowans are the descendants of angels. I am an Angel...or I should say that I *aspire* to be one."

"So you are my angel after all," she murmured.

Dante contemplated her curiously, as though he was not completely sure whether or not she was joking.

"From the first time I saw you, remember when we turned around and looked into each other's eyes? I thought I was looking at an angel because you were so beautiful. I've been calling you an angel ever since." Emilie couldn't bring herself to look at him while she spoke the words. As soon as they were out, she felt her-self blushing. She chanced a glance at him to gauge his reaction. She felt embarrassed that she had interrupted his revelation with her sentimentality.

Dante wore the most mysterious smile on his face. "I've been called a great many things in my life, but that has to be one of the sweetest things anyone has ever said to me."

She had obviously taken him off guard, and he had lost his original train of thought. "I'm sorry I interrupted you. You were telling me about angels," she prompted.

"Right…Now I need you to take a deep breath and try not to freak out on me here." He paused as though he was trying to decide if he should continue.

Emilie was already overwhelmed, and having him warn her not to get upset just made her more apprehensive.

"Beyowans are called 'enemies' because we are thought to be the children of Satan and his follow-ers," Dante explained, bracing himself for a negative reaction.

Emilie could feel the smile slipping off of her face. He wouldn't have been so hesitant to tell her about him-self if everything was all sugar and spice. There had to be a down side for him to have described his world as something out of her worst nightmares.

"Satan was originally an angel right?" she asked as her heart filled with dread.

"You're right. Satan was the most beautiful of God's angels, but he rebelled. God punished him for his sins by casting him out of Heaven with all of his followers. But it didn't end there. We believe God cursed them all by turning them into mortal creatures that were not quite angel and not quite animal. Our species are the descendants of those Fallen Angels."

"Wow..." Emilie muttered, staring.

"Not surprisingly the first of our kind were angry and vengeful, especially against humans, because you're considered God's children. We have changed a great deal over the millennia. We've evolved alongside you and have become more integrated into human culture. We've even been interbreeding. Most of us just want to live our lives and mind our own business. We don't want trouble with you humans."

"So you consider yourself an angel. What does that mean exactly?"

"We're considered Dark Angels because we're not Heavenly Angels. We try to live our lives in peace and harmony, particularly with humans. We try to follow more of a religious lifestyle. Not in the same way as Judeo Christians, but with a similar mentality. We have a separate theology from humans. As a student of anthropology you must know that there are many common veins of belief between different religious doctrines."

"So you're a descendant of Satan, but you're trying to become more of a child of God," Emilie attempted to summarize.

"Basically..." Dante replied, shrugging hopelessly. "If I had known I was coming here to explain our whole history and philosophy, then I would have brought over a few books for you to read. It's a long and complicated story. The short version is that I'm not human, I'm Beyowan, and I'm a descendant of angels. I'm physically similar to you in some ways, but I also have very different abilities."

"What else can you do?" Emilie asked apprehensively.

Dante grinned. "There isn't anything else I can demonstrate for you. We're basically the same inside and out. But our physiology is far superior to humans. It's not easy for us to bleed to death because our bodies can channel blood to and from different areas more efficiently. We also have regenerative abilities, so we heal very quickly." He stopped and patted his injured shoulder to make his point. "Plus we can lapse into various states of hibernation if, for example, we get too injured, hot, cold, oxygen deprived, hungry, or thirsty. We can conserve energy almost indefinitely until conditions improve.

"We're also stronger and faster, plus we can see, hear, and smell far better. We have camouflage, which I've demonstrated. Plus many of us with purer blood have other...special abilities. Do you follow?" he asked. Dante was forced to stop at this point because his phone was ringing.

"I don't know. I think so. We can always discuss it further if any questions arise. Right?"

"Hmmm...Yes...Of course." He was distracted, playing with his phone. "Anything else?"

"I have a hundred questions!" Emilie announced. "I just can't think of any of them at the moment. My mind is reeling." *How could Dante be an inhuman descendant of Satan?*

"Maybe it would be best for us to stop here for today. You probably need some time to process all of this. Once you've accepted everything then we can move on from there, and I can answer any other questions as they arise."

She nodded, still trying to absorb what he had revealed. Dante hesitantly reached over to take Emilie's hand. As she looked into his nervous face, she couldn't help feeling sorry for him. He had taken a huge risk by telling her the truth, and now he might be worried that she was going to reject him. She took his hand in hers and squeezed it gently. She was grateful he had chosen to discuss these things before they had become physically intimate. This would have been a much more awkward conversation if there had been any...inappropriate touching.

He smiled at her self-consciously. "I will be honest with you about my life, but it's going to take time. We have much to discuss, but I don't want you to get overloaded. We still don't know each other very well, and we shouldn't rush."

Emilie couldn't agree more.

Dante checked his watch. "I'd really like to stay, but maybe I should go. I haven't been out of the hospital for that long. I should be taking it easy after being shot and all."

Emilie had completely forgotten about his injury. *How inconsiderate of me*, she scolded herself. It was difficult to imagine him in any pain because he looked so normal, but he had to be uncomfortable. Plus he may have been up for most of the night and needed to rest. "Yes, of course," she said. "I'm sorry for keeping you so long. Thank you for coming over here in your condition, especially since you got shot because of me."

Dante snorted angrily. "I got shot because of me! You were in danger because of me. It was the least I could do."

Emilie was confused. "What do you mean?"

He rubbed his hand across his face. "I guess I owe you an explanation. The truth is that Ethan was like me." Dante watched her reaction but quickly continued. "Well...not exactly like me, but that's another story. He was probably only interested in you because he knew who and what I am, and he was curious about my involvement with you. You were in danger because of me."

"So Ethan is an angel?" Emilie asked uncertainly.

Dante snorted much more disdainfully this time, then stated in a confident tone, "Absolutely not...far from it. I would call him something else, but that would be rude." He paused and sighed almost regretfully. "You never would have had anything to worry about from a Dark Angel. You could have been the only human in a room full of Angels and you'd never have known any different."

"Why would Ethan want to hurt me because of you?"

"I don't know anything for sure..." Dante had an agonized expression on his face. "We have a more complicated social class system than you humans. I think he was jealous of my social position and wanted to hurt you because he knew you were important to me."

Dante closed his eyes and breathed deeply, as though trying to calm himself down. "I'm sorry. We are so much more instinctive and have trouble with our emotional control. We have to struggle more to think before we act. The pain I feel here…" He paused and patted his shoulder, "…is nothing compared to the pain of knowing you suffered because of my carelessness. In that sense, Ethan knew very well how best to hurt me."

Emilie was touched. She slid over toward him on the couch, wrapped her arms around his shoulders, and hugged him gently. He squeezed her gently and snuggled his cheek against hers.

"Thank you for coming to my rescue," she whispered into his ear then kissed his cheek.

Dante held her firmly and whispered back, "I'm sorry I left you there with him. I should never have left you. This was *all* my fault."

"It wasn't your fault. You can't blame yourself. Let's just put the whole thing behind us," Emilie soothed. She ran her hands up and down his back in an attempt to make him feel more at ease.

She tried to let him go, but as she pulled away, he had a very determined look on his face. She wasn't surprised when he tightened his grip on her and kissed her. She was still feeling uncomfortable with everything, but his lips felt too good on hers.

Emilie was confused. She had wanted him to kiss her for so long and here he was…kissing her. He looked, smelled, and tasted human. No matter how much trepidation she had been feeling, the fact of the matter was that she was simply unable to resist him. She ran her fingers into his hair and kissed him back with all of her heart.

They held each other for a long time. Finally Emilie pulled away. She was concerned about Dante's injury.

He let her go with considerable reluctance. "I'm sorry about that too…" Dante admitted sheepishly. "We have trouble with all sorts of control."

She had to laugh. He was still the same man even if he wasn't a man. Emilie laughed again. *What nonsense.* She needed to rest as well. She was obviously more confused than she thought. "You need to go home before Jude and Colin come over here and drag you off," she scolded.

"You're right," he conceded. He stood up and walked over to the closet for his coat. Emilie followed right behind him. "Are you okay with all of this?" he asked, running his fingers through her long hair.

"I don't know yet. I think I'm still in shock."

"That's understandable." He put on his coat. "I'll call you soon."

"Do you mean it this time?" she teased.

Dante smiled roguishly. "Yes…This time I mean it."

"Good. I'll see you soon."

"I hope so," he answered as he reached for the door. He opened it and turned around to face her. She smiled and kissed him good-bye properly.

Emilie watched him walk down the hall then closed the door, shaking her head in bewilderment. She had a great deal to process.

ﷲ

Dante walked into the stairwell. It was always safe and quiet in here. It would make coming to visit his girlfriend a lot more convenient, especially as the weather worsened.

Dante smiled. *I have a girlfriend,* he thought cheerfully to himself. Why then did he feel as if he had just walked up the gallows and was waiting for the noose to be fitted around his neck?

He had told her the truth...most of it anyway...the important stuff. He couldn't believe that she had kissed him after everything. He was relieved though. He didn't know what he would have done if she had panicked. He would have had to knock her unconscious and call in reinforcements. It would have been such a shame if he had been forced to take drastic measures. It would have broken his heart, but he couldn't have risked a potential security breach, no matter how deeply he felt for this human girl.

He was teetering on a slippery slope. This was a dangerous situation and had to be handled with delicacy. He still wasn't sure if he'd made the right decision, but he was determined to ride this out and see where it took him.

The biggest problem would be keeping his hands off of Emilie while she was still human. That was going to be a serious challenge. He just couldn't be alone with her for long. Unfortunately they would be forced indoors much of the time because of the awful weather in this city. There was only so much eating and talking that two people could do together. She would eventually want more privacy with him…and he wouldn't be able to resist her for long.

If he still wanted to call himself an Angel, he had to follow the rules of his religion. He was already bending them enough with this little experiment of his. Did he really have a future with Emilie or was she so tempting because she was technically forbidden to him?

He would have to reconcile these issues as they arose. Dante didn't know what he was going to do about Jude and Colin. Colin, in particular, would be furious with him for involving himself with a human civilian. *Angels and humans don't mix. Am I completely out of my mind?* Dante asked himself.

He came out of inter-dimensional space in the entrance of his condo.

"So how did she take it?" Jude asked. "Was there crying and screaming?"

"Keep your fantasies out of my love life. I didn't tell her anything," Dante lied.

"What? You're not supposed to have a love life, you idiot," Jude snarled. "I thought this was going to be over with once and for all."

"I couldn't do it…It wasn't the right time," Dante lied again.

"You're just stalling, Romeo. You're only going to make this more difficult for yourself, you do realize…I hope."

"I know. I know. I'll take care of it. Don't worry," Dante grumbled as he headed into his bedroom.

"What are you up to now?" Jude demanded, following closely behind.

"I was shot, remember? I need to rest."

Jude dropped back and let his friend go. *He can cut me some slack*, Dante thought, although he expected Jude to keep a watchful eye on him. When it came to Emilie, Jude didn't trust him—and with good reason.

Dante lay down on his bed face first. He already missed Emilie, but he also felt optimistic for the first time since they'd met. He would be able to see her more often, and he could be more honest with her, but not completely honest. Not yet. She needed to be eased into his world, especially if he wasn't entirely sure if he wanted her to be a significant part of his life.

One thing was certain: he was looking forward to basking in Emilie's affection. Beyowan women were not particularly affectionate. They were passionate, but that wasn't the same. Dante growled to himself, thinking about how nice it had been to get a good taste of her today. Emilie had responded like a race car to his touch. It was going to be impossible to keep himself in check. Even today, he had been thankful that Jude had called when he had. Things could easily have gotten out of hand. He laughed to himself. *Poor choice of words,* he thought. He would have to be more inventive. Maybe he could bend the rules here and there, to both of their satisfaction. It would be difficult but manageable.

He yawned and shifted himself around uncomfortably. Bone injuries always healed too slowly. Hopefully it wouldn't be too much longer. He needed to be in better health to deal with his new and complicated life.

ॐ

Emilie was exhausted. It had already been a long day and it was only late afternoon. She sat on her couch thinking about what had happened to her in the last twenty-four hours. It was incredible, and she didn't know what to make of it all.

She needed more sleep. Talking to Dante had taxed her physically. Her headache had returned with a vengeance. She decided to take a nap before supper. Then she had to try to get some studying done. As she lay in bed, she thought about Dante. *Be careful what you wish for,* she thought. She had wanted him with all of her heart, and now that he had made himself available to her, at great personal expense, she was uncertain how she felt about having a relationship with him. Despite everything, her heart didn't seem half as confused as her brain.

She decided to distract herself with some more pleasant memories. She couldn't believe what an excellent kisser Dante was. Technically she had kissed him the day before, but that was different—wonderful but different. Today she had felt his kiss in a completely unclouded manner. When he looked into her eyes, her heart had skipped a beat, but when he touched her, it pounded. There was something very special about Dante Ashton, in so many ways. He had a magical hold over her. *I wonder if he's doing it on purpose.* Maybe he had that kind of power. She didn't have any idea what his limitations were, but she was excited to learn more about him.

Chapter 11

Emilie woke from her nap feeling worse. Her headache had almost disappeared, but she didn't feel rested. Her sleep had been disturbed by strange dreams, memories, and images.

Dante wasn't human. He was a real angel. It was shocking, but she wondered why he had used "nightmarish" to describe what he was. She supposed the whole child of Satan thing could be seen as quite frightening, but after all, it was ancient history. How bad could it be today?

Then she remembered that Ethan was one of his species. Ethan was definitely not the same as Dante. She thought about Ethan's actions and was confused by her memories. Nothing had made any sense at the time, but now Emilie tried to sift through the events and look at them in a different light.

What she was most confused about was the bizarre pain she had felt in her neck before Dante had come charging down the stairs to save her. She brought her hand up and ran her fingers gently along her neck. She found two tiny bumps on her skin. Nothing that would normally have attracted her attention, but now she wanted a closer look.

Emilie jumped out of bed and rushed into the bathroom. In the mirror, she could see two small, scabbedover dots. It looked like she had been poked with some kind of sharp, two-pronged fork. Why on earth would she have something like that on her body? Did Ethan do this and, if so, with what?

Emilie walked slowly back to her bed, rubbing her neck some more. Her muscles were very sore and stiff. Ethan had really yanked her head hard over to one side. What had he been trying to do? Emilie tried to concentrate on what Ethan had said to her. She remembered some nonsense about her smelling good. Emilie shuddered at the thought of how close she had come to being raped by that animal.

She paused for a moment. There had been something odd about the words Ethan had chosen. *Wait*…she realized. *It wasn't good. He said…delicious.* And he hadn't used the word in a way a man would with a woman he was planning on having sex with. His tone of voice had been hungry in another way. It had sounded almost like something a man would say smelling a pan of cookies fresh from the oven.

Emilie stood frozen next to her bed, lost in thought. She had to sit down. Something disturbing was starting to creep into her imagination. Had Ethan been trying to bite her? She hadn't been able to see what he was doing. Now if Ethan was human and tried to bite her, Emilie would have written it off as perverted. Dante had told her that Ethan wasn't an angel. What was he? And did they eat people?

Emilie ran back into the bathroom and examined the marks more closely. The spacing of them was suspicious. Was Ethan something else? Dante had even alluded that he would use a different term to describe Ethan. What if that something was a...*vampire*?

Hadn't he disappeared into dust? Didn't vampires disappear into dust when they died? *Wait a second*, she thought. Dante had been talking about Ethan in the past tense. Was Ethan dead?

Another disturbing idea occurred to her. If Ethan was like Dante and Ethan was a vampire, would that make Dante a vampire too?

He was descended from angels. He hadn't said anything about vampires. Wouldn't he have just come out and said he was a vampire if that was in fact what he was? Maybe if Ethan wasn't *exactly* like Dante, then Dante wasn't a vampire. He couldn't be a vampire. Could he?

Emilie began sorting through all of the strange things Dante had said and done in the weeks since they'd met. Dante was the only person she knew who didn't like sunlight. Not a good sign. He ate a great deal of raw or bloody meat. Dogs acted very strangely around him. He also made a great deal of little comments with double meanings. Hadn't he made some joke about not biting her?

Then Emilie remembered the glimpse she had caught of Dante's glowing red eyes during their chasing game on St. Helen's Island. She had dismissed it as a trick of the light. But now...And wasn't Dante hungry right after the game? Even though they had just had a fairly large lunch together?

Emilie swallowed hard. She was having a hard enough time accepting Dante as an angel. Angels were sweet, gentle, and protective creatures. In many ways he really was her guardian angel. But a vampire? It couldn't be possible. It just couldn't.

Dante had said that she should be terrified of him. Why would he have said such a thing if he was simply an angel? Angels didn't come from your worst nightmares. Vampires did.

Emilie felt nauseous. None of this was possible. What was she supposed to believe? She started to shake and had difficulty breathing. She went into the kitchen to get herself a glass of water. She sat down on one of her kitchen chairs and tried to calm herself. She had to think about this more carefully. It was too important. She needed answers and she needed them immediately.

She didn't know if she should talk to Dante about her concerns or if she should leave him alone to rest and heal. He was hurt, and she felt selfish asking for more of his time. But if he was going to be at work all week long then she wouldn't be able to talk to him about any of this for days. Emilie didn't think she could wait a week to get the answers to these questions. She decided to text him. She got her phone and typed:

Working tomorrow?

It would be convenient for her if his injury kept him home for the day, but knowing him, he would go to work. Her phone went off. She read:

Don't know. Y?

Emilie sent:

We need 2 talk.

"Oops," she hissed. Saying those words, in that manner, often implied something bad. She didn't want to stress him out, but she needed to know. *Nothing to worry about*, she thought sarcastically. *I just have a few minor questions that'll give me nightmares if I don't get them answered right away.* Her phone went off again.

Good or bad talk?

Emilie sighed heavily knowing that she had sent him the wrong message. She had to laugh but replied.

Need 2 know more about what u r.

She wanted to ask him outright if he was a vampire, but she thought it sounded too crazy. Part of her wanted to find out from a distance, because it was too horrifying to imagine. Another part felt it was personal enough that they should talk about it face to face. Her phone rang for real this time.

"Hello," she squeaked. She felt like such an idiot for bothering him, in his condition, about something so insane.

"How are you?" he asked delicately.

"Anxious," she replied. She didn't know where to begin.

"Do you need me to come over again?" he asked, sounding tired.

Emilie felt horribly guilty. "I'm so sorry...I know you're already in trouble with your friends and recovering from a serious injury, but I have one important question nagging at me, and I don't know if I can wait to get it answered."

"Really? Is it life or death important?" he teased, laughing softly.

"More like life or *undead* important," Emilie replied, but her own laugh was distinctly uncomfortable. There was silence at the other end of the line. Emilie sat with dread, waiting for his response.

"I'll be right over," he said in a deeply serious voice.

"Okay..."

"Bye."

He had hung up before she could say anything else. Emilie took a deep breath and let it out slowly. For the first time ever, she wasn't sure if she was happy that Dante was on his way over.

§

Emilie decided to eat something and had just put some frozen stew in the microwave when there was a knock at her door. She ran to open it and looked into Dante's anxious face.

"Wow...You must have flown here," she exclaimed, leaving him in the entrance to take care of himself.

"Something like that," he mumbled as he took off his shoes.

Emilie was already halfway back to the kitchen and hadn't quite heard his comment. She was too distracted to think much of it either. "I'm starving, so I'm going to eat something," she explained. "Do you want some stew?"

She turned around to say something else and ran right into him. Emilie was surprised. She hadn't heard him walk across the floor at all. Normally a person couldn't get around so quickly and quietly on the old wood floors of her apartment.

"You sure sneak up on a person, don't you?" she said, backing away from him a bit nervously.

"I was just standing here. I didn't do anything," he replied defensively with his hands up in the air.

Emilie busied herself taking care of her dinner. She took the microwave dish out and dumped everything into a pot on the stove. "I don't like to microwave meat for long. It tastes better warmed up slowly on the stove," she explained over her shoulder. She turned around slowly this time, expecting Dante to be right behind her, but he was gone. "Where did you go now?" she called.

"I'm here," he answered from the living room. "I didn't want to be in your way."

Emilie walked into the living room and found him looking at some of her parents' photographs.

"You weren't in my way, silly. I'm just used to being alone in here, I guess." She wanted to put him at ease. "Why don't we stay in the kitchen until the stew is ready? I'll need to stir it so it doesn't burn."

He shrugged and followed her into the kitchen.

"Would you like to turn up your nose at another bottle of my wine?" she asked playfully. "I might be able to mix you a drink if you prefer something else."

He laughed and shook his head. "I can have whatever you're having. Don't trouble yourself on my account."

Upon further reflection, drinking alcohol after everything might be unwise. She had been trying to be polite for Dante's sake. *Maybe I'm just stalling*, she thought critically to herself.

"I'm fine with water myself, but you can have whatever you want. I might have a beer in the back of my fridge somewhere. Let me have a look for you." Emilie opened the fridge and started rummaging around. She triumphantly pulled out a bottle of beer, handed it to Dante, and quickly turned her attention back to the pot on the stove.

"It smells good in here," Dante said conversationally, twisting the cap off of his bottle. "Did you make the stew yourself?"

"Yes, I like to have comfort food handy for emergencies. I freeze a lot of food because it isn't much fun cooking for one person. You're lucky to have Jude and Colin for company."

Dante made a sour face. "I think it must be nice to have your privacy."

"Yes...It is," she replied. She was becoming aware of just how large the elephant in the room had become.

"You wanted to talk?" he insisted.

"I do."

"What's this all-important question burning a hole in your soul?" he asked, looking like he dreaded hearing it.

Emilie stared at him for a moment, uncertain how to proceed. "Dante...I was wondering...About Ethan..." she stammered. She hesitated, and Dante waited quietly for her to finish. "Does your species eat...people?" She felt the color draining from her face and she couldn't bear to look at him. She compensated by busying herself stirring the pot.

Even with her back to him she could hear Dante take a deep breath and let it out slowly. She turned herself slightly and glanced back at him. He was rubbing his hand across his face and looked reluctant to answer.

The stew was ready. Emilie divided it into two bowls and handed one to Dante. She picked some papers, books, and a half-case of Coke off of her little kitchen table and sat down. Then she jumped up again to get them some cutlery out of the drawer.

"I didn't make a salad because I know how you feel about salads," Emilie teased, trying to calm her thundering heart.

"I can take them or leave them really," Dante said, stirring the stew around in his bowl. "Do you really want me to answer your question before we eat?" He wore a rather sickened expression on his face.

Emilie was busy fanning her mouth, trying to chew a scorching piece of stew. "I don't honestly know if there will ever be a good time to hear the answer to that question," she mumbled.

Dante blew delicately on a piece of meat. Emilie was always impressed with his manners. He sat up straight and chewed with his mouth closed. He was chivalrous, polite, and well spoken. He had style and class. He also came across a bit pretentious every now and again, but she was still at the stage in their relationship where she found it somewhat charming.

Emilie was staring at him, thinking to herself about how beautiful he really was, when his face became an unreadable mask. Based on her recent experience, this meant he was going to try to hide something from her. She braced herself.

"I think I know where your line of questioning is headed," he said evasively.

Emilie waited and chewed another mouth full.

After a few seconds he continued, "I was really hoping to talk more about this later. I'm not sure if now is the best time."

"So are you hinting that I'm on the right track but telling me not to pursue this any further?" Emilie asked. His presumptuousness irritated her. Did he actually believe she would accept that?

Dante smiled devilishly. "I'm smart enough to know better than to expect you to listen to me if I tell you something you don't want to hear, even if I am right about it."

He's cute but definitely arrogant, she thought to herself. "Are you now?" Emilie challenged. She wondered what he hoped to gain by talking down to her in this way.

Dante rolled his eyes. "I'll tell you whatever you want to know," he soothed. He paused as though assessing her level of irritation. "I'm not deliberately trying to hide anything from you. I don't want to throw everything we could possibly have together out the window because we've rushed into this without thinking."

"I wish the lack of thinking was my problem, Dante. I would be a lot happier if I wasn't burdened with all of these nagging thoughts," Emilie countered, even more offended. He did have a valid point, they shouldn't rush into anything. But there were some matters that needed immediate clarification before they could move forward.

Dante rubbed his hand across his face. "You've misunderstood me. I'm not suggesting you haven't thought things through. I'm just warning you to watch out how much you bite off because you might not be able to chew it all." He smiled mischievously as she swallowed another huge mouth full.

His sense of humor was one of the things she loved most about him. Her current behavior wasn't very ladylike, there was no denying. But she was starving and wanted to finish eating before they got to the blood-thirsty part of the conversation.

Dante continued, "Perhaps if you're having doubts about what's going on between us, you might want to reconsider finding out anything else. You could save us both a lot of time and trouble if you would just decide whether or not having a relationship with me is going to be worth it, knowing that it will be extremely complicated." His expression was cold and hard. "Believe me, what we have between us now will only get more difficult the more you find out about my life and my world."

Emilie sat for a minute, gazing into his stern yet beautiful face. There was no misunderstanding him.

He was preparing her for some bad news and wanted to give her the opportunity to walk away. She needed to think carefully about this. Would she still love him if was a vampire? She didn't know. How could anyone answer a question like that?

"I understand all of your warnings, but I'm afraid I'll need more information before I can make any decisions."

"Are you sure you've thought through how you're going to react to any more…information? Do you need to have your fears validated so you can walk away guilt-free or do you want to know more because you're feeling receptive to different, maybe more disturbing ideas?"

"I don't know," Emilie snapped, throwing her hands up in the air. "You're frustrated because you tried to warn me about this from the beginning. You've had all the information and expected me to be upset. I chose to stay with you regardless of what you said to me, but I was grossly unprepared for what you were about to tell me. I'm still unprepared for what I suspect you're going to tell me next."

Emilie's conflicted emotions were overwhelming her. She was tired and had not fully recovered from last night's events. Plus she was feeling terribly overloaded. She hardly knew Dante. Yet her feelings for him were incredibly strong, and she couldn't imagine her life without him. *Why am I so drawn to him? What kind of hold does he have over me?*

"Have you cast some kind of magical spell on me or something?" Emilie accused.

He shook his head with a surprised expression on his face. "What?"

"Why do I love you so much?" Emilie mumbled, blushing bright red and locking her gaze into her bowl.

Dante laughed softly. "You think you've been bewitched? By me?" he asked incredulously. He was staring at her as though he couldn't believe his ears. "My little devil...You have no idea how long I've been wondering the same thing about you."

Emilie raised her eyes and looked him over carefully. He was serious too. They smiled at each other across the table and then the mood started getting awkward again. There was too much unsaid. This was an impossible situation. Emilie wanted him to tell her everything, and somehow she knew it wasn't going to change the way she felt about him. She would be afraid and she would be confused, but in the end she would still love him.

"I'm ready for the truth now," she announced. She closed her eyes and tried to calm her pounding heart. This was going to be difficult and she had to be steady.

"Are you sure?" Dante asked dubiously.

Emilie opened her eyes. He looked sad. He knew how important this was and what was at stake.

"Let's go and get more comfortable," she suggested. She took their dishes off the table and put them in the kitchen sink, then led him into the living room by the hand.

I wish I hadn't eaten so quickly, she thought. *I'm suddenly not feeling very well.*

As they sat on the couch together, Dante took her by the hands and looked deeply into her eyes. "I need you to try your best to stay calm." His attempt at comforting her only made her more anxious. He took a deep breath and continued. "As I've said before, I'm not human. I'm Beyowan and I'm descended from angels." He paused and took another deep breath. "This is the hard part. Although I'm considered an Angel, most of my kind are not. Another definition of a fallen angel is a…demon."

Emilie was taken aback. She had been expecting something else. "A demon? You mean some kind of beast with horns and a tail?"

Dante laughed. "I've never seen anyone with that description."

"Well, I…I don't know what to say," she stammered. "And here I thought you might be a vampire."

Dante winced and his eyelids fluttered in annoyance. "Please don't ever call me that."

"Why?" Emilie asked fearfully. "Do you also have vampires in your world?"

"Let me be very clear about this," he began with an almost angry expression on his face. "You humans have always had your own names for us. 'Vampire' is just one of many. It's not our name for ourselves. Over the years some have come to embrace it for reasons I can explain later. It's not a term that I, and others like me, embrace, but it might help you to better understand what I am."

"You're a vampire…" Emilie croaked, having trouble finding her voice.

"Please…Please don't call me that. It's very offensive. It's the human equivalent of a racial or religious slur against me and others like me. Let me try to explain it to you." He looked a bit ill, as though he regretted getting himself into this conversation.

Emilie was having a difficult time processing Dante's revelation. Could he sense the fear pouring off of her? He paused and looked at her tentatively. "I'm not going to hurt you," he soothed in a smooth and velvety voice.

"But you could…" she squeaked, staring at him suspiciously.

"But I won't!" he insisted. He backed away as discreetly as possible. "Do you remember this?" he asked, touching his finger to the golden angel around his neck.

She nodded again, waiting for him continue but still watching for any sudden moves.

Dante's frustration was apparent. "It's against my religion, as a Dark Angel, to harm a human in any way. It goes against what I believe. What I've believed my whole life, even before I met you."

"Vampires are religious?" Emilie asked, confused.

He rubbed his hand across his face. "Please…Don't call me a vampire. I'm not a vampire!"

He was getting angry, and she didn't want to see him angry. "Sorry," she whispered, swallowing hard, eyes wide in fright.

"No, I'm sorry," he replied. "I'm having trouble with this too, I guess…The answer to your question is that some of my kind try to live a good life and others embrace evil. Most are somewhere in the middle. Same for humans, if you think about it."

"I guess," she replied sceptically.

Dante looked as though he was bracing himself for some kind of outburst.

"I don't know what to say…" Emilie mumbled almost incoherently. Then she thought of something awful. "Dante, I think Ethan bit me. Am I going to turn into a vampire?" She rubbed her hand across the spots on her neck and stared at him in anguish.

She was surprised to see him smile at her as though he found her utterly ridiculous. "Let me see," he insisted. He reached over and tried to remove her hand. She felt nervous about exposing her throat to him and had to suppress a shudder.

"I'm not going to try to bite you, silly girl," he muttered, laughing softly.

She took her hand away slowly. He smiled mischievously as he examined her. He ran his fingers gingerly over the bumps and announced, "He barely got his teeth into you. I'm glad I got there when I did."

He backed away from her, the smile fading from his face. "Turning a human is a very complicated process. You don't have anything to worry about."

"Really?" she whispered hopefully.

"Turning humans into creatures like ourselves is thought to be our revenge against God," Dante explained. "It's one of the most unforgivable sins in my religion."

Emilie thought she heard a deep sadness in his voice. Then he turned away and continued, "You see, we all used to be venomous, like snakes. Only through a venomous injection can a human be changed. There's a catch though. It only works if the human victim is actually willing to change. Otherwise it's simply fatal. It can be a long, painful process, and if you don't understand what's happening to you, your body shuts down from the stress.

"The stories about selling your soul to the Devil are true, and they arose from this process. To get whatever it is you want in this life, you have to make a deal with him to become his servant for the rest of your life. Although, if you really think about it, your soul always belongs to God. It's your behavior and beliefs that ultimately determine what happens to your soul. But we can have that discussion another time."

"So I would have to want to become a vampire in order to be changed?" Emilie asked, rubbing her neck.

"Stop using that word!" he snapped, but paused and took a deep breath before continuing. "You'd have to want to become a changeling. You would have to work hard to gain a reputation as a vampire." Emilie thought she saw the sadness creep back into his eyes again before he said, "The Angels believe it has to be written on your soul. Perhaps some people are born to be damned. But even many who believe they want this life die from the venom. It's very dangerous."

"Wow..."

"Not many of us are venomous anymore either. Venom is rare and expensive." He sighed heavily. "Do you have any other questions?"

"How many of you are there?"

Dante laughed. "I'm a messenger. I don't work for the census. These things are kept very secret. There aren't many of us anymore. At least not many Beyowans."

Emilie was redefining her world today. "What do you mean?"

"Remember when Ethan called me a prince?" Dante asked, looking self-conscious. Emilie nodded and opened her mouth to say something, but he interrupted her. "Now don't go and get yourself all excited," he warned with a crooked grin. "We don't have royal families like you humans have, but we do have noble families.

"Beyowans are not very social creatures, and living in large groups is often difficult for us. We're self-governing in that we have groups of more powerful and influential individuals who control all of our kind within certain geographical areas. They're called councils, and most major cities around the world have them. We fit into your world, but we have our own culture.

"Our social structure has two different branches. There are those who were once humans and have been changed, and there are those like me, Beyowan. Those who were born. For Beyowans everything is about blood. Being born is very special because we have always had serious fertility problems. As a matter of fact, it's becoming a real concern that our species might be going extinct."

"Really?" Emilie interrupted.

Dante just nodded and continued. "Anyway, what makes me special beyond being born is that my mother's blood line is ancient and well respected. So therefore I'm considered of noble birth, like a prince. Ethan was calling me a prince to ridicule me, not to compliment me. He was jealous of my wealth and social position, so he was essentially calling me a spoiled brat." Dante paused and added, "As a matter of fact, I believe he did call me a spoiled brat. He was a changeling and would always be considered lower class. Beyowans, like nobility everywhere, are rich and spoiled, and changelings are, in general, the equivalent of our working class. We employ changelings to do everything for us."

Dante had to stop his narrative and smile because Emilie was busy dissecting him with her eyes. He shook his head. "What?"

"You look so human. I can't believe that you're..." She stopped herself before she said what she'd almost said, "...something else."

He laughed, knowing full well how close she had come to insulting him again. He appeared grateful for her effort anyway. "Is there anything else before either Jude or Colin discover my absence?" Dante asked, rubbing his injured shoulder vigorously.

"Speaking of Jude and Colin, do they work for you?"

"Jude is like a brother to me. He's older than I am, but not by much. My father wanted me to have a companion as well as a bodyguard, so we hired Jude. Colin is a different story. He's my spiritual advisor."

"Which explains why Colin doesn't like me very much," Emilie declared with relief.

"It's not that he doesn't like *you*. He doesn't like the risk you represent to my body and soul. It's not advisable for someone like me to become involved with humans. He's also of purer blood than I am and has a harder time understanding my attraction to you. To him, it's like the fox wanting to kiss the rabbit instead of eat it."

Emilie appreciated that Dante was being careful not to hurt her feelings or gross her out, but he really needed to try harder.

"Any other life or undead questions?" he teased. "Because I'm not coming back here tonight."

Emilie was not sure how to ask a particularly delicate question.

"What?" he encouraged.

"Can you explain to me why it bothers you so much to be called a vampire?"

"It bothers me because it's not true! The word 'vampire' is a human creation and has been mostly reserved for and embraced by changelings. What's most frustrating is that we've been labelled vampires for one reason and one reason only: because many of us choose to drink human blood."

"What do you mean choose to?"

"A vampire, by definition, is driven to drink blood and has to have it in order to survive. Beyowans have never needed to drink blood, we just enjoy it," Dante explained and then made a face as if he regretted ever opening his mouth.

Emilie backed farther away from him. "Did you just say that you enjoy drinking blood?"

Dante put his hands up and out in front of him. "Why don't I explain why Beyowans started drinking human blood in the first place?"

"Okay," Emilie squeaked.

"The first Fallen Angels drank blood to show their contempt for humans as the true children of God and also to prove their dominance over humans as a species. As in many human cultures, drinking blood was even seen as a way to absorb your enemies' power. It was even thought that a person's soul was found in his blood and therefore drinking all of someone's blood meant you could absorb his soul. For thousands of years, humans desperate for money have sold small quantities of their blood to us, and in a sense, selling your blood is like selling your soul, thereby enhancing the myth of selling your soul to the Devil.

"Plus we have always been incredibly envious of human fertility. It didn't take long for it to become popular to drink human blood as a way to increase one's virility and fertility. It's still considered an aphrodisiac. It's similar to the way in which many humans have been taking remedies made from animal body parts for medicinal or magical purposes."

"I guess," Emilie replied squeamishly.

Dante just grinned. "Remember, the word 'vampire' was invented by humans. It's meant to strike fear into your very souls. It's supposed to represent everything evil. You have given vampires unbelievable power. Plus you have made them undead and immortal. But even with that in mind, those of my kind who embrace evil are still insulted to be called vampires. They should be called demons.

"Vampires were once human. A changeling is related to a Beyowan through venom alone. Beyowans are related to each other through blood and birth. The true blooded descendants of Satan are demons...or in some cases angels." He patted himself on the chest and tapped his angel charm again to stress his point. "If you look it up, you'll find that one definition of a demon is an angel cast out of Heaven for having sex with a human."

Dante inched slowly over to Emilie. "Let me show you something." He lifted his sweater, yanked the shirt out of his pants, and took her hand in his. She stared at him suspiciously, but he was smiling in such an impish way that she felt foolish fearing him. He slid her hand under his shirt and placed it over his heart. "Can you feel my heart beating?"

"Yes," she answered, dazzled by his beauty.

"Can you feel the warmth of my body?" he continued.

"Yes."

He released her hand and inched slowly back to his original spot on the other end of the couch, tucking in his shirt on his way. "You see. I can't be a vampire. I'm a living being, and I can assure you I'm not immortal. We're impressive creatures, far superior to you humans. Please don't take offense, it's simply the truth. But we're very much like you in so many ways. We feel. We think. We live. We're not all mindless killing machines. There are always exceptions. Even you humans can be monsters."

Dante was lost in thought and didn't even look at Emilie before he continued. "I can accept that some of the mythology of vampires could have originated from Beyowans, and how they have been perceived by humans over the millennia, but in my opinion there really isn't much of a comparison."

"I think I understand a bit better now."

"I'm glad."

Emilie started to feel nauseous as she asked her most delicate question, "Dante, do you drink blood? Because I've seen you eat real food." She swallowed hard and waited for his reply with bated breath.

"Blood *is* real food," he answered, eyes sparkling.

He was only teasing. She could tell by the silly grin sneaking onto his face, but she couldn't help wondering. "You know what I mean."

He laughed softly. "We have to eat more food, more often, to fuel our high metabolisms. We have to eat, or we have problems with…control. But as I've mentioned before, we don't have to eat blood. And it's not what you think. Like many other blood-drinking creatures on this planet we don't have to kill our prey to get blood. It's much harder to stay unnoticed if you run around killing animals—and especially people. We can be more discreet about it. We have all sorts of systems in place to accommodate our needs. Most of us just want to fit in with you and live our lives. We don't want trouble."

"That's all fine and good, but you didn't answer my question," Emilie said impatiently.

Dante looked confused. "I thought I had."

"Do *you* drink blood?" she asked again, more slowly.

"I have drunk the blood of many creatures over my lifetime," Dante answered nervously.

"Have you drunk any human blood?" she asked, feeling her poorly chewed and hastily swallowed meal churning in her stomach.

Dante paused, looking really guilty. "It's against my religion to drink human blood."

Emilie narrowed her eyes at him. "I've personally met Jews who eat bacon, Muslims who drink beer, and Catholics who eat beef on Friday. Have you ever drunk human blood?"

Dante brought his beautiful brown eyes up and whispered, "Yes."

That was it for Emilie. She was going to be sick. She actually startled Dante with the suddenness of her leap off the couch. She ran to the bathroom as fast as she could go. She slipped on the wood floor in her haste, but managed to get to the toilet in time.

She emptied her stomach, flushed the toilet, and sat miserably on the floor. She had thought she could handle this, but obviously she couldn't.

The man she loved was a bloodthirsty vampire...or demon. Whatever he was, he was bloodthirsty. Try as she might, she couldn't get the word "vampire" out of her head. Emilie burst into tears. She sat wretchedly on the floor, shaking and crying.

There was a gentle knock on the door. "Are you okay in there?"

Dante's magical voice sounded pitiful and dejected. Emilie unrolled a fist full of toilet paper, wiped her eyes, and blew her nose. She didn't know how to respond. "No, give me another couple of minutes. Okay?"

"Can I get you anything?"

"No…Just give me a minute."

Emilie rose unsteadily. She splashed cold water on her face and rinsed out her mouth. She felt horrible, and her reflection in the mirror looked as good as she felt.

She took a deep breath and opened the bathroom door. She searched for Dante, but he wasn't there. She walked back into the living room and found him sitting on the couch, playing with his phone. He glanced up with concern. "How are you?" he asked.

"In shock," Emilie answered in a rough voice.

Dante sighed. "Would you feel better if I left… Umm…Or do you want me to stay?"

She stared at him in amazement. He looked so human. He was sweet and considerate. Why did he have to be a blood-drinking demon? Why couldn't he be her angel? "Maybe you should go. You're probably in double trouble with Jude now, plus I'm feeling awful and would rather just go to bed."

Emilie walked over and sat down on the couch as far away from Dante as she could. He nodded sadly and said, "Sure." He stretched up his injured arm and twisted it around a couple of times. Then brought it down again and rubbed his shoulder vigorously.

"Does it still hurt?" she asked, forgetting her own discomfort for a moment.

"It isn't so bad. I messed up my shoulder blade pretty badly, and bone injuries are always a pain to recover from," he answered, snickering at his little joke. "It's mostly itchy right now and I have trouble reaching."

Emilie smiled and found herself saying, "Turn around. I'll scratch it for you."

The smile slid off Dante's face and he looked uncertain, but he quickly turned around.

She slid right up behind him. "Tell me if I hurt you."

He snorted as though he didn't believe it possible for her to hurt him. "You can be pretty rough with me."

"Fine." Emilie brought her hand up to scratch his back. She was still nervous. He did have a gunshot wound after all. He had on his sweater so she knew there would be a lot of fabric between her nails and his skin.

She scratched him gently for a minute, feeling awkward. Dante sat quietly. "I'm not being rough enough, am I?" she asked hesitantly.

"I'm not complaining."

Emilie laughed and scratched him harder. He twitched and groaned. She instantly stopped. "I'm sorry," she said sheepishly. She hadn't intended to make him feel worse.

"No, don't be…It feels great."

Emilie smiled and scratched him some more, making a larger circle around the injury. Then she brought up her other hand and rubbed his shoulders. Dante groaned happily and started leaning forward the more he relaxed. Emilie shook her head in amazement. He might be a huge, viscous wolf of an animal, but right now he seemed so much more like a cute little puppy with sharp teeth.

Emilie's emotions were rising again. Tears welled up in her eyes as she rubbed and scratched Dante's back. He really wasn't much of a big, scary monster. She wiped her tears onto her shoulders without stopping what she was doing. But Dante seemed to sense her change of mood. He straightened up and tried to look back at her over his shoulder. She slid her hands down his back and wrapped her arms around his waist. She leaned against his back, hugging him and sniffling.

Dante rubbed her arms and whispered over his shoulder, "Are you okay?"

"No," she mumbled into his sweater. She snuggled her face against him and breathed deeply, enjoying his unique scent.

"Maybe I should go," he said hesitantly.

Emilie held on to him for a bit longer. Then she reluctantly let go and stood up. He followed her to the hall closet.

"Will I ever see you again?" he asked guardedly, his hand on the door knob.

"Yes," Emilie answered with confidence. "But right now I need time and space to absorb all of this."

He smiled pensively. "Okay. Whatever you need."

"Thanks."

"Listen. I'm really sorry about—" Dante began.

"It's not your fault," Emilie interrupted. "Don't worry about it."

"Goodnight," he said as he opened the door and walked out into the hall.

"Goodnight, Dante."

Emilie shut the door behind him and closed her eyes. She would feel so much better if she could either love him or hate him. Feeling both at the same time was making her sick inside.

ॐ

Dante found himself once again in the hallway outside Emilie's apartment. He had a bad feeling about how well she was handling this shock. He snorted in irritation. He wasn't a vampire. Of course she would panic if he called himself that.

He had hoped to avoid this conversation until after they'd had a chance to get to know each other better. Once she had become more emotionally invested, she wouldn't want to walk away from him as easily. He wasn't a physical threat to her. Once she understood, she wouldn't be afraid. He hadn't had a drop of human blood in over half a century. He wasn't a blood-thirsty killer. As a matter of fact, he had never killed anyone for blood.

Things were out of his control now. He opened the door to the stairwell and hesitated. He decided to double back and check on Emilie. Just out of curiosity. He stepped into inter-dimensional space and walked quickly back to her living room, staying hidden behind the threshold. She wasn't there. His heart sank. He found her in the bedroom, crying miserably in her bed.

Dante was unsettled, standing there watching her. It hurt him to see her in pain. He had never loved a woman like this before. He had always tried to avoid this kind of emotional attachment. He felt helpless. He didn't like being helpless any more than he liked being emotionally attached. He wanted to do something to comfort her, but he knew better than to pop out of inter-dimensional space in her bedroom at this moment in time. He would have to think of some way to make her understand that if she loved him when she thought he was human, then she could love him as a Beyowan. He was the same person. But what could he do?

He reluctantly left Emilie in her apartment. He would give her some time. Perhaps she would reconcile her feelings on her own. She had rushed into this, and there was no point rushing anything else. He could be patient. He could afford to have patience because time was on his side. He expected to live for four hundred years.

Dante had a sick feeling deep in his soul. Maybe he had made a serious mistake telling Emilie about his world. If she chose not to be with him, he might have to have her killed. Even if he chose not to be with her, the result would be the same. She was a civilian, and if she revealed his secret to anyone then the council would have her immediately exterminated. If she was going to die, he was determined to be the one to do it. He would be sure to make it quick and painless. The method of execution chosen by the council would probably be less than pleasant.

Dante returned to his own room and slipped into bed. While Emilie had been in the bathroom he had notified Jude of his whereabouts. Poor Jude, this relationship was going to be hard on him. He wasn't used to Dante running off and needing so much privacy.

Dante was exhausted. He wasn't giving his body the time it needed to heal properly. His shoulder ached horribly and he was getting hungry. He would rest for a while and then he and Jude would go out to eat. He had to get back into a more regular routine, or Jude and Colin would get suspicious.

He might take a few days off from work. He had been shot, after all. They already knew at the council office. They would be expecting him to need some time. Dante had a lot of soul searching to do. Perhaps he would go to the temple to pray for guidance.

He could give Jude the day off. Maybe Jude would go out somewhere on his own for a while, then Dante would have a chance to see Emilie again. He had to think of something to do or say to make this whole situation easier for her to accept.

Chapter 12

Emilie sat in the library trying to pay attention to the chapters she was reviewing. She'd had a rough night. Caroline had come over to check on her, and Emilie had had quite a struggle keeping track of all of the little half-truths and outright lies she had been forced to feed her friend in order to protect herself and Dante. Caroline hadn't stayed late, but Emilie had laid awake long into the night thinking of Dante's revelations, and when sleep finally came it was restless and full of nightmares.

She was still uncertain about her feelings for him. She wanted to trust him, but he had been hiding so much. *How do you trust a monster anyway?* To add to her confusion, she didn't even know what exactly he was. A Beyowan. *How odd.* At least he wasn't a vampire and he wasn't exactly a demon. But he was no angel. Angels didn't drink human blood. Whatever he was, she was going to have to sort out her feelings for him.

Her phone started vibrating. She discreetly picked it up and peeked at who was calling. Speak of the Devil! She read:

We need 2 talk!

Emilie wasn't sure if she was ready yet, but she was done with her work for the day. She had lost track of time studying and found that it was essentially supper time. She typed:

When? Where?

Dante must have stayed home from work. Now that she knew he was still in Montreal, her uncertainty seemed less significant and she found herself hoping to see him. Her phone buzzed again and she read:

Anytime! Anywhere!

She smiled. He wanted to make this easier for her. She wrote him to meet her at the main entrance of McGill's arts building as soon as possible.

Emilie packed up her books and walked down the hall, chatting to a classmate who had also stayed late to catch up on some work. She spotted Dante standing at the main door. He was leaning casually against the wall looking magnificent, even though he was simply playing with his phone again. She excused herself from her classmate and walked over to him. He looked up and smiled. He held his index finger up, silently telling her to hold on a minute, and went back to his poking.

Emilie was reminded of the movie they had seen. At that time she would have given anything to have him kiss her. Tonight he might be willing to kiss her, and she was feeling uncertain about the whole affair. It was disconcerting to think of kissing someone with sharp teeth. Dante did have beautiful teeth, even if they were sharp.

Emilie wasn't sure how they should greet each other. She decided to leave it up to him. As she got closer she smiled nervously. She wondered if he was feeling awkward as well. He might be hesitant to be physical with her in public, especially until he had a chance to gauge her level of fear.

"Hello, handsome," she said playfully as he put away his phone.

He didn't seem to know what to do with her either. "How are you feeling?" he asked, looking at her tenderly.

"Tired," she replied.

He reached over tentatively and took her hand in his. It was a simple gesture, but Emilie felt it was appropriate. She smiled shyly and allowed her eyes to flick up to his for just a moment. He was looking at her rather intently, and she felt herself blushing. She glued her gaze onto her shoes while he laughed softly to himself. Electricity was definitely passing between their fingers.

Emilie glanced back in the direction she had just walked and noticed that her classmate had company. There now were three girls standing against the opposite wall, trying to look like they were minding their own business. They were obviously speculating about her and Dante. She squeezed his hand somewhat possessively.

She leaned toward him and whispered, "We're being watched."

He laughed. "Oh, I know." He tapped his ear. "They have interesting things to say as well," he added, then rolled his eyes.

Dante leaned closer and murmured in a husky voice, "I'd really like to give you a proper kiss and give them something worth talking about."

Emilie's thoughts flashed to how nice it felt to kiss him. Her doubts about him didn't seem as significant all of a sudden. She was preparing herself to let him kiss her when he said, "We should get out of here before we attract any more attention."

Emilie chuckled. Dante let go of her hand and took a step away. Somehow she felt disappointed. She was standing right next to him and yet she wanted to be closer to him. He looked down the hallway, lost in his own thoughts. Emilie glanced back toward her classmates and found that they were walking away but looking back occasionally.

"You really do attract a lot of attention, my angel," she said without realizing she had been thinking aloud.

He looked down at her in surprise, and then a beautiful smile spread across his face. "I like it when you call me that."

Emilie blushed. She felt incredibly foolish. She had spent the previous night worrying about dating a demon and now she found herself standing in a public place, lusting after him and calling him her angel. How confusing. She was positively enamored with him, and there seemed to be no escape.

"What did you want to talk about?" she asked.

Dante's brown eyes bored into hers. Emilie's heart started pounding from having those eyes of his looking at her in such an intimate way.

"I don't know…I just wanted to see you," he began, severing his gaze from hers. "You were so upset last night, and I was worried about you."

Despite her previous trepidation, she was deeply touched by his concern. "Thank you…How thoughtful." Then she managed to remember her own manners. "How are you feeling today?"

He smiled broadly and stood up taller. "I'm almost as good as new."

"I'm glad."

Emilie wondered what to do next. Her stomach growled. "Are you hungry?" she asked, smiling mischievously.

"Always," he answered, mirroring her grin.

Emilie had never given their words much thought before, but they certainly had a darker and dirtier meaning when you considered the fact that he was a demon. *Well…not exactly a demon,* she thought, feeling slightly more generous toward him this evening. "Maybe we can get something to eat. I've been neglecting myself today."

"Listen, I think we still have a few things to talk about," he said, looking uncertain.

"Don't worry, I'm not in any hurry. Do you want to sit down?" She gestured to a vacant bench against the wall.

"I would rather go somewhere more private."

"We could go back to my place," Emilie suggested.

"I have a better idea," Dante replied with a crooked grin. "There's something I'd like to show you."

Emilie looked him over suspiciously. "I don't know. What are we talking about here?"

"I have a special ability," he began. "Remember how I brought you home from the club the other night?"

"Barely..." Emilie quipped. Blurry images of a strange corridor flashed through her mind.

"I can travel through inter-dimensional space," Dante explained. "We call it travelling in mesay. It means 'in between' or 'middle' in Aramaic."

"You've got to be kidding me, right?" Emilie demanded.

"No, I'm dead serious."

Poor choice of words, she thought. *Why do I have to be in love with a demon?* "And you want to take me somewhere through inter-dimensional space?"

"Yes."

"I don't know..." She looked into his familiar face. The face that she had been dreaming of for so long. "Where are we going?"

"It's a surprise," Dante said, his smile broadening. "I don't know what the weather is like today, so if it doesn't work out, we'll just go back to your apartment. Okay?"

Despite her initial trepidation, Emilie felt a rush of excitement. The thought of travelling almost instantly to anywhere in the world was hard to resist. "Let's go!" she exclaimed.

"I can't just disappear anywhere I want," Dante corrected. "Let's find somewhere less obvious."

She took his hand and followed him to an empty lecture hall. Once in the entrance and sheltered from view, he turned to Emilie and said, "Hold my hand tightly and don't let go for any reason. Okay?"

She complied and followed him carefully. One second she was at school and the next she was back in

that strange, claustrophobic corridor with walls of ruffling papers. She had a hard time focusing. All of the
ruffling papers were making her feel dizzy. It was too
small, tight, and dark inside. Plus there was absolutely
no sound or smell. Everything was blurry and hazy, as
though she had some kind of film covering her eyes. She
blinked hard, trying to improve her visibility, but nothing helped. Emilie felt nauseated. As she looked behind
them she could see the papers folding into each other
as they passed through them. She couldn't see anything
in front of them either, because the papers were folded
together as well. The sheets seemed to ruffle easily aside
for Dante. There was nothing but the emptiest of darkness above and below them. She was having a hard time
walking while looking down into the void. She couldn't
shake the feeling that she was about to plummet to her
demise.

Emilie closed her eyes and let Dante guide her. She
squeezed his hand harder. He was already holding her
hand tight enough to cut off the circulation to her fingers. Having her eyes closed did give her a great deal of
comfort. *Talk about blind trust,* she scolded herself.

She didn't know how many minutes they walked
together in silence. The passage of time just didn't feel
the same here. It was all very disorienting. Finally they
walked out into the real world again and Emilie opened
her eyes.

They were in a jungle.

Dante was smiling broadly, waiting to see how she
would react. They were standing under an ancient stone

gazebo, covered in vines, in front of a small lake completely surrounded with dense vegetation. The stone floor beneath their feet was littered with leaves and dirt. It was a spectacular day. The air was warm and tropical and the view was unbelievable.

Dante brushed off a stone bench, took off his leather jacket, and sat down to admire the view. "All of the wildlife has been scared off for now," he said. "If we sit here quietly for long enough then some of the creatures will come back. We both smell too much like predators. Me especially." He laughed softly then continued, "This is my land. I own a small piece of this nature preserve in Thailand."

"We're in Thailand?" Emilie squealed. Some birds hiding in the tall grass near the water's edge erupted into the air at the shrill sound of her voice.

Dante nodded his head, smiling. "Yes, this is Thailand."

"Why did you bring me here?" she asked as she dropped her backpack on the ground, stripped off her own coat and joined him on the bench.

"I wanted to find someplace where it was daytime, where we could have some privacy and where we would be relatively safe."

Emilie nodded and studied the view. Her gaze finally fixed on Dante. He was wearing black jeans and a white, slim-fitting long-sleeved shirt with the outline of a black and red Chinese dragon printed over one shoulder and around the back. "You look good enough to eat," she murmured, running her eyes over him suggestively.

He laughed softly and replied, "Thanks. You do too."

Then something dawned on Emilie. "I get it now! You and Jude were laughing so hard the other night at the club because I suggested that Caroline would like to eat Colin alive…and Colin is a demon."

Dante laughed even harder. "Yes, it was rather funny. But Colin is far from a demon. He's much closer to being an Angel than I am, or ever will be, for that matter, so I would appreciate it if you didn't call him a demon."

His voice was soft and friendly, but Emilie could tell he was serious. She leaned in closer and ran her fingers through his hair. "Promise me you won't cut your hair short."

He laughed self-consciously and ran his own fingers through her long hair. "If you want…"

"I love it the way it is."

Dante laughed self-consciously again. "Thanks."

No matter how sharp his teeth were, he was irresistible. Emilie wanted to kiss him. She leaned toward him and brought her lips to his. He seemed just as eager as she. Even if he was a fallen angel, it was evident that he was an experienced lover. His lips felt wonderful, and as he slid closer to her and deepened their kiss, a little shiver of pleasure ran through her body. Emilie wondered what other delightful talents she could look forward to from her demon of a boyfriend.

He released her and slid back to his original spot with a mischievous smile on his handsome face. "So," he said. "Have you thought of another hundred questions for me today?" He looked as though he was trying to get himself comfortable for what promised to be a long discussion.

"At least," she replied, breathing deeply to savor the heady smell of the tropical jungle. She was glad that she had trusted him enough to come on this adventure. What an incredible experience.

"Where would you like to begin?"

His ability to travel through inter-dimensional space, or mesay, as he called it, was a remarkable thing to say the least. He truly was a magical being. "How did you ever get used to travelling that way? It must have been terrifying."

"It was," he exclaimed with a little chuckle. "It took me more than ten years to truly master my ability. I was afraid of getting lost. Getting in is the easy part. Getting out again is much trickier. I had to start off in my own house and slowly work my way around the neighborhood and so on. Plus I can't just pop out anywhere. Remaining undetected is absolutely essential.

"I can stand at the threshold of a mesay doorway and look out before I exit. Sometimes people who share my ability can see into an open doorway and tell if someone is on the threshold, but they have to look very carefully. I should mention how incredibly lucky I am to have the ability. Not only because it's rare in any Beyowan these days, but also because my father isn't Beyowan."

"What?" Emilie demanded. This was the first she'd heard of this. "What is he?"

"My father is a changeling. He was born human and had himself transformed in order to marry my mother.

He's only about forty something years older than I am. He's getting to be an old man now. That's part of what I'm doing here in Montreal. I need to keep an eye on him. He'll be retiring soon, and I want to enjoy as much time with him as I can."

Emilie could sympathize. She had lost both of her parents and knew how hard it was. His father was going to live to a ripe old age; they were both lucky. *Wait a second*, she thought. "Dante, how old are you?"

"I was born September 18, 1896," he answered, watching her reaction carefully.

"That makes you over a hundred years old!"

"I'm only a little more than a quarter of the way through my life expectancy. I'm still young. Do you think I'm too old for you?" he asked, although he didn't look too concerned. "You're probably already through more of your life than I am."

"I don't know about that!" Emilie retorted. "Anyway, you don't *look* too old for me." Yet he could make himself appear even younger if he wanted, she knew. "Are you going to live for four hundred years?" she asked, wide-eyed. It was hard to imagine living for so long.

"I hope so," he answered, watching her struggle with the idea. "But no one really knows for sure."

Everyone said life was too short. A great many things could be seen and done with such a long life. "How come your father doesn't get to live as long as you do?"

"Changelings are different. They only get to double their expected human life spans. Sometimes they get lucky and can live quite a bit longer. It depends on how old they are when they're changed and what kind of life they live after their change. Beyowans live longer the purer their blood. I was lucky that my father was not human when I was conceived, for many reasons. It's all very complicated."

She glanced around again, struck by the beauty of the jungle. "How long have you owned this land?"

"I bought it almost eighty years ago from the government. I paid a huge price for it and pledged it back as part of the nature preserve. I wanted the land because there has been an Angel Temple here for over fifteen hundred years. I've paid to have the temple restored and renovated. Other than the temple, there's only a small cabin. The rest is wild."

"How much land do you own?"

"Here in Thailand or all over the world?"

Emilie stared at him for a second, thinking carefully about his question. "Let's start with here in Thailand."

"I only own about a hundred square kilometres of this jungle. Just a little piece, but it's special."

She was impressed.

Dante looked around peacefully. "We shouldn't stay long. I can mostly tell if anything is hunting us, but I'm not comfortable sitting here for too long by the water's edge. This is real jungle and there are real predators out there. Plus the bugs get annoying after a while. I don't have to worry about tropical diseases, but I doubt you've had all your shots."

"It's really beautiful here," Emilie sighed, sliding closer to him. "I think it's great that you own a piece of a nature preserve. It's very ecologically friendly of you."

"There's definitely no poaching on my land," he mumbled darkly.

"How do you know?" she asked apprehensively.

"I pay property taxes on every inch of this land and have a deal with the government to manage it privately. I also have a deal with the Bangkok Council Office to take care of poachers for me."

"How?"

Dante sighed deeply. "I don't know if you're ready to find out about this kind of thing."

"Why not?" Emilie asked defensively.

"You don't know me very well and may not be prepared to hear about the world I come from," he answered in a soft and gentle voice.

He was trying to protect her again. "I want to understand more about your world," she argued.

"My world is very dark. You won't like what you hear, and I don't want to frighten you."

"How bad could it be?" she asked, forgetting that she was speaking to a demon.

"To a human civilian it can all be very shocking," Dante answered evasively.

"I'm a big girl. I can handle it," Emilie assured him, her voice more confident than she actually felt.

"Okay..." he replied with scepticism. "As I mentioned to you before, most of the major cities in the world have council offices, which organize and govern all of my kind. It's also where we can go to get anything we need." He paused to think carefully about how to proceed with his explanation. "I have an arrangement with the Bangkok office to rent out my cabin for hunting and eco-tourism expeditions."

"You allow hunting on your land?" she asked, her tone a bit more judgmental than she had intended.

Dante sighed deeply with a sheepish smile on his face. "They don't hunt the wildlife," he explained, leaving the words hanging dangerously in the air.

Emilie swallowed hard, realizing what happened to the poachers. "I see," she whispered.

"I have warnings posted all over the perimeter of my land, and as far as I'm concerned, anybody trespassing is...umm...fair game."

There wasn't a trace of shame or guilt in his voice or on his face. Emilie cast around nervously. Dante laughed softly, obviously picking up on her unease. He said, "I receive notices whenever any hunting trips are planned. There isn't anybody out here today. I checked before bringing you here."

"How do the people who live at the Angel Temple feel about you encouraging human hunting right in their back yard?"

"I don't kill any humans," he answered casually. "I've helped lead a good many expeditions, but I've never done any hunting. I leave that to the paying customers."

"You didn't answer my question," Emilie replied somewhat irritably.

"I guess not." Dante smiled. "I believe they understand their need for protection."

"Do Angels need to be protected from humans?"

"There was an incident at the temple a long time ago." He sighed heavily before continuing. "Some armed men decided to take over the temple for their temporary hunting camp. They were…unkind…to the monks and the worshipers living there." Dante paused, his expression hard and angry. "Those idiots had no idea just how dangerous the Angels actually were. It was their religious choices that prevented them from protecting themselves. The Angels may be forgiving, but I'm not."

Emilie looked carefully into Dante's cold eyes. He didn't look like the kind of man you risked crossing. Some of her initial suspicion was creeping back into her mind, making her wonder if she had made the right decision in coming to a place like this with him.

He continued, "The poachers probably don't realize that they're safe at the temple. There's no hunting on temple property, but I pity the man who takes refuge there. He better be planning to pledge his life to the temple, because the second he walks off their property, his life will be forfeit."

Emilie was uncomfortable with the turn this conversation had taken. "I find the whole idea quite disturbing."

Dante snorted with contempt. "It's not like the world will miss a few humans."

"That's not the point," she argued.

He looked unconvinced. "What's the point?"

"The point is that hunting is wrong," she stated, but she didn't feel entirely comfortable or confident about her answer.

"Is it?" he replied with a devilish grin. "I thought hunting was acceptable as long as you ate what you killed."

Emilie felt nauseated. "I don't know…" was all she could manage after she processed what he was implying. Why would he say something like that to her? They barely knew each other, and it wasn't instilling her with confidence about his intentions toward her.

"You eat meat," he argued.

"Yes," she agreed, not quite understanding his point.

"Just because you didn't kill the animal yourself doesn't make it any less dead."

"We raise animals for eating. It's different."

Dante rolled his eyes and turned away.

Emilie grabbed him by the arm. "Are you saying that your kind raises people for eating?"

"I didn't say anything." He laughed, making a show of looking anywhere but in her eyes.

"That look says it all."

"Let me just say…it isn't common practice," Dante explained with hesitation. "But it's easier to hide certain activities in some countries."

"Gross," Emilie whimpered.

"If you really think about it, it's the same. We raise a different species for food."

"Do you actually approve of that kind of thing?" she snapped. Now she really wished to be back in Montreal.

Dante looked affronted. "No! Absolutely not. It's against my religion to eat people."

"But you have. You told me so yourself." Emilie eyed him nervously.

He just laughed. "Yes, but that was different."

"Oh really? How was it different?"

He shifted uncomfortably. "I don't know if I can explain it to you without upsetting you even more."

"Really?" Emilie asked, laughing darkly to herself. "This gets more upsetting, does it?"

Dante rolled his eyes. "Yes, it does. Why don't we leave it there?"

"I don't think I can, at this point."

"That's what I was afraid of," he grumbled. "Umm… Remember when I said that my kind can go to the council office for anything we need? Well, access to human blood is just one of many services available."

"Where do they get it from?" she inquired, dreading the answer.

"There are humans who sell their services to the council. Some people just sell their blood. It's complicated. Normally, no one dies."

Dante was beginning to look irritated, but Emilie didn't care. She wasn't prepared to let this drop. "Normally?"

"You can buy *anything* from the council."

"Anything?"

Dante nodded and examined her curiously. He was probably wondering how she was handling this glimpse into just how dark his world really was.

"You can go to the office and pay to drain all of the blood out of a human even if it means killing them in the process?" she asked.

Dante nodded again, and Emilie just stared at him incredulously.

"You have to understand. It's considered a special request. They may not have anyone on hand for that purpose. They may need to find someone for you, so you might have to wait." His explanation was cold and casual, as though it was really no big deal.

"That makes it better," she remarked sarcastically.

Dante shrugged his shoulders. "Why do you ask me these questions if you don't want to hear the answers?"

Emilie sighed. He was right. She had asked him. He was just being honest with her. He had repeatedly warned her. She just hadn't realized how dark his world really was.

"I'm sorry." She paused because her mind was still reeling. "I'm not angry with you. I'm just trying to wrap my mind around all of this. It's all so shocking."

"I told you so," he mumbled.

"That isn't helping," she growled, punching him hard in the arm.

His eyes narrowed. "You shouldn't hit me. Remember?"

Emilie was temporarily confused and then she remembered something about that kind of gesture being considered sexual. "We're dating now. Can't I be playful with you?"

"I guess so...We're in private, but you're basically giving me an invitation, and I don't think this is the time or the place for it."

Emilie laughed. He was right again.

Dante slipped his arm around her. "Are you okay?"

"I'm fine," she answered dismissively, but she felt uncomfortable with his touch. She stood up so as not to make her need to escape him obvious. "Don't worry about me, but thanks for asking."

"Sure..."

"Maybe we should get going," she suggested, hoping that he wouldn't get suspicious.

He stood up and stretched, looking relaxed and comfortable. "Whatever you want. I'm entirely at your service."

His response made Emilie feel more at ease. "Can I ask you something before we go?"

He smiled warmly. "Of course you can."

"What happened to Ethan?"

His brows furrowed as he sat back down. "I'm not exactly sure myself. I think he was killed by venom." Dante wore a pensive look that was difficult to read.

"The same venom necessary to transform a human?" Emilie asked. Her curiosity made her resume her seat next to him.

"No. We have two types of venom: one that transforms and one that kills."

"How does it kill?" she asked.

"In humans, it causes heart attacks or brain hemorrhages. For us, the venom disables our regenerative capabilities and then attacks on a cellular level. It's like allowing time to catch up to our bodies so they simply disintegrate. There's no antidote, and it's always fatal.

"Ethan disappeared into dust just like you saw, but how he got injected with the venom is unclear. I have a theory, but he was most likely darted by someone. That's the most common way it's done. Venomous Beyowans don't have to be bothered biting anyone personally anymore. They can easily live long and happy lives selling their venom to the highest bidders. You see, we can be milked like snakes."

"Gross," Emilie replied, sickened.

Dante shrugged. "It may be gross, but wouldn't it be worth it if you could be obscenely rich?"

"No," Emilie replied firmly.

His eyes locked to the floor of the gazebo. "Listen, there's something important I need to tell you before we leave."

"Go on," Emilie encouraged, but the expression on his face was worrisome.

"In my world, in order to for someone like me to be involved with someone like you, I need to apply for a license."

"Really? How odd…What kind of license?"

"A hunting license."

"What?" Emilie barked.

"It will protect us both," Dante began quickly. "Once I have the license, it becomes more difficult for anyone else to make an application for you specifically, and our involvement isn't seen as such a security risk. Therefore the council will leave you alone. Trust me, the last thing in the world you should want is to draw the notice of the council."

Emilie wondered if this was part of the reason he had brought her to this place. So she wouldn't be able to get angry and order him out of the apartment or stomp off in a huff. *Very sneaky*, she thought resentfully. *His world isn't just dangerous. It's crazy!* "You're going to get a license to hunt me. How romantic." She glared distastefully at Dante as though he were covered with bugs.

He glanced at her apologetically. "I'm so sorry. I know it sounds horrible, but it's a good idea."

"You've gotta be kidding me, right?"

"There are those, like Ethan, who would just love to get someone like me into trouble, not only because of my social position but because of my religion. It would be disastrous for me to be accused of hunting humans when I claim to be an Angel. I'm lucky that I can obtain a license without it becoming public knowledge."

"Sounds to me like you're trying to cover your ass with the skin of my hide."

Dante sighed heavily. "Emilie, I'm trying to protect you too, but I can't afford to have anyone using you to get to me. You really do complicate my life."

"Not half as much as you complicate mine," Emilie snapped harshly.

He looked hurt. This wasn't going very well at all. She needed to stop thinking about *what* he was saying and try just *listening*. He wanted to protect her. If he wanted to hurt her then he just could. There would be nothing that she or anyone else could do about it. She glanced around again. This was the perfect place to dump a body. She swallowed hard and tried not to panic. Something did occur to her though. "Do you have to have a license to have sex with humans, or is it just for drinking blood?"

A sickened expression crossed Dante's face. "Umm...I would need the license to protect me and the people I work for from the possibility that I could kill you by having sex with you or drinking your blood, either deliberately or by accident." He looked as if he expected her to start screaming. He had inched himself away to the far end of the bench, trying to act as non-threatening as possible.

His words did nothing to alleviate Emilie's fears. "Is there a possibility that you could kill me by accident while having sex with me?"

Dante swallowed hard and fumbled for a response. "Umm...I have never, and could never, kill anyone in that way." He appeared to be regretting ever starting this conversation. "Please, try to remember...just because I look like you doesn't mean I am like you. Keep in mind we are a lot stronger than humans and have a difficult time with our instincts. Also, as a woman, you must realize that rape isn't always about sex. It's often about pain and power. These licenses are designed to protect human civilians from men of my kind who prefer...that. The rest of us are covered even if we don't need to be."

"Does it happen often?"

"Having to have a license makes it a lot less regular. You humans are more protected from us in some ways than we are from you. The fine for hunting without a license is very expensive. If you can't pay it, and you can't barter some kind of services in exchange, then the penalty is death. And trust me, death can come in a number of very unpleasant ways. The council offices get a lot of unusual requests. There is zero tolerance for troublemakers in my world. Either follow the rules or you pay—no excuses and no exceptions. Otherwise raping humans would be an Olympic sport by now."

Dante had finished his explanation with a silly smirk. Emilie didn't appreciate his humor, but she could appreciate his effort to make light of a serious situation. "I see."

"Anyway, not that this is going to make things better for you, but there is easier access to sex with humans, and even drinking fresh blood, without having to go after civilians. You don't have to get a license, you just have to know where to go and be able to pay for it. It's tightly controlled and monitored. Everything is made as safe as possible for all parties involved, but there are always exceptions. You can buy anything in your world or mine. Desperate people are willing to do or pay almost anything to get what they need. The council offices take cash, credit cards, and service contracts."

Dante looked into Emilie's hard and serious face before he continued. "I told you that my world would be out of your worst nightmares. We're talking about organizing demons here. You would think of evil as chaos, but if you really think about it, it's much easier to be evil than it is to be good. You just have to be careful or you're dead. Simple, really."

Dante was beginning to look frustrated. He could probably sense her escalating discomfort. She just sat there staring off into the distance, occasionally shaking her head.

Emilie had wanted to be part of his world. She had wanted the truth, and she needed to take responsibility for her decision to go against all of his many warnings. He was being honest with her, and she had to be understanding for his sake. He was, after all, a demon, and it wasn't his fault.

Unfortunately, now she didn't know if she really wanted to be part of his world after all. Perhaps this was more than she could handle. She stared into Dante's beautiful face, but somehow he didn't look the same. She had always thought of him as her angel, but now, something was different. Somehow, he just seemed very dark and dangerous.

One thing was certain: it was time to leave. "Can you take me home now?"

He didn't look eager. "I don't know. You have a strange expression on your face, and I feel like you don't understand my intentions toward you."

"I don't think I do either," Emilie admitted.

"I would never hurt you."

"Not on purpose anyway," she retorted.

Dante sighed heavily. "You want me to be honest with you, don't you? This type of attitude will not go far toward promoting honesty in our relationship."

"What do you expect from me?" Emilie snapped. "You just told me you were going to get a license to hunt me and that you demons drink blood and rape women. How do you expect me to react?"

"I'm not a demon!" Dante roared with a resonating growl emanating from deep within his chest. His normally beautiful eyes even had a bright flash of red in them, making him even more intimidating.

Emilie was immediately snapped to attention. What was she thinking, provoking him in such a manner? In a place like this...*I must be completely out of my mind*, she chastised herself. She needed to do something to diffuse the situation quickly. "I'm sorry, Dante," she soothed. "I wasn't thinking. I didn't mean to offend you."

He rubbed both hands over his face and sucked in a slow, ragged breath. "No, I'm sorry. I shouldn't have snapped at you. It's just that I'm feeling quite helpless as to what to do to remove the look of absolute terror from your face."

Despite herself, Emilie smiled.

Dante's face softened as well. He walked over, put his thumb under her chin, and brought her eyes up to his. "I will never hurt you, and I will do everything in my power to make sure that no one else does. I promise you."

Emilie didn't know what to say. Her heart was still thundering in her chest. She just nodded blankly like some kind of simpleton.

Dante rolled his eyes, swept her into his arms, and squeezed her against him. "I thought bringing you here would make you feel more comfortable with me, but obviously I've just made everything so much worse."

Emilie had a frog the size of a badger in her throat and was unable to reply. She hesitantly brought her arms around his waist. She drew in a ragged breath of her own and then her eyes began to overflow. She didn't want Dante to notice her tears, but it was obvious that nothing ever escaped his notice.

He pulled away and looked down at her uncomfortably. "Oh God," he mumbled. "I'm so sorry. I'm such a rabid animal."

He wrapped her back into his embrace and kissed the top of her head. Somehow, instead of comforting her, he only made her cry harder. *Why do I have to be in love with a demon*, Emilie demanded of herself. "Please, Dante. I want to go home now."

He reluctantly picked up his jacket and slipped it on. "Okay," he whispered, his voice deep and sad.

Emilie quickly put on her own coat and secured her backpack over her shoulder. She reached out her hand and tried to smile encouragingly.

He took her hand in his and they headed back to her apartment.

ॐ

Dante was practically trembling as he stepped out of mesay into the entrance to the Angel Temple in

Thailand. He had left Emilie sobbing into her pillow again. *I just seem to make that woman cry,* he thought miserably. *What have I done? And, more importantly, how can I get myself out of this mess?*

Dante nodded a greeting to the monk on guard at the entrance. Dante needed to pray for guidance. His world was unravelling fast. He had made such a mistake telling Emilie the truth about himself. *What have I done?*

If she balked and told anyone about him, then the council would come after her. He couldn't allow that to happen. Despite his self-deprecation, he loved Emilie and didn't want to see her suffer.

His reputation would be ruined though. He would surely be tried and fined for hunting without a license. Her death would be on his shoulders and he would never be able to set foot in this temple again.

He glanced around nostalgically as he made his way to the prayer room. Even though it was still early, many monks were up and about their daily business. He nodded politely to everyone but tried to make it clear that he didn't have time to stop for a discussion. He would never be able to look any of these people in the eye. Not with what he had just done and what he might be forced into doing.

The prayer room was crowded at this time of day. Dante decided to take a detour. He headed for his master's office. Michael Enasvant was almost never at the temple. He led a very complicated life, and each visit was a precious gift. Dante would use the office to pray in quiet and solitude.

He said a little prayer of thanks to God that he hadn't run into Colin. Dante closed the door and locked it. He stood in front of his master's desk and remembered all of the lessons he'd sat through in this room. So many years, so much wisdom, wasted.

Dante's shoulders slumped and he sighed heavily. He stomped over to sit in the comfortable chair behind the desk but stopped short. *I'm not worthy of sitting in this chair*, he realized. He turned and took the uncomfortable seat in front of the desk instead. He put his elbows on the desk and sank his head into his hands. *What have I done?*

He lost track of time as he immersed himself in prayer. He was finally starting to find some inner peace when a familiar voice drew him back into the room. "What can I do for you today, my son?"

Dante glanced up quickly into his master's serene visage. He jumped out of the chair in complete shock and stood like a small child, fidgeting and stuttering. "M-Master, I-I didn't know you were here at the temple. Please forgive the intrusion. I just wanted a little solitude."

"Do not apologize, Dante. You are always welcome. Normally my door is never locked." He shot Dante a disapproving glance.

Dante rushed to unlock the office door. "I'm sorry, sir."

"I told you not to apologize." Michael gestured for Dante to resume his seat.

"I didn't mean to bother you," Dante began. "I know you must be busy. It's been such a long time since your last visit." He turned quickly to leave.

"Dante!" Michael insisted. "Please...have a seat."

Dante froze in place, uncertain how to proceed. He was feeling too volatile and ashamed to face one of the oldest and purest Angels in existence, yet he craved the opportunity to unburden himself. His guilt was such a cumbersome thing to carry.

"Dante?"

Dante turned and sat in the seat across from his master but couldn't bring himself to look into Michael's eyes.

"Have you anything to talk about, my son?"

Dante marvelled at the tone and resonance of Michael's hypnotic voice. He really sounded like one would expect and angel to sound. Dante's eyes flicked guiltily to his master's face, but he just continued fidgeting in his seat.

"What have you done?" Michael asked, sounding far more concerned this time.

"Oh, Master...I've made such a terrible mess."

"Go on."

"How do you know if you've met your soul mate?" Dante asked, finally looking into his master's face, with desperation written all over his own.

Michael smiled. "You will know it in your heart. If God binds two people together then nothing but death will keep them apart. Have you met someone?"

Dante sighed. "I've made such a mess, and I don't know how to fix it."

"Tell me about this girl."

"Would God really bind me to a…human?" Dante asked with serious trepidation.

Michael looked visibly shaken. "A human, you say?"

"Yes…" Dante was forced to sever his gaze from Michael's and lock it into his lap.

"In a way, I would not be surprised."

Dante was suddenly offended. "What? Why?"

"Your mother was bound to a human. Maybe it is your destiny as well."

"My destiny…" Dante grumbled sceptically. "How I am supposed to know what to do?"

"What kind of mess have you made, exactly?"

Dante was so embarrassed. He really didn't want to talk about this, but he needed some advice. "I've fallen in love with a human civilian, and what's worse, I made the mistake of telling her what I am. Now she's terrified of me, and I'm afraid that she'll never see me again. If she blabbers to anyone, she'll get herself killed. I can't let that happen, but what am I supposed to do?"

"You are your mother's son, are you not?"

Dante laughed sadly. His mother and father had gone through a great deal in order to be together, only for her to die in childbirth. "I hope I can avoid her fate."

"Some people would give everything they owned for one day with their soul mate. If you have truly found this woman, you should consider yourself fortunate."

"How do I know if she's the one for me?"

"You say you love her. Are you sure?"

"I have no idea!" Dante muttered, his agitation clear as daylight. "I've never felt this way before. It's horrible yet wonderful at the same time…"

"Hush now," Michael scolded. "It is obvious that you are in love. Now what are you going to do about it?"

"I have no idea. I'm drawing a complete blank."

"I've known you since your birth. You have never loved anybody but your closest friends and family members."

"People make mistakes, Master. I could be deluding myself to everybody's detriment."

"If God has bound you to this woman, you will be together. Enjoy what time you are given. You never know how long it will last. Look at your parents. They loved each other fiercely, but they only had a short time together. Why not try speaking to your father about how he found his soul mate?"

Dante practically shot out of his chair. "I can't talk to him about this!"

"Really? He should be able to advise you from personal experience."

"He would never understand." Dante punctuated his statement with a derisive snort. "He wants me married to a princess and making babies. He would never accept a girl like this into our family."

"Are you sure?"

"Of course I am. My father was born human, but he sticks to the rules of our world more strictly than many of us do. I'm a man of noble blood and much is expected of me. I'm the last of my line. I have a responsibility to my whole family."

"I am certain that your father loves you and wants you to be happy."

"Unfortunately he wants me to get married and have a baby first."

"What do you want?"

"I don't know!" Dante growled. "Why does everybody keep asking me all of these questions? If I had the answers, I wouldn't be so miserable."

Michael laughed softly.

"Master, will God forgive me if I have to kill my soul mate?"

"What?"

"If Emilie becomes a security risk, the council will take her, and I can't just leave her to suffer at their hands. I could make her death quick and painless."

"Angels are not allowed to take human lives, Dante."

"But you understand what they will do with her! She will know suffering that no creature in this world should have to endure. I couldn't live with myself knowing that she died because of me."

"You have to have faith, my son."

"Faith..." Dante muttered. "It's so hard to believe that God would actually allow such a thing. It shakes me to my core."

"Have faith. You will see. If she is meant for you, then you both will know it. Otherwise it would be best for you to separate yourself from her as quickly as possible. No matter what the cost. Humans are God's children. Leave them to Him. Remember, if there was no suffering in this world, there would be no joy."

"Your words are wise, but they give me little comfort," Dante admitted.

"Come and see me later and let me know what happens with this woman."

Dante felt a rush of hope. "Are you staying for a while?"

"I believe I will. My presence may be necessary, for a while at least."

"Thank you, Master. I feel better knowing you'll be here just in case."

"You should seek guidance from God, my son. But I will be here to offer you any support I can."

Dante rose from the chair, bowed to Michael, and turned to leave. As the door clicked shut, he saw Colin marching purposefully down the corridor toward him.

"There you are!" Colin called. "Karan told me you were somewhere in the building. I need to have a word with you." The expression on Colin's face implied that he had been speaking to Jude and didn't like what he'd heard.

"I was just in with Michael," Dante said quickly. This distraction would allow him to escape without having to endure one of Colin's lectures.

The stern look slid instantly off of Colin's face and he started almost glowing with excitement. "Michael's here? Is he in his office right now?"

Dante nodded and stepped aside. There were many people who needed to speak to Michael. At least Dante could avoid Colin until he could figure out what was happening with Emilie. He turned and walked slowly back to the entrance. The temple was beginning to swarm like a hive of bees around their queen. Michael's presence would be a good distraction, and at least his words would offer many others the comfort they deserved.

Chapter 13

It was Thursday afternoon and Emilie was just finishing up her class. She was finally done for the day and felt drained. She hadn't been sleeping well. Every night she was plagued with nightmares about Ethan. As much as she was uncertain about her feeling for Dante, she was glad that he had come back to save her. He could be a guardian angel, even if his halo was somewhat tarnished.

She hadn't heard from him since their visit to Thailand. She didn't know what to think. Part of her thought she had finally given him the chance to walk away and that he wasn't coming back. Another part thought that he was giving her the space she needed to sort through her feelings. She had picked up the phone at least a hundred times but had been unable to dial. She didn't know what to say to him. She didn't know how to make things right between them. But most importantly, she didn't know if she wanted to make things right. What was she to do?

One thing was certain, she missed him. He had become such a constant fixture in her thoughts. Removing him was far more difficult. If she managed to distract herself during the day, then he would appear in her dreams. Only a few days had passed since she had seen him last, yet it felt like weeks.

As Emilie waited for a friend to ask the professor a question, she finished packing up her school bag. She noticed a commotion at the doorway to the classroom and got up to see what was going on outside.

It was Dante, of course. Emilie smiled as she saw him leaning against the wall a short distance from the door. He was wearing a fabulous medium grey business suit with his hair slicked back. He looked like he was posing for the cover of *GQ*.

Emilie wasn't the only woman to notice how gorgeous he was. Many girls were openly ogling him and giggling amongst themselves. *Little do they know*, she thought. *Fallen angels are beautiful and beguiling creatures, but they live in a tenebrous world.*

Dante seemed to sense her presence and looked up from his phone just as her own phone started vibrating. She took it out of her pocket and saw a text message, which read:

We need 2 talk.

Emilie smiled and put her phone away. She walked over to him, much to the excited whisperings of the other girls in her class.

"You look good enough to eat," she teased.

He laughed and cocked his head flirtatiously. "You too, I'm not ashamed to say."

He was being generous, as usual. Emilie looked horrible, and she knew it. She had been so unhappy lately that she had been neglecting her regular beauty rituals. Her clothes desperately needed laundering and she hadn't bothered doing her hair or makeup. She felt frumpy next to Dante, all pressed and proper.

He made no move toward her, much to her disappointment. *How confusing,* she thought. She wasn't certain of her feelings and yet she still wanted him to make a small gesture of affection. What exactly did she expect of him? But she was too embarrassed to make any gesture toward him.

"So how did you find me this time?" Emilie asked.

"You once told me you had class on Thursdays at four. Some information is easily obtained by individuals with the proper motivation."

"How long have you been waiting this time?"

"Only for a few minutes. I really hate hanging out here," he grumbled, glancing around the hall distastefully. "It's all very distracting."

"Are you hungry?" she asked with a crooked grin.

"Always."

She chuckled. "We could go and get something to eat while we talk."

Dante checked his watch and then looked off into space pensively. "Do you like French food?"

"Sure," Emilie answered. "I love snails."

He made a sour face. "Yuck."

Emilie snorted. "This coming from the man who drinks blood."

Dante laughed softly under his breath. "To each his own, I guess."

There was an awkward pause and she scrambled for something to say.

Dante beat her to the punch. "Listen, do you want to come with me to look at some art and then we can get something to eat? I know of a great place not too far from the art museum."

"Are you interested in art?" Emilie asked in surprise.

"My father and I have made donations to the museum here in Montreal. I've even donated a piece or two. Every once in a while I receive a special invitation to view a collection. I assume that the museum doesn't keep all of their donated art. They must sell some of it to raise money for other things."

Emilie's curiosity was engaged. "Do you collect art?"

"Not really...I've inherited a good amount of it though. I do enjoy art, and if I see something I like today, I might buy it. I'm a little obsessive-compulsive about clutter though. I don't like my spaces to be too visually busy." Dante looked at his watch again. "I have an appointment to see a particular piece from a recent catalogue."

"Well, sounds like fun. Let's go," Emilie said, smiling enthusiastically.

Dante turned toward the door. "I didn't bring the car. We'll have to walk."

"The weather's so nice. It'll be good to get some exercise," she replied, following closely behind.

The air was cool and fresh. The October sky was already darkening, and a gentle breeze was blowing. It was a beautiful fall evening even if the trees were bare and eerie against the sky. Emilie and Dante walked casually toward the main gates. The museum was only a few blocks west of the university.

As they walked along, they chatted about their favorite artists and their different tastes in artistic styles and media. Emilie had taken an art history course as an elective and was surprised to find that Dante knew far more about art than she had expected.

A thought occurred to her as they approached the museum. "Did you ever go to university?"

"No." Dante smiled sadly. "My father is annoyed about my lack of formal education. I was privately tutored when I was younger, and then I started working when I was only sixteen. I just haven't had time to go to school. I do read a great deal though."

"Well, maybe you should take some time off to study," Emilie suggested.

Dante smiled sadly again and shook his head. "There are a lot of people wishing I would take some time off. But I'm going to have to work through the weekend to make up for the deliveries I had to reschedule from my day off on Monday. If I miss one day, then I have to work like a dog to make up for it. I can't imagine taking four years off. More if I want to be a graduate student like some people."

He fished a piece of paper, the museum's invitation, from his coat and checked it to see exactly where they should go.

Emilie had to laugh. She was impressed that someone as young as him would be so dedicated to a career.

Truth be told, he didn't seem to be suffering financially for his lack of education. Most people attended university in order to obtain career opportunities from which to gain eventual financial independence. She could see how university might seem somewhat frivolous to Dante.

They walked up the main steps, and Dante spoke to a girl at the ticket counter. "My name is Dante Ashton. I have an appointment with Thomas Maine."

"One moment, sir," she said as she picked up her phone. "I'll see if he's ready."

"We're a bit early. We may have to wait," Dante explained to Emilie.

In only a moment's time, a man came rushing toward the desk. "Dante Ashton, I presume?" said the tall, thin, middle-aged man with short, greying hair.

"Yes…Sorry, we're a bit early."

"Not a problem. You called about one of the pieces from our most recent catalogue?" the man continued pleasantly. "I'm Thomas Maine. We spoke briefly on the phone." He extended his hand to Dante.

Dante shook Thomas's hand. "This is my good friend, Emilie Latour."

"Pleased to meet you," Thomas said politely, shaking Emilie's hand. "Please follow me. I'll take you to the room where we have all of our catalogued items on display."

Thomas led the way down a long corridor. "Could you remind me which piece you wanted to see, Mr. Ashton?"

"I'm interested in the painting of the poppies."

"Ah, yes. I remember now. That is a nice piece. It's still for sale as well. We've been fortunate to have sold quite a few of the items from our catalogue."

They arrived at the room, and Thomas unlocked the door, opening it for them. Dante held the door for Emilie and waited patiently for her to enter ahead of him, then followed her inside.

Thomas said, "If you have any questions, I'll be right outside the door."

"Thank you very much," Dante replied as Thomas closed the door behind him. "Let's have a look around," Dante whispered.

Emilie was impressed with the tasteful arrangement. It wasn't a large room, but the high ceiling made it seem more spacious. She was surprised at how much art could be displayed in such a small space. The room had no windows, but it was very well lit. There were many paintings on all four walls and some pieces of sculpture displayed on a few white cubes of various heights in the center of the room.

Dante started with the first wall immediately to their left. Since they had gotten together earlier, he hadn't deliberately touched her, but their bodies had brushed against each other on numerous occasions. It was as if they had some kind of magnetic charge drawing them together.

They finally came to the piece that Dante had come to see. It was done on a canvas about two feet by four feet in size. It was very bright yet richly colored, mostly done in red and black.

"Why would you want to buy a painting of flowers?" Emilie asked. She didn't see him as a floral painting kind of guy.

Dante snickered while carefully examining the painting. "This would look great in my bedroom," he said almost to himself. "I have one red wall and dark furniture. I also have a particular fondness for poppies. They're my favorite flower. I especially like the traditional oriental-style poppies, which are red and black, my two favorite colors."

Emilie found the painting beautifully done, but somehow it just didn't seem to be something she would expect to capture the interest of a young man. She noticed that Dante was contemplating the painting as though he saw something else.

He leaned over and whispered to her in a seductive voice, "Poppies are a bit obscene I'll have you know."

A little shiver ran through her as she savored the closeness of his body. "Really?" she replied with obvious scepticism.

"Seriously. The pods in which the flowers develop look like fuzzy little testicles." Dante's beautiful brown eyes sparkled with mischief.

"I don't believe you!" Emilie declared. Her heart skipped in her chest as she looked longingly into his eyes. He was just so breathtaking.

"I swear to you," he asserted, staring at the painting with a huge grin on his face. "You Google them when you get home. I'm telling the honest to God truth. You'll see."

"What are you smiling so devilishly about?" she asked. Before she knew what she was doing, she reached out her hand and traced her fingers down his arm from his shoulder to his elbow.

Dante seemed hesitant to say anything, but then he smiled. "Beyowans have enjoyed the recreational use of opiates for more than five thousand years. The only good thing about being shot is the morphine." He laughed softly and rubbed his shoulder.

"So you like poppies for opium?"

"Oh, you don't get opium from this kind of poppy, but it's one of the reasons I like them," he replied, refreshing his devilish grin.

Emilie was suddenly concerned. "You don't have a drug habit I should be worried about, do you?"

"No! Don't be silly," he scolded with a dismissive wave of his hand. "Beyowans aren't affected by drugs in the same way as you humans. Drugs aren't as powerful for us. They don't last as long and they aren't as addictive. Don't get me wrong, they can still be a problem, but it isn't the same. Drugs can seriously damage a human's body. We heal too quickly for any lasting effects."

Dante paused, running his eyes thoughtfully over the painting. "I'm going to buy this. Why don't we go and tell Mr. Maine."

Emilie had an idea. "Listen, I have to use the little girls' room. Why don't I tell him on my way out and you two can get started without me?"

"Sounds fine. I'll wait for you here then," he answered, turning toward some of the pieces they had missed.

Emilie walked out of the room and found Mr. Maine standing off to the side of the door talking on his cell phone. When he saw Emilie open the door he hurried himself off the phone. As soon as he had hung up she announced, "He wants to buy his piece."

Mr. Maine smiled broadly. "Excellent. I'll get started on the paperwork."

"Excuse me. Could you point me in the direction of the ladies' room, please?"

"Of course. Down this hall and to the right. It's not far."

Emilie started on her way and called back over her shoulder to him, "Thank you."

༄

On her way back, Emilie noticed a very handsome young man talking to Mr. Maine at the far end of the hall, and it wasn't Dante. The stranger started walking down the corridor toward her. He had on matching dark pants and shirt, with a dark mid-length jacket that was open and flowing out behind him as he walked with the confidence of a model on a catwalk. As they drew closer together, she found that he had a striking resemblance to Jude. He had lighter skin than Jude and was shorter, smaller built, and younger. But his face was the same as Jude's. He had the same bone structure, the same dark eyes, and the same short dark hair. He was incredibly handsome, and Emilie was sure he was Beyowan.

He reached the viewing room before her, and as he grabbed the door handle, he winked at Emilie in the exact same way Jude had done on the day she had met him. She hurried to see if Dante knew this man. She reached the door just as it started to close behind the mysterious stranger.

As she came through the door, she saw the man just inside the room. He reached under his coat and pulled out what looked like a gun. Dante was examining a painting on the opposite wall and hadn't turned around. He must have assumed that it was her coming through the door and not anyone else.

The man pointed his gun at Dante's back. Time seemed to stop ticking for Emilie. Her heart raced. In that terrifying instant, her mind and body felt as though they had become detached. She lunged forward and shoved the stranger in the back as hard as she could. The gun fired, making hardly any sound. Emilie screamed Dante's name at the top of her voice.

The impact of her body hitting the stranger's back had barely budged him at all, but she hoped it was enough to have slightly adjusted the angle of his shot. The stranger took one unbalanced step forward and then twisted himself quickly away from Emilie. He took another step and disappeared into thin air. Unfortunately her body continued along its original trajectory. She toppled forward and crashed into one of the display cubes. She stared at a sculpture of a ballerina as it rocked back and forth, giving motion to its normally frozen form. The statue teetered for a few moments but safely came to rest on the cube again.

Emilie looked up at Dante, who had quickly turned around at the sound of her voice. He had narrowly missed being hit by the stranger's shot. Her relief was overwhelming. It was not just that she didn't want Dante injured because he was a living being and she didn't wish that type of harm on any living creature. It was because she didn't want to lose him and couldn't imagine her life without him. She loved him deeply, no matter what he was.

ॐ

Dante was shaken. He had turned at the sound of Emilie's voice and seen Karim Kahal pointing a dart gun in his direction. For a heart-wrenching instant, he was certain that he was done for. He had tracked the dart's trajectory in the air and it had missed him by the smallest of margins.

Any brush with death is unnerving, but there was something different about this time. As his life flashed before his eyes, he realized his one regret was that he was going to be leaving Emilie. And it was not just because she might find herself in trouble with the council. It was because there was still so much he wanted to say to her and do with her. Despite all of their problems, he still wanted to build a life with her.

He looked down at Emilie, crumpled and trembling on the floor, and hurried toward her. She stood up unsteadily and fell right into his arms. She held him with all of her strength and sobbed into his shoulder.

He smiled to himself as he stroked her hair and kissed her forehead. "You just saved me from a fast and painful death," he whispered to her gratefully. Emilie couldn't reply because she was weeping so hard and could barely catch her breath.

"Is everything okay in here?" Mr. Maine's anxious voice came from the doorway.

Emilie seemed unaware of Mr. Maine's presence and didn't even look in his direction. "My friend is not feeling very well. Could we please wrap this up as quickly as possible?" Dante's tone had made it clear that he wasn't really asking. He held Emilie tightly and continued stroking her hair. "She could use a glass of water, if it wouldn't be too much trouble."

"Of course. I'll be right back," Mr. Maine muttered as he turned and left the door to close on its own.

Dante guided Emilie slowly toward the door but stopped right in front of it. "Are you okay?" he asked, peeling her off of himself so he could look her in the eyes.

"How do you think I am, you idiot?" Emilie replied tersely, punching him in the arm to stress her irritation. "Somebody just tried to kill you, right in front of my eyes!"

Dante wondered if she would ever stop slapping him. He smiled broadly but hushed her. Then he held his index finger over his lips. He pointed above the door frame. Emilie followed his gaze and noticed the security camera.

He leaned down and whispered, "Jude will be so proud of you for saving my skin."

"That man looked just like Jude," Emilie commented as she leaned her trembling body against him.

Dante hushed her again. "Don't say that to Jude. He'll be offended."

"Did you recognize him?"

"Yes, unfortunately."

"Why did he try to kill you?"

"Like I said before, there are many people who'd be happy to see me take some time off work. That's all I can say for the moment." Dante rubbed his hand across his face and pointed up at the camera again. The council would be reviewing these tapes and he couldn't allow Emilie to say anything to incriminate herself. So far, only Karim had broken with protocol and would be the one in trouble for this incident. "We're standing in the camera's blind spot, but it could still have ears."

He walked back across the room and pulled the dart out of the wall opposite the door, making sure his body blocked the view of the camera. He walked casually back to Emilie, took the invitation out of his pocket, and folded the dart inside of the paper, then put the package into his coat pocket to examine later.

Mr. Maine returned with a glass of water for Emilie. She took it gratefully saying, "Thank you so much. I'm starting to feel a bit better."

"You're very pale, my dear. Perhaps you should sit for a moment. Why don't we finish the paperwork in my office?" Mr. Maine suggested helpfully.

"Excellent idea," Dante stated, gesturing for Emilie to follow Mr. Maine.

They walked silently down the hall together. Mr. Maine's office wasn't very far away. Emilie sat down in one of the two chairs in front of his desk. Mr. Maine glanced nervously at her and then into Dante's smooth and unreadable expression. "Right. I have the paperwork for you to sign right here. Did you want to pay now or later?"

"If it would be convenient, I would like to take care of it later. I can call to arrange payment and delivery. I'd really like to get Emilie home as soon as possible."

"Not a problem. Can I just ask you to sign here?" Mr. Maine put a paper in front of Dante and handed him a pen. "We'll be in touch later."

"Thank you so much for everything, Mr. Maine. It was a pleasure meeting you," Dante said politely as he signed. Then he rose and extended his hand.

"The pleasure was all mine, Mr. Ashton. I sincerely hope that you're feeling better soon, Ms. Latour," Mr. Maine replied, shaking hands with both Dante and Emilie.

As Dante prepared to leave the office, he held his hand out for Emilie to take. He helped her up and waited for her to leave the office in front of him. He wrapped his arm around her waist as they walked to the exit. He stopped in the hallway and carefully scanned the area. He would take them back to her apartment through mesay. Hopefully the museum didn't have a camera on the other side of the door. Or else they would be seen walking out the door but not reappearing on the other side. He couldn't afford to draw any more of the council's attention, but he also didn't have any time to lose.

"Hold my hand very tightly. Don't let go for any reason," Dante commanded. Emilie appeared more than happy to oblige. It only took a minute to walk through to her apartment.

"That other guy disappeared into thin air as well. Do all of you demons travel through inter-dimensional space?" she grumbled.

Dante wondered if Emilie would ever stop calling him a demon. He shook his head; at least she hadn't called him a vampire. He was annoyed and offended, but this time he made every effort to remain composed. "Please don't call me a demon," he scolded, his voice gentle. "I'm definitely not perfect, but I'm not a demon."

"You didn't answer my question."

"We all have different abilities." Dante paused and took a deep breath. "Listen, I hate to ditch you before we've had a chance to eat, but I need to get back to Jude. We need to take care of some business about this… attempt on my life."

Emilie glowered at him, her irritation radiating from her body in tangible waves. She reached over and took him firmly by the hand. "I have a thousand questions for you, mister. You can't just run away now!"

Dante contemplated her with amusement. She was so beautiful, with her aqua eyes sparkling in anger and her full lips pouting. He reached over and ran his fingers gently along her jaw line. His intentions were affectionate, but he only managed to annoy Emilie even more. She brushed his hand away from her face and glared up boldly into his eyes. "Don't try to distract me, mister. I know what you're up to…"

Dante's adrenaline levels hadn't returned to normal and Emilie's aggressive body language was only stimulating appetites he was already struggling to harness. Unfortunately he was too agitated to have the control required to keep himself in check, and before he could stop himself, he had grabbed her. She tried to back away from him, but he tightened his grip, smiling devilishly. She made a playful attempt at breaking from his grasp and he had to hold his breath as he fought the urge to pin her to the floor. He loved a good struggle and was primed and ready to enter into whatever sexual games she desired, only he knew he couldn't. That didn't stop him from kissing her. He felt her shiver in his arms as his lips locked onto hers. He practically choked himself, swallowing the growl of arousal building within his chest.

Emilie made one last attempt to escape him, but it was all in vain. Dante squeezed her body tighter and kissed her even deeper. Luckily for her, instead of renewing her attempts, she simply melted in his arms. He was beyond pleased that she was kissing him with as much enthusiasm as he felt.

It took a while for Dante to loosen his grip. He brushed his lips tantalizingly on her ear as he whispered, "Thank you for saving me."

Emilie had to clear her throat before she could even speak. "I guess this makes us even. That's all."

"Okay..." he murmured as he brought his hungry lips back to hers. He would love to stay with her, but it was imperative that he report in to the council.

"Are you sure I can't convince you to stay?" Emilie murmured between kisses.

*Oh God...*Dante thought to himself. *I wish you hadn't said that, you evil little temptress.* "Hmmm...I'd really like to," he replied, running his hands down her back and squeezing her bottom firmly in both hands. Then he sighed heavily and released her. "But this is important and I'm already going to be in trouble for waiting so long to report...the incident."

"But I won't see you again for days and days," Emilie whimpered, trying to snuggle back into his embrace.

Dante was pleased with her response. She had gone from cold and uncomfortable to eager and affectionate. Hopefully this incident had changed the way she felt about him. He hugged her quickly and said, "I'm sorry, but I really have to go. I'll see you soon. I promise."

"Don't get yourself killed," she scolded, looking up at him with the deepest affection glowing in her eyes.

"I won't," he soothed, kissing her forehead. "I'm a tough creature."

"I love you, my angel," she whispered, squeezing him tightly.

Dante was taken aback by the flood of emotion he felt upon hearing her heartfelt words. He couldn't believe how wonderful they sounded. He pulled away and took her face in his hands. He kissed her again, this time very softly and sweetly. "I love you too, Emilie."

She sighed dreamily, and he had every confidence that she was being sincere.

"Good-bye." He backed slightly away from her, then winked playfully as he took a step toward her but disappeared into mesay before reaching her.

Dante came out of inter-dimensional space in the entrance to his condo and found Jude sitting on the couch.

Jude's anger and frustration were billowing off of him like smoke. "Sneaking out again, lover boy?" he accused.

"Yeah, sort of...But listen! I just took Emilie to the museum where your little brother Karim showed up and tried to dart me," Dante blurted. He took a deep breath in an attempt at reigning in his agitation. Luckily he didn't have to be brave for Jude in the same way he did for Emilie.

"My half-brother," Jude corrected. "Did you kill him?" he added hopefully.

Dante had to laugh. He carefully pulled the dart out of his pocket and unwrapped it for Jude.

Jude stared at it uncomfortably but wouldn't come any closer. "Looks like a venom dart to me." Jude watched Dante nervously as he examined the dart. "You be careful with that thing. It wouldn't take much venom to make you a pile of dust," he scolded.

"I know," Dante mumbled, focused on his task. "I'm just curious. I'm going to keep this as a souvenir. It isn't every day that someone tries to kill you."

"Luckily for you and me both. I would call Karim a little bastard if only he actually was. I'm the bastard between the two of us."

Jude sounded as if he was about to go off on a rant, and Dante wasn't in the mood for Jude's family politics, so he just continued with the facts. "Emilie was coming back from the washroom when Karim came in. She saved me," Dante declared proudly.

Jude glared at him. "Are you trying to tell me that your insignificant human mistress saved you from my hotshot little brother?"

Dante didn't appreciate the tone Jude was using to speak about the woman he loved. "Emilie is not my mistress. You better be more careful how you speak about her to me."

Jude shot Dante a disapproving glance. "I shouldn't be talking to you about her at all. You promised both me and Colin that you were going to take care of this whole Emilie situation quickly and quietly."

"I know. I know. It's complicated. Give me a break," Dante grouched and started pacing around the room.

"So what did Wonder Woman do to my brother?" Jude sneered resentfully while he tracked Dante's movements around the room.

"I believe Karim thought I was alone and assumed Emilie was just one of the museum staff members. She came in behind him and screamed. Then she shoved him from behind or something. He fired off this one shot." Dante gestured at the venom dart. "He'd lost the element of surprise, and Emilie had alerted the whole museum of the situation, so he just disappeared. Smart guy. I would have killed him if I had to."

"What did Emilie say about you, a humble messenger, having an assassination attempt? For that matter, what did she say about my brother disappearing right in front of her eyes? She must have freaked out."

Jude looked as though he already knew what was coming. "I told her—" Dante started sheepishly.

"You know what?" Jude interrupted. "I don't want to know! Don't tell me anything!" He clapped his hands over his ears and marched away.

Dante stopped in his tracks and watched his friend leave the room. He walked over to his favorite chair and flopped down miserably. He felt guilty about putting everyone and everything at risk for his relationship with Emilie. She was a human civilian.

Dante's chest hurt. *I didn't ask for this!* He didn't even like being in love. *Love is Hell!* he hissed under his breath. He wanted to be with Emilie every second of the day. *How inconvenient.* He was only happy when he was touching her. He was a busy man and couldn't afford to spend much time with her. It wasn't practical, and it wasn't safe for him to get too predictable or too vulnerable.

It wasn't safe for her either. Someone would eventually recognize the opportunity to use her to get to him. She was human, and he couldn't protect her. Maybe he could hire someone to watch over her. He resolved to look into it as soon as possible. He was going to have to arrange a lot of things to protect himself as well as her. Emilie knew she was risking her life to be with him. He had warned her, but she probably didn't appreciate just how serious he had been.

I'd better get used to Hell, Dante thought miserably. He was going against all of his religious beliefs. He was supposed to avoid humans as much as possible, not get romantically involved. The physical risks to human women involved with men of his species were terrible. Killing humans, no matter how unintentional, was not a pathway into Heaven.

While he was thinking long term, he had to admit that to marry Emilie he would have to become what he had been trying to avoid his whole life: a true Child of Satan. And as if that in itself was not bad enough, he would have to endure enormous social and family pressure about his choice of bride. He was within his legal rights, but everyone, *everyone* would make his life…Hell.

Jude came out of his room and announced, "We have to go to the council and report the assassination attempt."

Dante just nodded. He knew the drill. This wasn't the first time, nor would it be the last.

"If anything, my little brother is going to have his hands slapped for trying to kill someone like you, someone heavily protected by the council. And in a public place on top of it all. It'll keep Karim away from you for a while at least. Ever since he turned twenty-one he has wanted to take on the challenge of being the one to kill you without getting caught. Many have tried and many have died." Jude chuckled proudly to himself.

"I need a new job and a new life," Dante grumbled. But he smiled cheerfully, imagining the new life he could build with Emilie by his side.

Chapter 14

Since Dante was already at the council office and finished with the incident report, he decided to see the chairman. Dante was grateful that his cousin could see him on such short notice. Now Dante was sitting in front of Purson's desk, waiting. The chairman had been called out of his office to deal with yet another problem.

Being a councillor was a lot of work. Many people thought they just sat around, made rules, and doled out punishments. It was serious business running these cities. There were many intricacies that were only noticed when things weren't functioning properly.

Maybe he should reconsider taking the seat in Thailand. He could at least expect to work predominantly in the city of the seat he held. *But no...*When he thought about it carefully enough, he realized that, because of his ability, he would be the member sent to all the meetings around the world. It would end up amounting to even more work than he already had, and it would be even more dangerous. Dante smiled. He also had an extra special reason to spend more of his time in Montreal.

Purson came back in and plunked himself in his chair. "I'm sorry," he began. "I've told my assistant to hold all of my calls, but I'm afraid I won't be able to give you much time today."

"Don't worry about it," Dante replied. "I appreciate whatever time you can spare."

"So what can I do for you?"

"I need a serious favor," Dante began.

"Listen, I can understand that you might be feeling a bit hostile toward Karim, but I can't authorize any retaliation."

"No, sir," Dante corrected. "This isn't about Karim Kahal."

"Is this about the shooting?" the chairman inquired. "I looked over the incident report and was surprised to see that you're having territorial disputes."

"Yes, well. Therein lies the crux of my problem," Dante explained.

"Angel or not, you can't expect to cruise through human clubs and not be targeted by scouts. That is part of their job, you know?"

"I didn't have a problem with the scout until he took an interest in the human girl I was with," Dante grumbled far too defensively.

The chairman stared blankly at Dante for a lingering moment. "You were out with a human?"

"Yes, sir. That's why I'm here."

"Is there a problem?" Purson asked anxiously.

"No, sir. The human girl is not a threat," Dante soothed, much to the obvious relief of the chairman.

"So what's the problem?"

"I need a hunting permit."

Again the Chairman gawked. "You…need a licence to kill a human civilian?"

"Yes, sir," Dante admitted. He felt dirty inside. He was supposed to be an Angel. All of his kind, regardless of social class, could buy blood and sex from the council, easily and conveniently. Only true demons actively hunted humans out of the general population. Only rich demons, because the licenses required were very restrictive and expensive. "I need to keep this very quiet," Dante added, only compounding his shame.

"Indeed," the chairman said. "This is out of character for you."

"I know." Dante was trying to appear more defensive than ashamed, but it was difficult under the experienced scrutiny of his much older cousin.

The chairman flipped open a file and pulled out a picture, which he handed to Dante. "Is this her?"

Dante swallowed hard as he examined the photo of Emilie. So they already knew. He wasn't surprised. Dante looked up into Purson's grinning face. He really was a good actor. Dante could fully appreciate why he had attained the position he held. "Yes, sir."

"I was shocked to discover that our spies were amassing a case against you."

"I know, sir. I was struggling with my demons. I did hope to lose interest in her."

"So your demons have won this battle?" The chairman was obviously pleased and continued before Dante could reply. "Don't look so downhearted. I've never understood why you Angels suffer and sacrifice so much for God's children. He made us first then left us all alone with them. What did He expect? In my opinion, we have every right to exercise our power over them. They're just lucky that they're such successful breeders, or we would own this planet by now."

"Yes, sir," Dante said, not wanting to enter into a religious debate. He felt like such a hypocrite already. No point in making things worse for himself by becoming indignant.

"Are you planning on keeping this girl as a mistress or are you finally trying to father a child to prove your virility and secure yourself a high-ranking wife?"

Dante winced. How could he explain himself? It was probably better if he just went along with what was expected. "I want her as my mistress."

"Well, then. I'm glad to see that you're treating your fall off the wagon responsibly." He paused and started laughing. "Oh…that's funny. You're an Angel and you're falling for a human."

Dante made every effort to chuckle along with his cousin, but he really wanted to reach across the desk and twist his head around. "Yes, sir…funny."

Once Purson had regained his composure, he continued flipping through the file. "Tell me about this girl, Dante."

The chairman obviously wanted to compare what Dante knew about Emilie to the intelligence collected by the spies. *She's the woman with whom I'm going to spend the rest of my life*, Dante thought to himself. Aloud he said, "She's nobody of significance. She's an orphan and she's here studying at McGill. It doesn't sound like she has a lot of friends or family."

"Well done, my boy," the Chairman cheered. "At least you know how to pick a good mistress. You would be surprised how many men want to take celebrities as their mistresses. Those licenses are ridiculously complicated, and it's incredibly difficult to make a high-profile woman die or disappear without raising flags."

"I see. Well, you should have no problems with this girl," Dante assured.

"I don't foresee any difficulties in setting this up for you, but it will take a bit of time. And you can be assured of my complete discretion."

"Thank you, sir," Dante said with a sigh of relief. "I really appreciate this, but there is something else."

"Really?"

"I can't move her into my condo, for obvious reasons." Dante paused, and Purson nodded his understanding. "I need someone discreet to keep an eye on her for me."

"Good thinking, son. I know just the man. I'll arrange everything for you."

"Thank you again, sir," Dante replied. At least Emilie would be somewhat protected. It wasn't much, but it was the best he could do, short of announcing to the world that he was becoming a demon and moving Emilie in with him under constant guard. *Like she would ever agree to that…*

"So tell me, why did this Ethan creature challenge you over this girl?"

"I wish I knew. It must have been a class issue. We were in a human club, and he knew that I was the one doing something illegal. Maybe Ethan thought he could play some kind of game with me because I had so much more to lose than he did."

"Did you have to kill him?" Purson scolded. "As twisted an individual as he may have been, he was fantastic at his job, and it will take us a while to get a suitable replacement."

"I tried knocking him out, but then he shot me and that just made me angry."

"Well, we certainly don't blame you. He was out of line. We just prefer not to have shootings in public places. Ethan's disappearance will become just another unsolved mystery. The humans have no security footage of you. Your blood will appear to be contaminated and will be dismissed as evidence. It was also smart of you to pick up all of Ethan's personal effects and scatter his ashes to the wind. Plus there were no witnesses with any reliable information. Except the one girl who swore she saw a man disappear into thin air. Ridiculous, eh?" The chairman winked.

"Yes, sir," Dante muttered. He was relieved to find that he wasn't in as much trouble as he had anticipated over the death of the scout, but he would have to keep a low profile for a while so as not to draw any more of the council's attention.

"Keeping a human mistress is complicated. That's why I've had so few over the years. Just remember the parameters of your license, and please don't kill her in a public place or take it upon yourself to dispose of her body. You'd be surprised how many messes we have to clean up every year. You just take care of her and we'll take care of the rest. Okay?"

Dante was getting more nauseous by the moment. He didn't have any intention of killing Emilie. He was hoping to avoid having to take such extreme measures. He wanted to build a future with her. He was only getting this license so that she would have the protection of the council from others of his kind and so they wouldn't dispose of her themselves. His license would guarantee him priority in a worst case scenario.

"Dante?" the chairman asked.

"Sorry, sir. I'll keep you posted on everything. I know I've never done anything like this before, but I'm going to be very careful, for everyone's sake."

"I have every confidence in you, son," Purson explained. "Now while I have you in my office, maybe we can talk about the possibility of you paying Jordano Gomez another visit. He has nothing but the highest praise for you and has been hounding me to set up another meeting."

Every deal came with a price tag. "Fine," Dante conceded, much to the satisfaction of the chairman. *Emilie is worth it.*

ψ

Emilie yawned and stretched. She had been studying for hours and was ready for bed. She was looking forward to a good night's sleep for the first time in days. She and Dante had finally resolved some of their issues, much to her relief. She was perfectly happy with him again. Demon or Angel, what mattered most was that she loved him.

Every couple had their rough patches. It was to be expected when you came from such different places. Emilie's confidence in their relationship had been renewed, and now it was in a position of strength. Now they would be able to overcome any challenges.

Her phone vibrated. *Who would be calling at this hour?* she asked herself. She had a message from Dante that read:

Need 2 talk.

Emilie didn't know how to respond. She typed:

It's late. In pjs.

Only an instant went by before she received his reply:

I know.

Emilie was almost startled right out of her seat as she heard a knock on her front door. Dante was obviously waiting. He had probably come in to check if she was still awake but had paid her the respect of asking her permission to enter instead of appearing in the middle of her living room. She stood up and straightened out her pyjamas. She was determined to make more of an effort to look good for him. He was always so well groomed. As she opened the door, she found Dante dressed in black jeans with a skin-tight black T-shirt covered in white skulls under his leather jacket. He looked fantastic.

"Trick or treat!" he exclaimed.

Emilie checked her watch. It was technically Halloween, but trick or treating normally started after sunset, not before sunrise. "Not much of a costume," she teased.

He laughed softly and brushed his hands down the front of his clothes. "I'm disguised as a human. Can't you tell?"

Emilie chuckled and gestured for him to come in. "Not very original. I'd rather see you in a long, flowing cape."

"I will never degrade myself by dressing as such a contemptible creature. Ever!" he declared, although he was smiling devilishly. "But I would rock in a cape."

"Yes, you would. Unfortunately I don't have any candy for you."

"I have sensitive teeth," he said, flashing her a toothy grin. "But you could give me a little sugar," he added in a sultry purr.

Before Emilie could protest, he had her tightly in his arms. She looked up into his big brown eyes and brought her lips to his. He was truly magical, and she knew they were going to have a wonderful life together.

ψ

It was the evening of Halloween and Emilie was getting ready to go out clubbing with her friends. She would have loved to bring along her demon, but he was in Asia on business. She missed him even though she had just seen him earlier that day.

She thought about his visit from the previous evening. He had acted rather strangely. He had clung to her as though it was her own life that had almost been lost. It had been so odd. He had been so tender and affectionate that it was impossible to imagine him being at all dangerous. She almost felt foolish for actually entertaining the idea he could ever hurt her.

Dante had only stayed for a short visit. They had laughed together and had kept their conversation light and easy. Before he left, he had insisted on tucking Emilie into bed, and at first she wondered if he was hoping to be invited to join her. Instead he had behaved like a perfect gentleman. He had kissed her goodnight and had disappeared into thin air, leaving her shaking her head in wonder.

Emilie found him absolutely amazing and was more enamored with him than she had ever thought possible. In reality, it was probably better if they didn't rush into anything physical. Understandably, she had a few concerns about having sex with a demon, but she couldn't help feeling a bit disappointed. Dante was so breathtaking, and the way he kissed her made her eager to discover what other talents he possessed.

There was a knock at the door, drawing Emilie away from her musing. Caroline had arrived to pick her up. They were going to walk together to the club.

"Hi!" Caroline said cheerfully as she stepped into the apartment. "Ready?"

"Almost," Emilie answered, heading toward the bathroom to stuff a few more things into her purse.

"You don't have any surprises for me this time, do you?" Caroline asked mischievously.

"What do you mean?"

"Dante isn't going to swoop in with his friends again, is he?"

"No," Emilie answered sadly. "He's working this weekend in Asia somewhere."

"So you've been keeping in touch," Caroline pointed out, but the implication was that something more serious was going on.

"Listen, Caroline, I want to tell you something," Emilie began, trying to sound casual. She smiled as she watched Caroline's facial expression change into something much more curiously excited.

"Is it about you and Dante?"

"Yes..." Emilie answered evasively. She wanted to build up the suspense at least a little bit.

"Well?" Caroline encouraged.

"We're keeping this very quiet right now, so I have to ask for your complete discretion. If that's even possible."

"I can try," Caroline replied impatiently, but she didn't seem offended.

"Dante and I are sort of dating—" Emilie started.

"That's great!" Caroline interrupted. She rushed over and hugged Emilie. "You must be so happy," Caroline cheered as she released Emilie and stood in front of her, waving her hands up and down like a child.

Emilie had to laugh. "I'm very happy, but I wish I could see him more often."

A crude grin crept across Caroline's face. "Exactly how much of him have you seen so far?"

"We haven't done anything like that yet," Emilie answered with a crude grin of her own.

Caroline patted Emilie's shoulder. "Too bad. You'll have to let me know if he looks as good without his clothes as he does in them."

Emilie sniggered. Caroline was such a naughty girl, but she was a great friend. "I'm looking forward to finding out."

Caroline headed for the door. "Let's go. You may have a man, but I don't."

Emilie grabbed her coat and purse and followed, thinking longingly about her angel.

COMING SOON

BOOK 2
IN THE LOVE IS HELL SERIES

Waiting At The Crossroads

After working hard to overcome all of the obstacles in their path, Emilie and Dante are finally able to get to know one another better and focus on their relationship. Or so they think. In order to ease Emilie into his world Dante has kept her in the dark about many aspects of his life and past. She believes the only remaining problem is how to seduce her reluctant demon, until an unlikely source close to Dante betrays his trust and reveals to Emilie just how high a price Dante will need to pay in order for them to have their fairy tale ending. Emilie is forced to decide if she can ask Dante to sacrifice so much for her.

For more information about the Love is Hell series, visit www.soniabranchaud.com.

Made in the USA
Charleston, SC
10 January 2012